RIVER MIST AND OTHER STORIES

RIVER MIST

AND

OTHER STORIES

by

Kunikida Doppo

Translated from the Japanese

by

DAVID G. CHIBBETT

Kodansha International Ltd.,
Tokyo, New York and San Francisco.

UNESCO COLLECTION OF REPRESENTATIVE WORKS
Japanese Series

This book has been accepted in the Japanese
Series of the Translation Collection of the
United Nations, Educational, Scientific and
Cultural Organisation (UNESCO).

English translation © Unesco 1982
Translated from the Japanese by David Chibbett.

*U.S. edition published by Kodansha International Ltd.,
2–12–21 Otowa, Bunkyo-ku, Tokyo 112 and
Kodansha International/USA Ltd., 10 East 53rd Street,
New York, New York 10022 and 44 Montgomery Street,
San Francisco, California 94104. First published in 1983 by
Paul Norbury Publications, Tenterden, Kent, England.*

LCC 82–84515

ISBN 0–87011–591–X
ISBN (Japan) 4–7700–1091–5
First U.S. edition 1983

*This book has been set in Plantin 10 on 11 point
by Permanent Typesetting & Printing Co., Hong Kong,
and printed by A. Wheaton & Co. Ltd., Exeter, England*

Contents

Preface

The classical literature of Japan, typified by the *Tale of Genji* and the *Pillow Book*, has always found a receptive audience in the west, not least because of its exotic qualities as a portrayal of a life so very different from our own. Modern Japanese literature, however, is much more of an acquired taste, beacuse it emulates western forms such as the novel and the short story but with such a different psychological approach and background that the westerner finds it hard to understand. However, the recent acclaim accorded to the works of Mishima and Kawabata suggests that this situation may well be changing with the consequence that other, equally talented writers will receive the recognition they deserve. Kunikida Doppo, though of a different era and perhaps lesser stature than Mishima and Kawabata, is an author whose works have recently been the subject of much critical re-appraisal in Japan, and although some of his works were translated into English by Arthur Lloyd and others shortly after his death, it is perhaps time for a new translation of some of his best works.

This volume comprises fifteen of the most widely admired Doppo short stories in Japan itself and is designed as an introduction to his work for those who may never have read any Japanese literature at all. If it encourages some readers to read translations of other of his works or even the works of completely different writers it will have achieved its purpose.

In order that the general reader may have some idea of the background of the stories, many of which are autobiographically based, brief notes have been provided at the head of each story and the introduction has been divided into two parts. The first part is an outline biography of Doppo and the second contains a brief analysis of his fiction for those who may wish to pursue that aspect of the subject.

Although this translation is entirely my own and any faults in it are mine, I should like to acknowledge the following persons for their considerable help: Mr S. Matsudaira, of the School of Oriental and African Studies, for his assistance over some technical points of language; Mr H. Yamanouchi, of Cambridge University, for identifying the Burns quotation in *Hoshi* (The Stars); and finally my wife who patiently read the manuscript and pointed out many faults in it. To her this book is dedicated.

David G. Chibbett   LONDON, MAY 1973

For Judith

Introduction

Very little is known about the early life of Kunikida Doppo,[1] his date of birth and even his parentage being matters of some controversy. Such information as exists is mostly in the form of reminiscences of childhood contemporaries sought out for publication after Doppo's death and consequently not altogether reliable. According to the most widely accepted tradition, Doppo was born on 30 August, 1871, in the small town of Chōshi in Chiba Prefecture where the Tone river flows out into the Pacific Ocean. His mother, Man-ko, came from the Awaji family who were tradesmen in Chōshi, and she had been married once before she met Doppo's father, Kunikida Sempachi.

It is on the fact of this previous marriage that doubts about Doppo's paternity rest.[2] The name of Man-ko's first husband is given in the Awaji family register simply as Masajirō (a given-name, not a surname), and in recent years a body of Japanese scholarly opinion, led by Sakamoto Hiroshi, has insisted that this man was Doppo's real father. Naturally this theory has thrown into question the validity of Doppo's traditionally accepted birth date and opinions have varied by as much as two years.

Whatever the truth of Doppo's paternity, and it will probably never be known for certain, such matters are of less importance in determining the pattern of Doppo's life than is the background in which he grew up. It is the environment which shapes the man. Although his mother's ancestry was not particularly distinguished, his father, Sempachi, was a *samurai* retainer of the Wakizaka family, feudal lords of Harima fief in modern Hyōgō Prefecture. In earlier days when the feudal system had still been in operation, his was a position of considerable wealth, status and power. But after the Meiji Restoration in 1868, the Japanese government embarked on the process of shaping the country along western lines, and one of its earliest reforms was the abolition of the very system on the basis of which men like Sempachi held their positions.

In common with many thousands of other dispossessed *samurai*, Sempachi was forced to search for some other employment which he eventually found in 1875 when he was appointed as a minor official in the judiciary to serve in the Yamaguchi court in South western Honshū (the main island of Japan).

As an ex-*samurai*, Sempachi would have been reasonably well

educated and aware of the importance of books and a good education.
His family would also have been used to some wealth, although during
Doppo's lifetime his father and mother seemed to have moved from one
financial crisis to another, so that Doppo himself always had to work
and struggle for advancement. However, financial considerations apart,
Doppo was in no real sense disadvantaged by his background. For some
years to come men of *samurai* descent were still widely respected in
Japan and not a few prominent politicians and writers came from a
similar class. By its very nature, Sempachi's employment on a court cir-
cuit involved many removals of residence and Doppo spent his earliest
years travelling from town to town with his parents in Yamaguchi and
Hiroshima Prefectures. However, in 1878 the family finally settled
down in the village of Nishi(ki)mi[3] in the Iwakuni district of Yamaguchi
Prefecture, and Doppo entered the Nishi(ki)mi Junior School.

It is clear from what he subsequently wrote that the Iwakuni countryside made a profound impression on the young Doppo and he subsequently used it as the setting for his story *Kawagiri* (River Mist). Many
years later he described this period in his life in the following
terms:

> 'I can never thank my parents enough for giving me the oppor-
> tunity to grow up in the country. If I had gone with my parents
> to somewhere like Tokyo when I was seven years old, I should
> be a completely different person. I believe that ... my heart
> would not have been capable of receiving and understanding
> the noble sentiments of poetry. As it was, I spent seven of the
> happiest years in my life roaming around the fields and hills
> near my home.'

These, however, are the reflections of maturity and any inference that
Doppo was a dreamy and introspective child is negated by two facts.
His childhood nickname was Garikame or 'Scratcher', given to him
because of his habit of using his nails in fights, and, secondly, it is clear
both from what he wrote about himself and from the 'boy' characters in
his stories that he was addicted to playing at soldiers. Like Shōsaku in
The Self-Made Man, his boyhood heroes were Napoleon and
Hideyoshi.[4] Fighting and playing at soldiers may be indications of imagination, but not of sensitivity. 1878, the year the family moved to
Nishi(ki)mi, also saw the birth of Doppo's younger brother Shūji who
was destined to be a stalwart companion to his elder brother, accom-
panying him on many of his journeys and even featuring, in a minor
way, in some of Doppo's stories.

Like many boys of his period, Doppo's opportunity to carry on living
at home was limited by the considerations of education. In June 1883
his father was transferred back to the town of Yamaguchi and Doppo
was obliged to enter a new school, the Kondō Junior School. Just two
years later in July 1885, when Doppo was not yet fourteen, Sempachi

was moved again to the town of Hagi, and to avoid even more disruption of his education, Doppo was obliged to stay on as a boarder at the Yamaguchi Middle School to which he had graduated earlier the same year. Little is really known about Doppo's performance at school, but it appears that he was gifted enough to get by without having to work too hard, and he also displayed some aptitude for art. More importantly, it was during his time at Middle School that he first came into contact with western literature in the form of Japanese translations of Defoe's *Robinson Crusoe* and Verne's *20,000 Leagues Under the Sea* which he read avidly alongside his favourite Japanese novels which seem in the main to have been the medieval war chronicles such as the *Taiheiki* and the *Heike Monogatari*. Such tastes seem not unusual for the son of a *samurai* warrior and it was these Japanese novels which gave him his first youthful ambition, as he later recorded in *Shinkobunrin*, published in January 1907:

'I was a boy possessed of fierce ambition. My whole aim was to become a great general and leave my name for posterity.'

There were, of course, many other boys in Japan at that time with precisely the same ambition, as there are likely to be in any country at any time.

In 1886 the Japanese educational system was reformed, one of the consequences of which was that the Yamaguchi Middle School where Doppo studied was closed down and re-established as the Yamaguchi High School. The direct result of this as far as Doppo was concerned was that it greatly extended the period he would have to study before he reached university requirements. Being young and ambitious, he made the decision that rather than wait the extra years he would leave school and travel up to Tokyo where he hoped eventually to make his career as a politician. In this he had his father's approval. Among the young men of his time this was a common ambition stemming directly from the resurgence of national consciousness after the initial period of westernisation, and like most of them, Doppo failed to realise his hopes. However, in going to Tokyo, he was unwittingly taking the road to a very different kind of fame from the one he intended. The decision to leave home and go to Tokyo is definitely one of the turning points on which Doppo's literary career revolves although it was to be more than ten years before it bore any really worthwhile results — a period in which Doppo had a variety of experiences which were ultimately to determine the type of writer he was to become.

Doppo arrived in Tokyo in April 1887. Like Victorian London, Tokyo was the Mecca for all young men of ambition in Japan. Although under the Tokugawa rulers it had (under the name Edo) been the *de facto* capital of Japan for more than 250 years, in 1887 it had been the titular capital for less than twenty. It was the political, social and cultural centre of Japan for the new class of young Japanese anxious to participate in the formation of the new state. It was a place where fortunes could be won and names made.

Sooner or later all Japanese writers or would-be writers gravitated to Tokyo to study their craft under a master in the traditional manner and most of them continued to live there. When searching the pages of Meiji literature, it is hard to find the names of any writers who worked anywhere else in Japan, with the exception of a few country-based writers such as Miyazawa Kenji and Nagatsuka Takashi. Doppo, of course, was well aware of all this and was resolved to make the best of his opportunities.

The first year after his arrival he spent studying at a private law school in Kanda, chosen for him by his father. Training in the law was considered to be one of the ideal methods of advancement for the prospective politician. At the same time he joined the Dai Nihon Seinen Kyōkai, a youth organisation which was one of many springing up all over Japan at that time, particularly in Tokyo. This organisation published a magazine called *Seinen Shikai* and it was in issue number eight of this (March 1888) that Doppo's first known work appeared. It was entitled *Gunsho ni watare*, and was a typical piece of juvenilia urging the youth of Japan to do great deeds for the country. There are no portents in it of anything that was to come.

Although Doppo left no clear statement of his motives for doing so, he decided to leave the law school in early 1888, joining instead the English department of the Tōkyō Senmon Gakkō. This college, later to become Waseda University, had been founded in October 1882 by the statesman Ōkuma Shigenobu and originally consisted of just three departments with seventy or eighty students. Although there were more departments in 1888, the college was substantially unchanged by the time Doppo became a student there.

It seems probable that he was dissatisfied with the value of his law school training and progress and thought that the knowledge of a foreign language such as English would in the long term be of more use to him. It is clear, however, that he was still determined on a career in politics, because after a year of study, he transferred in September 1889 to the department of English and Politics. Whatever his ultimate intentions, however, Doppo used his time at college well, although in the end he left before receiving a degree. He read widely and omnivorously, ranging from books on the English constitution and the speeches of Gladstone to the works of Carlyle, the novels of Tolstoy and Dostoyevsky, and the poetry of Wordsworth.

In such time as he had left over from his college work and his reading he went for strolls in the Tokyo suburbs where he first became familiar with the scenery he was later so graphically to describe in *Musashino*. What we know of his life at this time is largely derived from *Ano jibun* (In Those Days), an autobiographical piece which Doppo published in

June 1906. It is from the pages of this work that we learn how he spent his time, what he read, and most important of all how he underwent the spiritual transformation which was to affect his whole life and his career as a writer.

Towards the end of 1889 he began to attend a nearby Christian church where he was taken by a college friend named Satō (re-named Kimura in *Ano jibun*). One should perhaps beware of statements of religious revelation, particularly when they are made in retrospect, but Doppo's account is convincing enough and indicates that he became a Christian, at first at any rate, rather through intellectual conviction than emotional. In *Ano jibun*, he says:

'I became obsessed with such questions as "Where have we come from? Where are we going? What are we? ..." The two of us (Doppo and Satō) were walking along one day discussing a multitude of things, although I don't remember what they were in any detail. In his usual grave voice Kimura (Satō) asked me:

"Don't you believe that Jesus Christ was born in Bethlehem to save mankind?" There is nothing very special in that question itself, but in my heart I felt that there was a kind of power in the word "Bethlehem" and I felt as I had never felt before.'

This account is perhaps vague enough to have the ring of truth (no high-flown construction has been placed on his earliest encounter with Christians and Christianity), and it seems a reasonable inference that his taste in western literature, particularly Wordsworth, would have tended to lead him in the direction of Christianity. Once his decision to join the church had been made, this would have had the effect of reinforcing his love of Wordsworth's poetry and the poetry would equally have reinforced his Christian beliefs.

After at least a year of attending church he was finally baptised on 4 January, 1891 by Uemura Masahisa who was the local minister. Earlier, in October 1890, Doppo had joined the Seinen Bungakkai (Young Men's Literary Society) which had been formed at the college. Every month some notable figure from Tokyo literary society would be invited along to give a talk which would later be published in the society's magazine along with members' own works. It is obvious that Doppo's interests at this period were beginning to direct themselves towards literature.

During the early part of 1891 there was trouble at the Tōkyō Senmon Gakkō with student strikes and this was no doubt a factor in Doppo's decision to leave the college at the end of March without graduating. On 1 May he returned to his parents' home (they had moved again to another small village in Yamaguchi Prefecture) where he spent two months of leisure in reading and going for walks in the mountains and on fishing trips with his brother. In addition to his beloved Wordsworth, Doppo began also to read the works of Byron, Emerson and Shakespeare.

This life of leisure could not last, however, for the Kunikida family was beginning to feel the pinch of lack of money and Sempachi could no longer afford to support his son. Doppo was obliged to look for employment. Bearing in mind Wordsworth's dictum 'I wish to be considered as a teacher, or nothing', he decided to open up a private school. This he did in October 1891 at the village of Matsushita where he taught English and mathematics to about thirty pupils. This venture was not a success, however, not least because Doppo continually pined for Tokyo life. By the beginning of 1892 he was beginning to weary of life in the country as he indicates in a letter to a friend dated 1 January, 1892:

'Last New Year I was in Tokyo and having a good time. This year I am in the country and it is not the same. It is almost as if the celebration of New Year is confined to city society, the reason perhaps being that country people are not yet used to the new calendar (i.e. the western calendar).'

In February Doppo closed down his school and in June returned to Tokyo, this time with his brother. This year in the country was, however, of great importance in Doppo's career as a writer and in his development as a man. It gave the leisure for philosophical speculation. He subsequently used this year's experiences as the basis for several of his short stories, including *Tomioka Sensei* (Teacher Tomioka) and *Shōnen no Hiai* (The Sorrows of a Young Man). His finances had also been replenished enough to enable him to live, modestly enough, for a fairly lengthy period without having to seek work. His preoccupation with religious speculation continued. In a letter to his friend Tamura Sanji dated 22 September, 1892 he wrote:

'How to live is the first question and the last. I mean this not in a physical but in a moral and ethical sense. In the words of Christianity, "Search for the kingdom of heaven".'

By the beginning of 1893 Doppo was in sore financial difficulties and had to borrow from friends to live. He was forced to live in the cheapest lodgings he could find and to search for work. Having had his fill of teaching for the time being and perhaps being subconsciously propelled towards a writing career, he succeeded in gaining a post as a reporter on the *Jiyū Shimbun*, the organ newspaper of the Jiyūtō political party. He took up his duties on 13 February, 1893, but it was to prove a disastrous mistake. We are fortunate in having a very accurate and detailed portrait of Doppo's life at this time and for the next four years, because from 2 February he began to keep a diary. This was published after his death as the *Azamuzakaru no ki* (Record of an Honest Man) and is a further indication of Doppo's desire to write. He was later to prove that he had the makings of a fine journalist, but evidently he had great personal difficulties with the staff of the *Jiyū Shimbun*, particularly

Kanemori, the head of the company which published the newspaper.
He had been working there for less than three weeks when he felt compelled to record his feelings in his diary (entry for 2 March):

>'Mr Kanemori is very cold towards me. He won't give me any
>responsibility, pays me no salary, and won't talk to me. It is
>reaching the point where there is danger of he and I being
>unable to work together.'

Having taken the job simply in order to earn a living, Doppo found
that the paper was giving him very little money at all, and even when he
did receive the salary of 3 yen on 31 March, it was not enough to keep
him going. Goaded by poverty and the frustrations of a job which, in
these circumstances at any rate, he did not like doing, Doppo reached a
momentous decision which he recorded in his diary on 21 March, 1893:

>'Last night was one of the most critical nights of my life. I
>firmly resolved to make my way in the world by writing. I will
>use all my powers to become "a teacher of mankind" through
>what I write ... I do not desire to become a famous author ... If
>I can just teach the world the truth about love, sincerity and
>labour, all my aspirations will be fulfilled.'

By now the career in politics was truly a thing of the past and in this
statement confided to his diary, we can see the fusion of two elements
which had been dominating Doppo's thought ever since leaving college,
the desire to teach and the desire to write. Four years were still to pass
before Doppo wrote his first work of fiction and even though the decision to become a writer had finally been made, the forces of economic
necessity still prevented him from taking up his pen in earnest.

At the beginning of April, Doppo resigned his post on the *Jiyū Shimbun* and went home for a month, returning to Tokyo on 8 May. The
rest of the spring and summer that year Doppo spent in earnest self-
examination and reading, living for the most part on borrowed money.
In his diary during the months of June and July, he recorded the titles
of all the books he had been reading, the most influential of which were
the inevitable Wordsworth and the works of Ivan Turgenev which he
encountered for the first time in the translations of Futabatei Shimei.[5]

Minor disaster struck in August when his father, Sempachi, lost his
job, making the financial downfall of the Kunikida family imminent
and the need for Doppo to find some remunerative work imperative.
Driven by necessity, Doppo turned to a friend whom he had met in his
days at the Tōkyō Senmon Gakkō. This was the critic and journalist,
founder of the Minyūsha publishing company, Tokutomi Sohō[6] whom
Doppo visited on 5 September.

Through an introduction given him by Tokutomi, Doppo secured a
post at the Tsuruya Gakkan school in the small township of Saeki in
Oita Prefecture, Kyushu. He was to teach English and mathematics to
about thirty pupils, together with a little German to those who wanted

to learn it, for which he was to receive the comparatively good salary of 25 yen a month. He arrived in Saeki with his brother at the end of September, and the year he was to spend at the Tsuruya Gakkan was destined to prove one of the happiest times in his short life, and perhaps the most important influence on his development as a writer.

As far as his teaching went, Doppo's time at Saeki was not particularly successful, mainly because the other teachers approved neither of his method (which was to be sharply critical and sparing of praise — the apparent opposite of his predecessor at the school) and, more importantly, because of his Christianity. At the same time, however, the job as such was sufficiently undemanding to allow him plenty of spare time for reflection and his favourite leisure pursuits of fishing and rambling in the countryside. And everywhere he took with him the poems of Wordsworth. In a later story, *Koharu* (Indian Summer), he wrote:

> 'It was during my time at Saeki that I read Wordsworth most fervently of all. I felt that, rather than a teacher, I was a pupil learning about nature with Wordsworth as my guide.'

In his diary entry for 15 January, 1894, he went even further in his praise of the English poet:

> 'Confucius, Buddha, Christ, Socrates, Plato and Wordsworth are all of the same type.'

In fact, references to Wordsworth occur frequently in Doppo's diary throughout this period and it is probable that he was never at any time, either before or after, quite so heavily influenced by him. He was also at his most fervent in his Christianity doubtless under the influence of the niggling persecutions he received at the hands of his colleagues at the school.[7] So wearisome had his life at the school become to him by the early summer of 1894 that in a letter to a friend, Ōkubo Yoshogorō, dated 27 June, he wrote:

> 'Rather than teach a hundred pupils at a salary of a hundred yen, I would find it much more rewarding to have just three pupils and be independent. Country people are a collection of fools and the beauty of the nature surrounding them does not necessarily reflect in their hearts.'

At the beginning of July 1894, just like the young teacher in *Old Gen*, Doppo moved to new lodgings near Katsura harbour, but the respite provided by this was short-lived and he finally left Saeki on 1 August, the very day that the Sino-Japanese war broke out. He was then twenty-three years old and still was no nearer to fulfilling his ambition to become a writer.

Tokutomi Sohō had helped him before and Doppo decided that he had nothing to lose by asking for his help once again. At this time Tokutomi was in charge of the *Kokumin Shimbun* (People's Newspaper) which he had founded in 1890 as a progressive, democratic paper for the middle classes. However, as reports came in of the worsening relations between Japan and China, the tone of the paper, under Tokutomi's influence, became increasingly jingoistic. Doppo's appeal to Tokutomi for help was for a second time not in vain and he was taken on the staff of the *Kokumin Shimbun* as a reporter, with the aim of making himself 'the ideal reporter'. Soon after his appointment he was sent to join the warship Chiyoda-maru[8] to act as a war correspondent.

The Chiyoda-maru was basically a patrol vessel and seldom directly involved in front-line fighting. Nevertheless it provided a golden opportunity for Doppo to demonstrate his talents both as a reporter and as a writer. He hit upon the idea of addressing his despatches in the form of letters to his brother which, on publication in the *Kokumin Shimbun*, had the effect of summoning public attention. After his death in 1908, all Doppo's despatches from the Chiyoda-maru (which was in fact the second ship on which he served) were collected and published under the title *Aitei Tsūshin* (Despatches to my Beloved Brother).

These reports have some historical importance, but a glance at the despatch headings reveals that Doppo was not entirely concerned with military matters, a considerable number of them being concerned with ship-board life and the customs of the people in the ports which the Chiyoda-maru visited. It would be understandable if a patriotic young Japanese such as Doppo engaged, but not actively, in a short and successful war, were to be carried away by martial ardour and jingoism. Such, however, was not the case with Doppo who above all else was a humanitarian. The prospect of human confrontation and sudden death had a numbing effect on his mind and soul. In his diary he recorded his feelings (entry for 6 November, 1894):

> 'I am forgetting all about my beloved nature ... As I engage in war, I am becoming almost devoid of feeling. I once took great pleasure in minute examination of nature, but now I have become indifferent to it.'

Speedy victory for Japan in the war with China meant that by March 1895 Doppo was back in Tokyo having resumed his job on the *Kokumin Shimbun* with increased reputation. In fact, so greatly had his reputation increased that when a post on the editorial board of the *Kokumin no Tomo* (The Nation's Friend), a periodical published by Tokutomi's Minyūsha, fell vacant, Tokutomi had no hesitation in appointing Doppo. This was in April 1895. This appointment was indirectly to lead him to the grand and tragic passion of his life.

At the beginning of June, Doppo, along with reporters from the *Mainichi Shimbun* and the *Kokumin Shimbun* was invited to visit a hospital run by a Dr Sasaki and his wife, prominent Tokyo socialites, near the Nihon-bashi. The Sasakis had a daughter named Nobuko who was born in 1878 and was destined to become a kind of *femme fatale* of her age.[9] Although only seventeen at the time of their first meeting, she quickly captivated Doppo who thereafter became a frequent visitor to the Sasaki home. They quickly fell in love and from July onwards Nobuko's name appears in Doppo's diary more and more frequently. She even visited him at his lodgings in one of the poorer parts of Tokyo, a very unusual thing for a girl in her position and indicative of a remarkably strong, or rather head-strong, character. The first revelation of his love appears in his diary entry for 1 August, 1895:

> 'My life has been set on a completely different path. We have fallen in love. Last night Nobuko came to see me. We talked about our dreams of life in Hokkaido and found that we are of the same mind. We vowed that we would be together for the rest of our lives.'

So much for young love, but Nobuko's parents had different ideas. Doppo and Nobuko may have set their hearts on making a new life for themselves farming in Hokkaido, but the Sasakis had their social position to consider and a newspaper man at Doppo's level was hardly a suitable match for their daughter. They also considered, rightly so as it was to prove, that Nobuko was not old enough to consider marriage, whoever proposed it. If she were to marry, they had more suitable candidates already in mind. However, with the ready support of Nobuko herself and friends the couple were able to defy Nobuko's parents and fled to Musashino where they spent August together 'in a dream of love'.

With the aid of Endō Yoki-ko, a close friend of Nobuko, the couple finalised their plans to go to Hokkaido, get land and set up their farm. They set out on the first stage of the long journey in early September 1895, but, unfortunately for them, Nobuko's father had got wind of what was planned and he set out in pursuit. However, it turned out happily enough, for the two of them were able to persuade him when he caught up with them that as they were so much in love, marriage was the only course open to them. Nobuko's father reluctantly agreed provided that she returned with him to Tokyo while Doppo set out for Hokkaido alone to see what the prospects were. And thus on 16 September he set out for Hokkaido with high hopes, totally unaware of the personal tragedy that lay ahead.

In the last days of the nineteenth century, Hokkaido was to the Japanese what Australia had been to the Englishmen of the eighteenth and nineteenth centuries. The second largest of the four islands which make up Japan, Hokkaido was at this period still largely an untamed wilderness of forest and river. Land was cheap and any young man who was prepared to work hard and endure the loneliness could make himself a good living from agriculture. This was a theme which Doppo later used in *Gyūniku to Bareishō* (Meat and Potatoes) where he was writing from personal experience. As soon as he arrived, he wrote to Nobuko in the most glowing terms about the land he found:

> 'This is a land you will love, a land for you and I to bury

ourselves in! Come! Come! As quick as you can. The land
awaits you!'

On 19 September Doppo arrived in Sapporo, capital of Hokkaido,
and shortly afterwards he visited Nitobe Inazō, Professor of Agriculture
at the Sapporo Agricultural School, armed with a letter of introduction
provided by the famous Christian thinker, Uchimura Kansō, with
whom Doppo had become acquainted a short time before. With
Nitobe's aid, Doppo surveyed and chose for himself a piece of land by
the Sorachi river. All looked set fair for the future, but in Tokyo things
were not going as he had hoped. He and Nobuko had been successful in
persuading her father to agree to their marriage, but her mother remained uneasy and as time went by her opposition hardened.

When Doppo returned to Sapporo on 27 September after surveying
his land, he found letters awaiting him from Nobuko's father, her friend
Yoki-ko and his brother Shūji. They bore disturbing tidings. Apparently Nobuko's mother had been so furious that she had gone to the in-
credible lengths of suggesting to her daughter that she commit suicide
rather than marry Doppo. Furthermore, the letters reported, Nobuko
was going to America. Worse was yet to come because that very evening
a letter arrived from Nobuko herself mentioning that she had indeed
contemplated suicide, but on reflection had decided to go to America.

Confronted with these hysterical letters, one can well imagine
Doppo's feelings. Forgetting all about Hokkaido and his prospects
there, he hurried back to Tokyo in the hope of sorting matters out and
prevailing on Nobuko to change her mind. All was not yet lost.
Throughout the last part of September and early October, Doppo bom-
barded Nobuko with letters urging her to reconsider, to remember their
love and to marry him. Nobuko herself, a creature of fragile and fickle
emotions, was quickly won over and eventually Doppo's persistence
melted away her mother's resistance. She agreed to their marriage but
on stringent conditions — they were to leave Tokyo and not to return
for at least a year, and during that time they were to have no correspondence with any members of Nobuko's family. On 11 November
Doppo recorded in his diary:

'At seven o'clock today, Nobuko and I were married. My love
has finally triumphed and I have made her my own.'

Uemura Masahisa, the minister who had baptised Doppo, performed
the wedding ceremony at the Sasaki home and shortly afterwards they
left for the honeymoon in Zushi. To complete the couple's happiness,
in January 1896 Doppo's first volume, the first part of an unpretentious
biography of Benjamin Franklin, was published by the Minyūsha. Now
he had published some articles and a full length book; yet with only
twelve years of his life remaining, Doppo had not written a single word
of the poetry and fiction on which his fame as a writer rests.

On the last day of 1895 Doppo recorded in his diary his aims and hopes for the year ahead, one of which was to reach a harmonious understanding with the Sasaki family. This hope he was indeed to realise but at the highest price possible, the loss of Nobuko herself. By March 1896 the couple were driven by economic necessity to break their promise to Nobuko's parents and return to Tokyo. A reconciliation was effected, but the pressures on the marriage from Nobuko's parents obviously had their effect on the girl herself. She began to quarrel with Doppo and was often in tears until finally on 12 April when she was with Doppo and his brother at a church service (the Sasakis also were Christians), she fled from her seat in tears never to return to him. This time Doppo, though heartbroken, was unable to prevail on the unstable Nobuko and in his diary for 24 April he recorded:

> 'Our relationship as man and wife has today ceased for ever. I met Nobuko yesterday and she confirmed that her only desire was for divorce.'

In this and similar passages from the diary, we can see the very pattern of thoughts and emotions which were to recur in *Daisansha* (Third Party), the story Doppo was to write seven years later in 1903. And so Nobuko passed from his life for ever, but she was never to pass from his heart.

In May 1896 Doppo went away to Kyoto where he spent three months with the help of Uchimura Kanzō in trying to get over his tragedy. However, at the end of August he returned to Tokyo to take up his old position with the Minyūsha and set up house with his brother Shūji in the village of Shibuya where he was to live for almost a year. This was the setting for *Musashino*, a later product of all his countryside rambles as he tried to forget Nobuko. In this he was unsuccessful as his diary entry for 15 September shows:

> 'This very day twelve months ago Nobuko and I were at Shiohara (on the way to Hokkaido). Now she has abandoned me. Her heart is cold towards me. Most of the tragedies of human life are a direct result of the human character and this, perhaps, is the greatest tragedy of all.'

Now Doppo increasingly sought to alleviate the anguish of his soul in writing poetry which was published in both the *Kokumin Shimbun* and the *Kokumin no Tomo*. Quite naturally this poetry was preoccupied with his thoughts of Nobuko:

> 'When I hear the patter of the rain and the distant wind sighing across the fields, it is of last year I think. All night through I think of it.'

And so the months of quiet seclusion and contemplation at Shibuya passed and as 1897 progressed and more and more of Doppo's poems began to find their way into print, so he began to acquire something of a reputation in a modest sort of way. At last from the roots of personal tragedy his literary career was beginning to blossom. Poetry, however, was not enough for Doppo whose experiences, he felt, were better recorded in prose. It seems likely that this conviction occurred to Doppo during the months of April and May 1897 when, in the company of his friend the novelist Tayama Katai, he went on a trip to the city of Nikko, famous for its shrines and cherry blossoms. Although essentially on a sight-seeing trip, Doppo spent much of his time in writing, the ultimate product being his first work of fiction, *Gen Oji* (Old Gen), which was modelled on an experience he encountered during his days in Saeki. This was published in the magazine *Bungei Kurabu* in August 1897, and it is with this work that we can say that Doppo's literary career truly began.

It was also during 1897 that Doppo met the girl who was later to become his second wife, Enomoto Haruko. While Doppo was away on his trip to Nikko, Shūji acquired new lodgings for them both in Tokyo and when he returned in June, Doppo discovered that Haruko and her father, an artist, were among their next-door neighbours. Haruko was in many ways similar to Nobuko, being of very emotional temperament, but had a stability which Nobuko lacked and it seems more than likely Doppo turned to her hoping to find again the love he had once experienced with Nobuko. Although they were eventually married in August 1898, Doppo found trouble again with his prospective mother-in-law who was as opposed to the marriage as Nobuko's mother had been. However, until the time of the marriage Doppo seems to have spent almost all his time in writing. *Wasure-enu Hitobito* (Those Unforgettable People), *Kawagiri* (River Mist), *Musashino* and a stream of other works flowed from his pen during 1898, but although these began to acquire him a reputation, one problem they did not solve — his financial problem. This was made worse after his marriage when he had a wife to support.

During the spring of 1899, through an introduction given him by the journalist Yano Ryūkei, Doppo obtained a post on the *Hōchi Shimbun* newspaper where he was given responsibility for the coverage of politics and foreign affairs. This post he held until April 1900, but although it provided him with the means to live, the year on the *Hōchi Shimbun* left him either with too little time or insufficient inclination to write very much. The main event of that year in his life was personal rather than public for on 29 October, 1899, Haruko gave birth to a daughter who was named Sadako.

By the standards of his output during 1898, the two years between 1900 and 1901 were unproductive for Doppo. After resigning his post on the *Hōchi Shimbun* in April 1900, he took a succession of jobs with different newspapers, but was never completely free of financial worries, at one time being forced to send his wife back to her parental home because he was unable to support her. His apparent lack of progress either in the field of journalism or writing began to wear him down. At the beginning of 1902 he wrote to a friend:

'The task before me is so long, and my life is too short.'

His eldest son Torao was born on 5 January, 1902, and shortly afterwards, with the help of two friends, Doppo took over a villa near the town of Kamakura. There, free for a while from domestic anxieties and financial worries, he was able to devote his time to writing. This was one of the most productive periods of his career and during the first few months of 1902 he wrote a whole series of what have come to be regarded as his best works, including *Unmei Ronsha*.

As the year went by, financial problems began to catch up with him again, and when, in December 1902, his friend Yano Ryūkei asked him to become editor of a new magazine he was planning, Doppo was only too willing to return to Tokyo and accept. Thus, in March 1903 Doppo became editor of Japan's first 'graphic' magazine, the *Tōyō Gahō*. The magazine did not do very well at first, but as time went by it became more and more popular especially during the period of the Russo-Japanese war in 1904-5 when the pictures and illustrations it was able to publish proved a powerful selling point.

During the course of 1903 the stories which Doppo had written during his time at Kamakura began to be published together with new ones such as *Jonan* (Woman Trouble) which was written on the basis of his experiences at Kamakura. Altogether this was one of the busiest periods of his life and the strain began to tell on his health to which the death of his father in January 1904 was an additional blow. The outbreak of Japan's successful war with Russia in February 1904 was the signal for a renewed outburst of work for the magazine from which there was to be no respite until the cessation of hostilities in 1905.

In April of that year Doppo went back to the town of his birth, Chōshi, to recuperate and doubtless had time to reflect on what he had achieved. He had had a modest success with his writing career which had gained him a reputation to be proud of even if it did not match, nor was ever to match, that of great contemporaries such as Natsume Sōseki; he had a good job which he enjoyed doing; and he had a loyal wife whom he loved and who had borne him, by then, three children. He was still young, being only thirty-four years of age, and could look forward to ever-increasing success and prosperity. That, at least, is how it must have seemed to Doppo during the April of 1905, but unknown to him he was fast sinking into an illness which just three years later would take him to the grave.

By the middle of 1907 the troubling lung condition which Doppo attributed to 'three or four years of the dust of the Tokyo streets' forced him to seek medical advice. One doctor suggested that there was something wrong with his throat and another that he was suffering from catarrhal congestion of the lungs. These were days in which many medical men differed over such matters, but these doctors concurred in one thing at least — that Doppo should do everything in his power to get out of Tokyo. He took their advice and rented a house from a friend named Sugita at Mito in Ibaraki Prefecture, arriving in September 1907 and staying there until November of the same year. Sugita came to visit him frequently and lent money to the still impecunious Doppo; writing, even modestly successful writing, did not pay well.

The last three years of Doppo's life were divided between writing yet more stories and holidays of various lengths in hot springs such as Yugahara where it was hoped that his health would improve. The improvement never came, however, and at the beginning of 1908 it became apparent that he would have to enter hospital where racking cough and soaring fever soon indicated that he was suffering from tuberculosis. There was no hope and on the evening of 23 June 1908 Kunikida Doppo breathed his last, at the age of only thirty-seven. Next day his body was cremated and five days later in an impressive ceremony copies of some of his best works were buried with his ashes.

Throughout the rest of 1908 and 1909 most of the literary periodicals honoured Doppo in the traditional way by devoting special memorial issues to the study of his life and work — a fitting end to one who though never a consistently great writer had done more than most to further the art of the short story in Japan, and one which Doppo himself would no doubt have appreciated.

★ ★ ★

It is quite possible that to the general western reader the Japanese short story or *tampen shōsetsu* will prove something of a disappointment in terms of the literature he is used to reading. There is certainly nothing even in the most heavily western-influenced Japanese short-story writing to put the reader in mind of a Somerset Maugham or a Mark Twain, both of whom were writing at roughly the same time as Doppo and stood very much in the centre of the traditions of short-story writing in their own respective countries.

The typical Japanese short story is concerned not so much with plot as with theme and very little attention is paid to such important western tenets as characterisation. For this reason it is often difficult to distinguish one story from another, and sometimes even to distinguish one writer from another. It is generally true that modern Japanese fiction, short stories in particular, has produced very few 'characters' which stand out in the memory and there are many reasons why this should be so, not least the fact that the Japanese as a whole are very little concerned with the western cult of the individual.

Psychological distinctions apart, it is important to consider that the short story in the west developed over many centuries, whereas in Japan it was virtually an unknown form until after the Meiji Restoration in

1868. This in turn meant that it was bound to be somewhat artificial in its development because there were no roots in native literary tradition onto which it could be grafted. In many senses, the nearest approach to the short story in pre-Meiji literary history in the form it developed after 1868 was the *zuihitsu* genre. *Zuihitsu* (random jottings) writing is basically concerned with the factual recording of travels and incidents and the writer's reactions and feelings about them. This strong strain of the autobiographical in *zuihitsu* writing, the concentration on the personal feelings of the writer, is one of the most evident features of the Meiji short story.

Doppo himself was primarily concerned with setting down his own experiences and feelings about life in a but thinly disguised fictional format where elements of the factual are constantly intruding. The characters which appear in his stories are nearly always real people known to him given assumed names and used as a vehicle for conveying the author's ideas and feelings. Characterisation and plot as they are understood in western terms are very much secondary considerations to the revelation of this personal experience and feeling. Before attempting a more detailed analysis of Doppo's fiction as it is revealed in this anthology, however, it is essential to gain some idea of the world in which he lived and the development of literature in his society.

Kunikida Doppo was born in and lived through the greater part of perhaps the most exciting period of Japanese history — the Meiji period (1868-1912) which takes its name from the Emperor who reigned during that time. For a period of more than two hundred years dating from the late 1630s, Japan had undergone a time of voluntary isolation, its only communication with the outside world being through contacts with China and a small colony of Dutch traders living on the island of Deshima in Nagasaki harbour.

Such books as the authorities allowed the Dutch to bring into Japan gave the government at least some idea of what was happening in Europe, but basically the Japanese were completely ignorant of the West until the early 1850s when an American expedition under Commodore Perry and subsequent similar forays by European nations at last succeeded in prising Japan into the modern world. Their motive was in the main that of self-interest, the desire to establish trading concessions for themselves in Japan as they had already done in China, but the Japanese showed from the beginning, unlike the Chinese, a desire to learn from the West and to compete with it on its own terms. Equal competition with the western powers in the latter half of the nineteenth century meant that the Japanese had to acquire some sort of equality in terms of what the West valued most — economic and military power.

The story of the history of the Meiji period is fundamentally, therefore, (although this is necessarily an over-simplification) the story of Japan's struggle to achieve equality with the West in the fields of economics, technology and armaments. Such was the success of this struggle that by 1904-5 Japan was able to defeat the armed might of Russia in war. No such process of modernisation and adaptation, however, can be achieved without repercussions in all aspects of society, and to achieve what they did (and what had taken the West many centuries to achieve) the Japanese were obliged to import a whole series of measures which were alien to the historical character of the nation, notably the introduction of a democratic or semi-democratic system of government.

Enthusiastic acceptance at first of western technology and ideas in the 1860s and 70s was followed by a short period of absorption and eventually by a fierce nationalistic reaction. Naturally these basically political trends were reflected in all other aspects of Japanese society which western ideas affected — not least the world of literature — creating a society which was in many ways immature, but always larger than life.

The writer of fiction and poetry in Meiji Japan was something of a social outcast in the sense that he was not making a positive contribution to the economic and technical effort so necessary to achieve parity with the West. His reaction to this was in part defensive manifesting itself in a desire to band together with others involved in the same field, where at least his thoughts and views would receive a sympathetic hearing. In literary terms, therefore, the Meiji period was the age of the *bundan*, or literary circle. Small groups of writers harbouring some particular literary theory would hold meetings and publish magazines, containing their own works, which quite often had no readership outside the members of the circle to which they belonged.

Confusing though the political situation may have been, the literary situation was much worse, although of course of much less significance to the fabric of society. In the early days of passionate enthusiasm for all things western, many western novels and books of poetry were brought into Japan and translated. These translations were often imperfect and naturally this impaired the Japanese understanding of them. Often too the works translated were not representative of their authors in any meaningful way.

Literary forms and traditions which had taken hundreds of years to develop in the West were introduced in waves and were rapidly superseded by new forms and traditions, even before the earlier ones had been properly digested and understood. This was bread and butter to the literary circles whose arguments about the validity of particular types of western literature often assumed the proportions of political diatribes. Tempers were easily frayed in such a manner that in 1905 Itō Sachio and Nagatsuka Takashi were able to indulge in a furious slanging match over such a seemingly minor issue as their preferences for a particular type of *waka* poetry. Moreover, these were men who were the best of friends and belonged to the same literary circle (the Negishi Tanka-kai). Itō's abuse of Nagatsuka was minor in comparison with what he had to say about the rival Myōjō poetry group of Yosano Tekkan.

The major problem for the student of Meiji literature which is raised by the arguments of the *bundan* is that this basically polemical approach to literature has led to the artificial categorisation of the literary history of the Meiji period. Japanese literary historians have in many senses subscribed to these categorisations set up in the first place by the *bundan* themselves so that their books are littered with terms such as 'Romanticism', 'Naturalism', 'Anti-Naturalism', 'Neo-Classicism' and 'Neo-Idealism' referring to writers whose works are very much less well-defined than the inclusion of them under such definite headings would lead one to suppose.

It would be tedious and impractical to attempt here a potted history of the Japanese novel in the Meiji period and readers who are interested in this are referred to Okazaki Yoshie's book *Japanese Literature in the Meiji Period* where a good outline is provided.[10] Some observations on developments up to Doppo's time, however, are perhaps not inappropriate. During the first few years of the Meiji period, western literature made little real impact, mostly because there had not been time to build up a representative and meaningful corpus of works translated into Japanese. Thus, many of the forms of fiction of the Edo period (1603-1868) (generically known as *gesaku* fiction — cheap, popular fiction for the masses) continued to flourish, typified by the works of Kanagaki Robun (1828-92) notably his novel *Seiyō Dōchū Hizakurige* published in 1870 which was a parody of a famous Edo period comic novel. It is difficult to say exactly when this type of novel died out, if indeed it ever did during the Meiji period up to at least the 1890s. It rapidly became apparent, however, as more and more western works were translated that these old literary forms and styles were not meeting the needs of the age.

Running parallel with the *gesaku* novel were two other general forms whose chief function was in effect to bridge the transition between the old-style novel writing of men like Kanagaki and the new styles which were to emerge in the 1890s. The first of these forms was the translated novel — translations of western novels which the Japanese considered representative and which were designed to serve as works of art in their own right.

A glance at the authors who were translated between 1875 and 1885 is sufficient to show how suspect the Japanese concept of the representative really was: Verne, Defoe, Lytton, Dumas, Disraeli and Pushkin were the main ones, although the works of Scott and Tolstoy were also translated. The second form was that of the political novel which flourished roughly between 1880 and 1890 and, loosely speaking, dealt with political life in its widest sense. Such novels were basically the by-product of an increasing concern with democratic rights and political ideology. It is evident that by the late 1880s any concept of the novel as a vehicle of genuine entertainment had been lost in a multitude of intellectual ideals derived from the ever-increasing volume of translations of western literature. During the 1890s there is no doubt that the main force in Japanese fiction, despite some reaction in favour of the novel styles of the Edo period, was that of what is generally termed 'Romanticism' by the Japanese literary critics. This was the period in which the influence of the English romantic poets such as Wordsworth and Byron and the French Romantic novelists was at its most marked. It is also the period in which Doppo himself began to write.

In any consideration of Doppo's works it is important to remember that unlike most writers of his time he was not a member of any of the *bundan*, although he had many friends such as Tayama Katai who were. In this sense his pen-name of 'one who walks alone' is very appropriate. He would most certainly have been aware of current ideas and theories of literature, but he was not as obsessed by them as many of his contemporaries. His approach to his writing was essentially intensely personal and not cluttered by any consideration of what was fashionable or proper in a literary sense. He has been described, rather meaninglessly, by Japanese literary critics as a 'Romantic' who was at the same time one of the 'Pioneers of Naturalism'. What this probably means in terms of his development is that by temperament and inclination he was a romantic who through a succession of embittering experiences was disillusioned into taking a more 'realistic' view of life. Certainly, inasmuch as nearly all Doppo's stories are autobiographical, it is only reasonable to expect them to reflect the increasing bitterness of Doppo's life.

For critical purposes Doppo's stories have generally been divided into two periods: those stories written up to the time of *Gyūniku to Bareishō* (Meat and Potatoes) in 1901 which are labelled 'romantic'; and those written afterwards which are labelled as 'naturalistic' or 'realistic'. Such a division is rather too neat, however, and ignores such stories as *Haru no Tori* (Bird of Spring) which although written in 1904 is closer in theme to those stories written before 1901 than to those written later. There is at least one theme running through all Doppo's stories and that is the powerlessness of human beings in the face of the universe and the forces of nature which it engenders. It is in terms of this theme that Doppo's fiction can best be interpreted and understood.

Takibi (The Bonfire) (1896), *Hoshi* (The Stars) (1896) and *Shisō* (Poetic Images) (1898) are properly not works of fiction at all. They are basically embryonic works which can best be described, although not entirely satisfactorily so, as 'prose poems'. They are lyrical expressions of Doppo's thoughts about the universe and, as such, are valuable pointers to his future works because they introduce three distinctly separate attitudes which were to recur in more fully developed forms.

Takibi introduces in the form of the old wanderer the idea of which Doppo was subsequently to make the most use — that of a man buffeted by fate and the powers of nature, wandering the countryside with no purpose as an abject failure. The attitude implied by *Hoshi*, however, is more hopeful for here Doppo presents a man who defies the universe as 'the very incarnation of freedom'. There is even the feeling that some of the powers of nature are on his side.

Shisō is a calmer piece, really no more than a collection of thoughts perhaps later to be developed into longer stories. The underlying thought behind the four pieces is basically Buddhist, carrying as it does the strong message of the transience of all life. There is, however, in the story of the seeds a ready parallel with the Christian parable of the sower which is perhaps indicative of Christrian influence.

Gen Oji (Old Gen) (1897), although Doppo's first work of fiction, is perhaps his fullest expression of the idea first put forward in *Takibi*. In this story the character of the old boatman is Doppo's nearest approach to the creation of the figure of tragedy, for although many of Doppo's other stories contain the same elements of tragedy, Gen is the only character of whom it could truthfully be said that the tragedy was not in any sense of his own making. The sub-plot figure of Kishū is equally tragic because he came to his plight not through natural disasters as did Gen, but through human unkindness and intolerance. Gen's tragedy is fulfilled when he hangs himself, but the last lines of the story indicate that Kishū's tragedy will continue for many years to come.

Gen Oji also introduces the theme of suicide which again was to recur throughout Doppo's works. In this case the suicide is not seen as a form of escape, but as the natural culmination of tragedy, the logical conclusion. This inevitability is the real stuff of tragedy whereas the other characters in the stories of this anthology who commit suicide seem to have only themslves to blame for their position and could find other alternatives. In this sense, and allied to the fine structure of the story, the economy of language and the lyrical beauty of the descriptive passages, *Gen Oji* was perhaps the most complete work Doppo ever wrote.

Musashino (1898) does not easily fit into any study of Doppo's work, because it is basically so unlike anything else he wrote. It is simply a *zuihitsu* style description of Doppo's rambles on the Musashino plain, and has little to recommend it to western taste apart from some fine passages of scenic description. It only gains poignancy when considered against the fact that Doppo wrote it only shortly after losing Nobuko. It is, nevertheless, much admired by the Japanese themselves possibly because it is only they who can truly appreciate its very 'Japanese' nature. In terms of Doppo's view of the universe, the other 'Saeki

period' works, *Wasure-enu Hitobito* (Those Unforgettable People)
(1898), *Kawagiri* (River Mist) (1898), *Shikagari* (The Deer Hunt)
(1898) and *Haru no Tori* (Bird of Spring) (1904) follow the general lines
laid down in *Gen Oji* with certain important additions. *Haru no Tori* is
included in the category of 'Saeki period' works because although not
written until 1904 it is set against the background of Saeki. All these
stories are basically autobiographical.

The new element of Doppo's view of the universe which appears in
these stories, particularly in *Kawagiri* and *Haru no Tori*, is that it is
possible to escape from the ravages of fate if only by suicide. Rokuzō in
Haru no Tori is every bit as unfortunate as Gen, but he is not depicted
as a character to be pitied, but as something which is almost heavenly,
'a messenger of the gods' in fact. *Shikagari* is fundamentally not a work
of tragedy, however, even though a tragic element is included. Tetsuya's
madness is quite irrelevant to a charmingly evocative story of a deer-
hunt and is in fact its only real blemish.

There is no doubt that Doppo's idea of the universe as portrayed in
these 'Saeki period' stories is derived very much from Wordsworth, the
most open admission of which is the account of his poem *There Was a
Boy* in *Haru no Tori*. The other basic theme running through *Haru no
Tori*, *Takibi* and other stories is the innocence of childhood which again
derives from Wordsworth and begins to disappear from Doppo's fiction
as the influence of Wordsworth waned after the turn of the century.

Strangely enough, however, the influence of Christianity (and it was
at this period that Doppo was most fervent in his Christianity) is absent
from these early stories which is perhaps an indication that Wordsworth
was more important an influence and what he believed of Christianity
was derived from Wordsworth. All the other stories in this anthology
are extensions of Doppo's view of the hostility of the universe with only
very subtle variations of style rather than theme.

The degraded hero of *Jonan* (Woman Trouble) (1903) is different
from Gen only in that the fate which befalls him can be seen as almost
entirely his own fault. It is in this that we can best see the development
in Doppo's writing over the six-year period separating the two stories.
Gen in *Gen Oji* and Toyokichi in *Kawagiri* are portrayed very much as
victims of circumstances, but even in *Kawagiri* there is the suggestion
that it is the weakness in Toyokichi's character which is responsible for
his final downfall. As the stories progress towards *Jonan* we can see this
emphasis on human frailty ever increasing, notably in *Maboroshi* (Phantoms) (1898) and *Daisansha* (Third Party) (1903). The watershed of this
development is to be found in *Gyūniku to Bareishō* (Meat and Potatoes)
(1901) which is Doppo's closest approach to a 'story of ideas'. It is not
Masao's fault that he became disillusioned and cynical, but the source
of his bitterness ultimately lies within him. *Hibon naru Bonjin* (The
Self-Made Man) (1903) picks up the other thread of Doppo's attitude

towards the universe in what is the only genuinely cheerful story in this anthology. Shōsaku is a man who is very much subjected to the bitter blows of fate, but he uses the power of human character to fight and successfully achieve the fulfilment of his ambitions.

Although obsessed by tragedy, Doppo's stories contain a certain humour, especially in such stories as *Daisansha*, *Gyunikū to Bareishō* and *Shikagari* all of which have several flashes of ironic wit used either to provide light relief or in some cases to pinpoint the tragedy. This is an element in his writing usually ignored by Japanese literary historians, but nevertheless one of his most charming qualities. Doppo's fiction, then, reveals him as a man who suffered more than his fair share of life's blows; more perhaps than with any other writer of his period, his stories represent the painful working out of his own philosophy, step by step, and we can thus gain from them an accurate picture of his development. The reader is left to draw his own conclusions.

1. Doppo is Kunikida's most frequently used pen-name and literally means 'One who walks alone'. His childhood given name was Kamekichi which in 1889 he changed to Tetsuo. For purpose of simplicity 'Doppo' is used throughout this introduction.
2. This short biography is based on two sources: Fukuda Kiyohito's *Kunikida Doppo* (Meiji Shoin, Tokyo, 1970), a well-balanced and illustrated biography; and Sakamoto Hiroshi's *Kunikida Doppo* (Yūseidō, Tokyo, 1969), an authoritative, but somewhat polemical work. Doppo's paternity is discussed in Fukuda pp. 15-21 and Sakamoto pp. 1-12. They reach opposite conclusions.
3. Authorities differ on the reading of this place name. Some have Nishimi, some Nishikimi.
4. Toyotomi Hideyoshi (1536-98). A warrior and statesman who played an important part in the unification of Japan.
5. Futabatei Shimei (1864-1909) was one of Japan's most famous novelists of the Meiji period and, with Tsubouchi Shōyō (1859-1935), is regarded as one of the best translators of western literature.
6. Tokutomi Sohō (1863-1957) was in his long life a figure of great controversy. Founder of the *Kokumin Shimbun* newspaper and ardent nationalist, he had a sensational quarrel with his brother Tokutomi Roka, a humanitarian novelist, and was a firm supporter of the military regime in Japan during the 1930s and 40s.
7. For the full details of Doppo's relations with his colleagues at the Tsuruya Gakkan see Fukuda *op. cit.* pp. 60-70.
8. 'Maru' is a term applied to Japanese ships and is loosely equivalent to 'H.M.S.' although it is not applied exclusively to naval vessels.
9. Arishima Takeo (1878-1923) later used Nobuko as the model for his famous story *Aru Onna* (A Certain Woman).
10. *Japanese Literature in the Meiji Period* by Okazaki Yoshie. Translated by V. H. Viglielmo. Tokyo, Ōbunsha, 1955. The whole of Meiji literature is covered in this book, but for the novel see pp. 111-316.

1

River Mist

Kawagiri (River Mist) first appeared in issue number 372 of the *Kokumin no tomo* in August 1898, and is arguably the best short story that Doppo ever wrote. Unlike most of his fiction, *Kawagiri* is told as a straight story without the intervention of a narrator or any other personalised element. In addition, Doppo was describing in this story the scenery around the village of Nishi(ki)mi in Iwakuni District where he was brought up, and the river of the title is the River Nishi(ki)mi which is famous for its river mists. This gives the story an authentic and graphic quality.

All the elements of Doppo's 'romantic' period are present: the innocence of childhood, the miseries of the wandering vagabond and the powerful, cleansing imagery of water. Heavily under the influence of Wordsworth and other English romantic poets at this period of his life, Doppo was never able to resist the tragic ending, but although in some senses the ending of *Kawagiri* is tragic, there is a definite feeling in the final lines that perhaps after all Toyokichi is escaping from the sorrows of his life. This same feeling is present in other Doppo stories, notable *Haru no Tori* (Bird of Spring) where the idea of 'escape' is explicitly stated, but in *Kawagiri* the reader is left to draw his own conclusions.

At the age of twenty-one, Ueda Toyokichi left home to seek his fortune. Since then twenty long years had passed .....

On the day of Toyokichi's departure all the townsfolk turned out to give him a good send-off and wish him good luck, and so, dreaming dreams of the golden future that was to be his, he left the old castle town that had been his home for so long, without any special regret. In his impatience to get started, he made straight for Tokyo without bothering to make the diversion for sight-seeing in Kyoto and Osaka, and when all his friends and relatives heard of his safe arrival, they held a celebration and congratulated each other on his success so far.

A discordant note, however, was sounded by an old man named Namiki Zenbei, who was known among the townsfolk by the nickname 'Whitebeard-of-the-cedar-grove', or 'Whitebeard' for short.

'That Toyokichi will never achieve anything,' he said. 'Give him five or ten years and I guarantee he'll be running back here with his tail between his legs. Just you mark my words!'

'Why do you say that?' asked one of Toyokichi's friends, but the old man did not reply. He just tugged at the snow-white beard which had earned him his nickname and laughed unkindly. It was a laugh which lacked any real sense of humour.

Let me tell you a little about this old man. As I have said, he was generally known by his nickname rather than by his real one and folk thought him a very peculiar character, as indeed his nickname implied. His beard was snowy white, but he was otherwise a small and rather grubby old man of hardy and robust constitution, for all his seventy years. All who saw him standing silently in the cedar grove with his small, round eyes glittering in the gloom could not help but think him weird and ominous. It was not just the man himself. The cedar grove which stood in the grounds of the old *samurai* mansion where Whitebeard now lived, had a reputation for the eerie dating way back before his birth. There was one tree in particular which over hundreds of years had grown so big that it took five men with arms outstreched to encompass the full extent of its roots. Standing in a corner of the grounds with other trees round it, it soared into the sky, forming a kind of melancholy focal point for the other, lesser, trees.

Ever since his youth, Zenbei had been noted for his sharp tongue and he was one of a family remarkable for their eccentricities and manner of speech which others found hard to understand. And the older he got, the sharper his tongue became.

'That wretch is not long for this world!' He made such gloomy prophecies about others without turning a hair, and, strangely enough, he was often right. If you wanted to make a mystery of it, you could say that he was endowed with critical eyes which could see into the world of the spirit, but to tell the truth, his powers stemmed rather from a sharp, intuitive faculty. Since the townsfolk thought him something of a marvel, he grew to take more and more notice of other people's characters and what befell them, so that his interest and confidence in such matters increased until in the end he became very skilled. But he never went in for divination or anything like that.

Well, Toyokichi had never had much to do with this Whitebeard, but even so Whitebeard had seen fit to make a prophecy about him — a prophecy which was to be fulfilled after the passing of twenty years. There were, if you remember, three ingredients to this prophecy: 'He'll never achieve anything'; 'Give him five or ten years'; and 'He'll come running back here with his tail between his legs'.

I have already described in a little detail how the ill-natured Whitebeard's eyes glared out from the gloom of the cedar grove like a weasel's, but it remains for me to say that Toyokichi himself was a good man. He had talent certainly, but he lacked staying-power. Or rather, he did have staying-power as such, but somewhere in the core of his being there was a weakness and he was apt to miss out on essentials. He was rather like a stick which, although struck against an object with full force, produces a dull thud rather than the clear crack you would expect. He was a good man, full of the best intentions, but he lacked courage, or perhaps it would be better to say that he lacked spirit.

For twenty years Toyokichi tried his hand at a succession of things, mostly working in the Tōhoku region around Tokyo, sometimes with success and sometimes failing, and in the end it was not so much that he failed as that the well-springs of his vitality ran dry. And so he went back to the place of his birth. It was not a case of drifting; it was a deliberate return to a home which he had never been able to put out of his mind. He was ruined, but even so he was not the man to live out the dregs of his life as anonymous dirt in the streets of the capital. Yet his return was not after five or ten years. In this Whitebeard had missed his mark, for it was a full twenty years before Toyokichi set his course for home. For all that, Whitebeard had been right in essence, if not in literal fact. He was wrong only in that Toyokichi was not the type of man to fail and run for the shelter of home while any other course remained open to him. His character was such that he would do everything in his power before admitting defeat.

And so, for the most part Whitebeard's prophecy had come true, but there was one more thing which he had overlooked altogether, and that was something which perhaps only the cedar grove itself could have known, with its many centuries' experience of observing the fates of mortal men.

* * *

At one o'clock on a mid-September afternoon, a man stood by the cedar grove, lost in his own thoughts. He was some forty years of age and had grizzled black hair and sunken cheeks in his long face. He wore a sweat-stained, faded, western-style shirt and the ties of his leggings and his sandals were discoloured and worn out. His was the typical garb of a refugee from Tokyo, and, yes, it was Ueda Toyokichi.

In his twenty years' absence the appearance of his birthplace had changed radically. Everywhere in Japan at this time the centres of castle towns were undergoing modern development, but the small roads radiating to the old-style mansions in the outer parts of the towns were slow to change. Toyokichi's home town followed the general pattern. The centre seemed in every respect part of the modern world with its new buildings and flashy shops, but the larger houses on the outskirts were just the opposite, retaining everywhere the traces of an ancient capital. A kind of indefinable tranquillity pervaded their every corner.

For a while Toyokichi rested beneath the shade of the cedars; timid man that he was, even though he had at last come back to his beloved home, he could not bring himself to proclaim the news of his return. He found himself unable to walk through the town with arms waved aloft; unable to go directly to the house where he had been born and where his elder brother now lived. Nervously he began to walk, wandering in a trance on the verge of old memories; yes, the place certainly had changed. And yet, in a way it was unchanged, for the holes which twenty

years before he had mischievously poked in the wall with a stick were
tonous chirruping of the cicadas. The steady rays of the sun were scor-
remembered them and the trees seemed more forlorn with the mono-
tonous chirruping of the cicadas. The steady rays of the sun were scor-
ching and it was so calm that it seemed just as if the grounds of the old
house were sleeping. He walked round the hedge which surrounded the
pond. A crape myrtle on the plaster wall reflected against the blue of the
sky and the wall itself was almost buried in ivy. To the side there was
the gate, over-shadowed by oaks, plums and orange trees, and just inside two or three hemp-palms glittered as their large, splayed leaves
flapped in the breeze.

Toyokichi bent down to examine the name plate, the letters of which
were as black and clear as of old. They read 'Katayama Shirō' — the
name of one of Toyokichi's childhood friends.

'Well, he's still going strong, it seems. Perhaps he has children by
now,' he thought. He peeped inside the gate and saw six or seven hens,
a rooster at their head, strutting leisurely towards the gate from the
direction of the mulberry plantation. Then there was a loud noise from
over by the well, followed by what seemed to be the voice of the master
of the house:

'O-yasu, bring the washbowl, please.'

Toyokichi stared nervously around him almost as if he feared a surprise attack, and then he hurriedly rounded a turn in the wall. There
was no one in sight.

'Shirō, Shirō,' Toyokichi muttered the name, lost in thoughts of days
gone by. He gazed unseeingly into the distance along the narrow road
which was shaded by many trees. His eyes were screwed up. Far away, a
shimmering heat haze hovered over the road. Suddenly, a dog emerged
from the bamboo hedge right beside the road where Toyokichi was
standing, and looked at him, its ears pricked suspiciously. A moment
later it was gambolling off in response to a whistle and call from behind
the hedge. Toyokichi opened his eyes a little as if awakening from a
dream; a sad smile was on his face.

An eleven or twelve-year-old boy, carrying a fishing rod, emerged
from the shade of a tree and made off in the opposite direction without
noticing Toyokichi. He was singing a military-sounding song in a low
voice and the dog was following at his heels, sniffing the ground.
Unable to help himself, Toyokichi followed a hundred paces or so
behind, concentrating hard on the boy's shadow, seeing as he did so a
graphic image of himself as he had been thirty years before. Suddenly
the shadows of boy and dog disappeared round a bend in the road.
Toyokichi rounded the bend himself and saw an old plum tree with
cicadas chirruping in the branches, just as he remembered it. He looked
up at the tree and laughed joyously.

'Of course, that's the way they must have gone!'

A little further on he came to a small stream shaded by willows
around which was a group of three or four boys. Grinning, Toyokichi
hurried towards them. This stream was a tributary of a great river and
had been a favourite boys' fishing spot from time immemorial.
Toyokichi sat down in the shade of a willow and for the first time in
many years saw his shadow looking up at him from the waters of the ancient stream. At this point in its course, the large river near by
broadened and depened and became darker and less turbulent. Golden
bars of sunlight filtering through the willows reflected in the crystal
water and the gravel in the stream bed glinted like silver and jewels.

Here and there among the willow roots boys were fishing, but they
turned to see the new arrival:

'Hey, Hiyama! Look what I've got!' said one of them, a boy of eleven
or twelve. He held up a red-bellied mountain dace almost a foot long,
laughing proudly and happily as he did so.

'You're a braggart, Ueda,' said one of the other boys.

Toyokichi stood up abruptly and stared at the boy who had been addressed as Ueda as if he were dazzled, with knitted eyebrows and nar-
rowed eyes. He went up to him.

'Would you mind showing me that fish?' he asked, his eyes never
leaving the boy's face. The boy looked at him suspiciously and reluctantly raised the basket lid for Toyokichi to see.

'Hmm. I see. To be sure,' he murmured, taking no more than a perfunctory glance into the basket before transferring his gaze to the boy
once more. He inclined his head speculatively.

'Isn't it huge!' said the boy abruptly, and taking the basket as if it
were some ill-gotten gain, he plunged it into the stream, gazing at the
bed as if he had already forgotten the man standing beside him.
Toyokichi was dumbfounded.

'You must be my elder brother's son. You're his spitting image and
when you spoke just now, it was just like hearing his voice.' As he spoke
his eyes never left the boy's face. They made a fine picture, the two of
them there together. The long leaves of the willows sparkled in the sun,
their black shadows mingling with every sigh of the breeze. In the chilly
shade at the water's edge, the plump little boy stood fishing, his eyes
fixed intently on the deep, clear water, while seated on the roots of a
willow a little way off, a traveller, his ruin and suffering evident from
the state of his clothes and face, looked on as if in a dream. Far away
across the tops of the willows he could see the crumbling stone walls of
the castle on Shiroyama. It was early autumn and the air was clear and
the sun bright. Yes, it made quite a picture — a picture, moreover, with
a profound meaning.

Toyokichi's eyes were brimming with tears, and although he blinked
and tried to choke them back, he was unable to prevent two or three
drops falling to the ground. His heart was filled with an indefinable

sense of longing, of yearning; 'This is the place I was born, and this is where I shall die. I am happy. At last my heart is at rest.' He felt somehow as if all the hardships and sufferings had been shed from him like a skin. he went up to the boy again and asked him kindly:

'Your father's name. What is it?'

He looked up at Toyokichi wide-eyed.

'Is it Kan'ichi by any chance?'

Now the boy stared at him in amazement. Toyokichi smiled.

'Is he well?'

'Yes.'

'I'm relieved to hear it. Truly I am. Has he ever told you about your uncle Toyokichi?'

The boy jumped to his feet in astonishment.

'Well, what's your name, then?' Toyokichi asked.

'Genzō.'

'Well, Genzō, I am your uncle — Toyokichi.'

Genzō turned pale and threw away his fishing rod; without uttering a word he ran away towards the mansion as fast as his legs would carry him. The other boys, rather taken aback by this strange development, looked at Toyokichi suspiciously. Then they wound in their lines, raised their fishing baskets from the water and beat a hasty retreat as a stupefied Toyokichi watched them, not knowing what to think.

★ ★ ★

The news of Toyokichi's return spread quickly and those who remembered him from the old days were very surprised to hear of it. His friends of twenty years before were now middle-aged and some of them even were grandparents. One after another they came to visit him, especially the women who had once been beautiful girls and were now grandmothers. Everyone was amazed at how decrepit Toyokichi had become, but they nevertheless rejoiced at his safe return. It did not matter to them that he had come home ruined for they looked kindly on him. They laughed. They wept. They said all they could to comfort him.

Home! Never once in his twenty years' absence had Toyokichi forgotten it, whether in success or failure. He had come back a ruined man and never had he believed they would be so kind to him. He was astonished by the sympathy shown him by everybody, from his elder brother on. And then he cried, not knowing whether the tears were of joy or of sadness. He was discouraged and suddenly very old, feeling that he had arrived from the seas of a hopeless ruin to an island haven of equally hopeless security.

His brother did all he could to look after this tragic castaway from the wreck of life and his children showed the greatest affection for their kindly uncle. There were three children: a fourteen-year-old girl called

O-hana; then there was Genzō whom we have already met; and finally there was the youngest, a charming little boy called Isamu. O-hana sought to console her uncle while Genzō played with him and Isamu played up to him, as very young children often do. Toyokichi used to lean against the window of the tea-room in a doze, listening to O-hana singing as she sat on the stone steps of the storehouse; in the same doze he sat on the river bank, fishing with Genzō. Sometimes Isamu used to ask his uncle to carry him round the room on his back, neighing like a horse, but Toyokichi would infuriate him and make everyone else laugh by mooing like a cow instead. Having plenty of free time at his disposal, be began to teach O-hana and Genzō to read the Chinese classics, also giving them lessons in English and mathematics. On the strength of this, people began to say that he was doing himself no good by just idling away his time, and that if he would open a private school for the children of the village, he would be doing both himself and others a good turn. Naturally his brother thought it a good idea and gave him every encouragement. Toyokichi agreed to do it readily and secretly was glad of the opportunity, because ever since his return, he had been unhappy about living without any real challenge. Not only that; he had been much troubled by the thought that he might end up by doing nothing, achieving nothing and being a burden to others.

Before he knew it, a month of this dull life of hopeless security had elapsed and he was no longer dozing as he listened to O-hana sing. On the clear autumn evenings when the stars shone brightly, he walked with her on the banks of the stream and as he listened to her singing some mournful air in her low voice, it penetrated to the core of his being and his heart leaped. It seemed to him that, despite past failure, how much more desirable it was to undertake some work into which he could put his whole heart and soul rather than living on in rest and security. Perhaps it was not his fault after all that he had gone to other parts and failed; his failure might have been the fault of the unkindness of the strangers among whom he had lived. If he could live and work among these kindly people of his birthplace, he might well achieve some kind of success or at least avoid those former ruinous failures.

But Toyokichi did not know himself, was not perhaps aware of his weaknesses, and it was thus that he was happy to accept the principle of founding a private school, because he had wanted to propose some suggestion of work he could do, but had found it difficult to broach the subject.

* * *

It was ten o'clock on a clear moonlit night and the river seemed to turn sharply away round the foot of Shiroyama. Toyokichi was alone, ascending a wooded path towards the hill-top, chasing his own shadow. Leaving the path which led through thickets of bamboo, he came to a graveyard where several mounds stood in a line on a slight slope, white under the light of the moon. He halted before the smallest of these graves by the roots of a small pine tree. It was the grave of Namiki Zenbei who had died seven years previously — the last resting place of 'Whitebeard-of-the-cedar-grove'. That day, Toyokichi's brother, Kan'ichi, and the others had been working on the preparations for the opening of the school, having decided to rent the Katayama household gymnasium for a classroom. This gymnasium, of generous proportions, had a wooden floor and in his childhood Toyokichi had often enjoyed a rough-and-tumble there with the Katayama boy on their way home from school. Before the Restoration, it had been used for *kendō**practice.

Everyone was very interested to help out and had collected sufficient desks and chairs for the use of twenty pupils. They had taken these things from the village hall lumber room and the primary school storehouse — things which were half broken and serving no purpose — and had repaired them just in time for the school opening. The opening ceremony was to be held on the following day and Toyokichi, who had all sorts of preparations to make on his own account, had just about got as far as writing a draft of his public address. All day long the mansion had been the scene of an abnormal number of laughing and talking voices and even the cedar grove, normally so melancholy, was somehow quite transformed. O-hana had arranged to sing the national anthem for her uncle and Genzō, now that his uncle was to be a teacher, was very proud of himself during these few days, even though in point of fact he attended quite a different school. Isamu, however, did not understand what all the fuss was about. It was in the evening that Toyokichi had been to the Katayama gymnasium to put the finishing touches to those preparations he still had to make for the next day, and on his way home he had decided to change direction and make for the river.

He sat on Whitebeard's grave and looked up at the moon. Now Whitebeard had no idea of what was happening to Toyokichi, and Toyokichi still knew nothing of Whitebeard's prophecy about him. He looked down at the waters of the river and gazed for a while in fascination at the scene of his home town. He sighed deeply. He felt a broken man, as indeed he was. His vitality had withered away and now he was feeling unbearably weary. He could no longer summon the strength of spirit to achieve the practical realisation of his private school. The hill, the river and the moon looked as they always had done, but he knew that some of his friends of earlier days must now lie in this graveyard where he was sitting. He felt that the river of his life had almost run its course to the sea and only a semi-transparent membrane separated him from his dead friends. It was not really true of course, just that he was

---

* The Japanese sport of wooden sword fencing.

exhausted and no longer had the strength even to look for a cup of water from the nearby river.

Calmly, he got up and walked down to the river bank, wearily beginning to trudge towards the lower reaches of the river. Under the superbly clear moonlight, Shiroyama cast its black shadow upon the water which flowed sluggishly at this point and was like a mirror. Where there was a current, the light of the moon shattered and glistened. Toyokichi walked in a trance.

A small boat was tied up to the bank. Toyokichi climbed aboard, cast off and applied the punting pole. His old-time skill acquired from years of messing about in boats as a boy had not deserted him and the boat slid smoothly into midstream. As he looked far off down river, the scene was bathed in moonlight and a mist floated over the water as in a dream. Toyokichi felt that he would like to be lost in this river mist and he steered the boat downstream towards it, but as he did so the mist gradually receded. Presently the river opened out into the sea.

Never again did Toyokichi return to his home to the great sorrow of everyone, but to none more so than to O-hana and Genzō.

2
Old Gen

Gen Oji (Old Gen), 'Saeki period' work, was first published in the magazine *Bungei Kurabu* in August 1897 and was regarded by Doppo himself as his first true work of fiction. Japanese literary historians today hold it, with *Musashino*, to be the finest of all Doppo's works. It is told in two distinct parts; the first through a narrator and the second, more successfully, as a straight story. The young teacher described in the opening pages is Doppo himself who did indeed come down from Tokyo to Saeki (September 1893) and left about a year later (August 1894).

In this story we have the creation of a true character in the form of the old boatman Gen and the first introduction of the wandering vagabond which was to haunt all Doppo's 'romantic' fiction. Hitherto, apart from several essays of literary criticism and general *zuihitsu* pieces, Doppo had concentrated on writing poetry and what might be loosely termed as 'prose poetry' typified by such works as *Hoshi* (The Stars), *Takibi* (The Bonfire), and *Shisō* (Poetic Images). Elements of these earlier 'prose poetry' works remain in the strong lyrical strain of *Gen Oji*, particularly in the scenic descriptions.

The story, which took Doppo a month to write, is a genuine tragedy of a man buffeted by a series of calamities which eventually destroy him by driving him to suicide. The suicide theme recurs in other stories in this anthology, explicitly in *Daisansha* (Third Party) and perhaps implicitly in *Kawagiri*, but it would be dangerous to deduce anything about Doppo's obsessions as a writer from this, because suicide is a common theme throughout Japanese literature and does not have the connotations of suicide in the West. In a later work (*Waga sakuhin to jijitsu* — The truth about my works), Doppo stated that the characters of Gen and Kishū were modelled on people he knew living in the district of Katsura harbour, but Japanese literary historians have been unable to identify positively who they were, and it is quite evident that the relationship between them is fictional.

O nce a young teacher of English came down from the capital to Saeki where he stayed about a year, arriving in the middle of autumn and leaving in mid-summer the following year. By early summer he had grown weary of living in the town itself and moved instead to a place near the harbour of Katsura about a mile away, commuting from there to his school. He lived there by the sea for about a month. During this time he made few friends, being of rather taciturn nature, and the only person he talked to at any length was the landlord of the house where he was staying. One rainy and windy evening when the waves were pounding roughly against the shore, this man of few words, normally so fond of his own company, felt strangely lonely. He came down from his first-floor room to the veranda where the landlord and his wife were enjoying the cool air. The lamp was unlit and they were talking in the dark, fanning away the mosquitoes as they spoke, but when they noticed the teacher they were quick to offer him a seat, his visit being something of an event. The evening wind was gently blowing the rain so that occasionally drops fell on their faces, but none of them minded this and they soon fell into easy conversation.

Late one winter evening several years after his return to the capital, the teacher sat alone at his table to write a letter to an old friend in his native province. His pale and anxious face had a touch of colour that night. Frequently he looked puzzled, as if he were searching for something that was enshrouded in mist. In this mist stood the figure of an old man. Laying aside his writing brush, the teacher re-read what he had written and then closed his eyes, but still he could see that same figure for although his eyes were shut, his inner eyes were still open. In his letter he had described what the landlord had told him that evening in Saeki.

'Among other things, the landlord told me of an old man named Gen. To tell the truth, there was nothing very extraordinary about his life-story and there must be many like it to be heard all over Japan, but somehow I can never forget him. I feel as if he were a box containing some secret which no one can open. Perhaps this is no more than my mind playing tricks as I admit it is prone to do, but whenever I think of him, I seem to hear the sound of distant music and there stirs in my heart the desire to wander in the land where I was born. I feel as if I have just read a poem filled with lofty sentiments and am looking up at the infinite sky.'

However, the teacher had been unable to discover the full story of that old man who so haunted him, and only knew the rough outline he had heard from the landlord. He remembered he had been unable to understand how the landlord knew even as much as he did. This was the landlord's story:

'This harbour is just right for a town like Saeki. As you can see, there are few houses here worthy of the name and only about twenty people. It is always as lonely as it is tonight, but think what it must have been like when there was only Old Gen's house standing on the shore. The pine tree by his house now stands at the side of that wide road you can see, offering travellers protection from the heat of summer, but ten years ago it stood right on the shore, its roots washed by the waves of the sea. People coming out from Saeki to take Gen's ferryboat used to sit on the rocks thrusting out into the sea by the shore, but they no longer exist. The authorities had them dynamited because they were so dangerous.

'Well, Gen didn't always live alone. Once he had a beautiful wife named Yuri, who was born on Ōnyū Island. There are all sorts of stories about them but one I know for a fact because Gen told it to me himself one night when he was drunk. Late one spring night, when he was twenty-seven or so, all the lights had been extinguished when there was a knock at the door. Gen got up to see who it was and discovered that it was a girl who said she wanted to be ferried over to the island. Looking at her more closely under the light of the waning moon, he recognised her as a girl named Yuri who he knew actually lived on Ōnyū Island.

'In those days', continued the landlord, 'there were many ferrymen hereabouts, but Gen enjoyed something of a reputation along the coast because he was a very fine young man with an obliging nature. But there was another, more profound reason for his popularity. How I wish you could have heard him sing as he did then! People used to take his boat just for the pleasure of hearing his fine voice as he rowed along. But even in those days, he was a man of very few words.

'It has been said that the girl Yuri asked for a boat late at night with some ulterior motive, but that is a secret known to no one save perhaps the gods looking down from their lofty heights. I asked him what passed between him and Yuri that night, but even drunk, Gen said very little. He just smiled and two deep wrinkles appeared on his forehead and it seemed to me that in that smile there was sadness. At any rate, they got married and the years passed in a fleeting dream of love until, when their son Kōsuke was six years old, Yuri died during her second confinement. Many people in the town offered to adopt Kōsuke and bring him up into their businesses, but Gen refused them all, saying that he could not bear to be parted from his son, least of all after losing his beloved wife. From that day forth, Gen became even more taciturn than before. He seldom smiled and hardly ever sang even when rowing, unless he was drunk. Even when occasionally he sang cheerfully as his boat smashed through the moonlight of Daigo Bay, his songs seemed sad. It may, of course, only be my imagination, but I fancy that the loss of his wife broke the heart of this once cheerful man. On misty days he used to take Kōsuke with him in the boat, saying that it was a pity to leave him behind in the lonely house. The passengers felt sorry for them, and several of the women gave to the lonely little boy sweets and cakes which they had bought in town for their own children. When this happened Gen always seemed not to notice and never thanked them, but no one felt at all put out by this seeming ingratitude.

'Two years passed. When work on this new harbour was half completed, my wife and I moved over from the island, built a house and set up in our business. A road was cut through the mountain, passing in front of Gen's gate. A steamboat plied across the channel twice a day, morning and evening, but the wild shore with the fishermen's nets hanging out to dry was the same as it had always been and Gen's ferrying business was unaffected. As before he ferried the people of the bay and the islanders back and forth, and when the new harbour was opened and the road completed, more people came than ever before. Compared with the old days it was a real hive of activity, but Gen did not know whether to feel happy about it or sad.

'Some three years had passed when one day while the now twelve-year-old Kōsuke was playing with some other children on the shore, he accidentally drowned. The other children ran away in fear without telling anyone and it was evening before it was noticed that Kōsuke was missing. Of course, by the time we began looking for him, it was too late, and by a strange coincidence we found his poor little body beneath his father's boat.

'Well, after that Gen never sang at all, and he avoided speaking even to his best friends. Silent, never singing, never laughing, the years went by until it seemed that Gen had been forgotten by the world. He continued to run his ferryboat, but as far as his passengers were concerned, Gen might just as well never have existed. They have forgotten him. Even I remember him only when I see him rowing his way home, with his eyes half shut. In fact you're the first man ever to ask me about him. I admit it's sometimes possible to get him to sing if you invite him in for a drink, but we don't understand his songs any more. He never grumbles or complains, just sighs very heavily from time to time. I think it's rather sad, don't you?'

That was the last the landlord said about Gen that night.

When the teacher got back to the capital, he found he was unable to put Gen out of his mind. Frequently as he sat beneath the lamp light listening to the night rain, his pathetic image would leap to his mind. He pictured him sitting alone by his fire with his eyes half closed, remembering the pleasant spring nights of so many years before, and thinking of Kōsuke.

Many years passed and all unknown to the teacher as still in the winter nights he sometimes thought of Gen, the sleet was falling on the old man's grave. Even as the young man was turning the pages of his memory in an attempt to write a poem about the man, a still sadder fate had befallen Old Gen and he was lost to the world. So the teacher's poem lacked its final stanza.

* * *

The year which had seen the young teacher move to Katsura harbour drew to its close, and one day at the end of the following January, Old Gen set out for Saeki before lunch, to transact some business. The sky was cloudy and it looked like snow. You can tell how cold it must have been for snow is something of a rarity in those parts. Normally at this time of day, the streets of Saeki would have been very busy for all the people of the surrounding mountain villages would have come by boat to town where it was the custom for traders to gather along the banks of the Banshō river. There would have been a great clamour what with the singing of the bay people and the abuse of the mountain men. That day, however, the streets were deserted and the rippling surface of the river reflected only the ashen shadows of the clouds. The main street was forlorn with its darkened shops and lack of people, and the stony lanes were frozen. The temple bell at the foot of Jōzan tolled to the clouds, its doleful notes spreading slowly over the whitened moss on the house roofs, hurled like a stone into a fishless lake.

At the wide crossroads where the stage should have been set up as for festival days, a group of ashen-faced children were playing half-heartedly with their hands in their pockets. A beggar came by and one of the children shouted out at him, 'Kishū! Kishū!', but Kishū, for that was his name, passed on without paying any attention. His appearance gave his age about fourteen or fifteen. His unkempt hair trailed down over his neck and his long face, with its sunken cheeks, made his chin seem sharp. His eyes were dull and almost lifeless. His tattered, saturated coat barely reached his knees and an elbow, thin as the leg of a grasshopper, showed through his sleeve, shivering in the cold. Just then Old Gen came by and met the beggar at the crossroads.

'Kishū,' he called, his voice soft but compelling. The young beggar raised his dull eyes and looked at Gen as if he were no more than a stone. For a while they stood looking at each other until at last Gen produced his lunch box from his sleeve pocket and offered the beggar a rice ball, Kishū taking out his begging bowl to receive it. Not a word passed between them during this operation, nor was there any emotion. When it was done, Kishū went on his way without a backward glance while Gen watched him until he had disappeared round a corner. Gen looked up at the sky and as he did so, two or three flakes of snow fell. Once again he looked towards the place where the beggar had just disappeared and sighed deeply. The watching children nudged each other, trying hard not to laugh, but Gen did not notice them.

In the evening he returned to his house. His windows faced out onto the road, but he never opened them. Despite the darkness he did not light a lamp, but just sat in front of the fire with his face in his large, thick-fingered hands, sighing deeply. He put a piece of wood on the fire where it burned with a candle-like flame until it was completely devoured, the room illuminated for a moment as the flames flickered up. His shadow flickered large against the wall where hung a colour print which Yuri had once brought back from a visit to her parents when Kōsuke was four or five. Now, however, the print was greasy and slowly had turned black through ten years or more of hanging on the smoky wall.

That night the wind was still and the murmur of the waves inaudible.

Gen strained his ears to hear the whispering sound of the sleet as it fell around the house. For a while he listened attentively, but then he sighed again and turned his attention to the house. When at last he picked up a lamp and went outside, the cold chilled his bones and he felt a shudder pass through him at the thought of rowing in the icy winter night. The hills were black and the sea was dark, but for as far as the firelight extended he could see the snowflakes glistening as they fell. The ground was frozen hard. Just at that moment two young men came along from the town, locked in earnest conversation, but seeing Gen standing at his gate with a lamp in his hand, they paused to ask him what he thought of the cold. Gen made some perfunctory reply and turned his eyes in the direction of the town. When they had passed on their way, one of the young men remarked to his companion that the sight of Gen's face was enough to make a young girl faint. The other replied that he would not be surprised if next morning Gen were found hanging from the pine tree next to his house. The hair on their heads bristled and they looked back, but the light from Gen's lamp was no longer to be seen.

The night advanced, the snow continuing to fall intermittently, occasionally alternating with sleet. The moon floated in the sky at the edge of Mt. Nada, its light enshrouded by the clouds. The ancient castle town looked just like a dessicated graveyard. Even now a wraith-like figure was passing the crossroads in the direction of a small bridge. A dog which was sleeping at the bridge approach raised its head and stared after the figure, but it did not bark. Was it a ghost to wander thus, escaped from the grave to meet and talk with someone? It was Kishū.

In the autumn of the same year that Old Gen had been bereft by Kōsuke's drowning, a beggar woman from Hiuga way had appeared in Saeki, bringing with her her seven-year-old son. Whenever they went out begging together, they were always successful and as the people of Saeki seemed more charitable than those in other parts, the woman must have thought it would be a good place to leave her son, which she did, the following spring. Someone said later that, on a pilgrimage to Dazaifu, he had seen this same woman in the company of a large wrestler, begging at the gate of the shrine. Hearing this, the townspeople hated the cruel-hearted mother and pitied the abandoned child even more than ever; and so it seemed at first that her plan had worked. However, despite the fact that there were many temples in the neighbourhood, the people's charity had its limits. Everyone felt very sorry for the boy, but no one wanted the responsibility of adopting him and bringing him up. Sometimes he was treated kindly and taken on to sweep people's gardens and so on, but this seldom lasted very long. At first he pined for his mother and wept so that people gave him things to comfort him, but as in time he came to forget about her, so the townsfolk's charity began to wear thin. They forgot about the mother themselves and thought only of the child who they said was a fool, liable to forget things, dirty and dishonest. They made all kinds of excuses to themselves, the result of which was that they labelled the boy a good-for-nothing beggar and shut him out of their human world.

In the early days, someone had taught him his alphabet and later another person taught him to read well enough to recite a couple of pages from the school reader. He also taught himself to sing by listening to the songs of the other children. In fact, he laughed, sang, talked and played like any other child and was in no way different from them. No one knew his real name, so as he came from the Province of Ki, the children nicknamed him 'Kishū', which just means 'Province of Ki'. In the end he just came to be regarded as some sort of natural appendage to the Saeki township.

As time went by and people ceased to take any notice of him, his heart just withered away without anyone realising it was happening. Although it seemed that he was living in the same world as others where the morning sun shone, where smoke rose from kitchen fires, where there were parents, brothers and sisters, friends and tears, he mentally transferred his miserable little existence to an unpopulated island, and there his heart perished. He no longer thanked people when they gave him things. He no longer laughed. Seldom did anyone see him angry or crying, for in his heart there was neither hatred nor joy. He just moved, walked and ate, and if anyone standing by him asked him if he enjoyed what he was eating, he said that he did, but without any real emotion. If anyone threatened him with a stick for a joke, he just moved slowly away with a kind of smile on his face, just like a dog running away with its tail wagging after a scolding from its master. He never tried to get things by flattery. The heart which looks on in pity at the beggars of this world never extended its warmth to Kishū, and the eyes which watch in pity the struggles of men drowning in the waves of this transient world, found it difficult to see him, for he had deliberately crawled beneath the waves.

Gen crossed the small bridge where he had seen Kishū go and soon reached the crossroads where he paused to look around him. He carried a small boat lamp and wherever he shone it over the ground, the snow glistened beautifully, the beam halting at the darkened entrance of every house in the square, where Kishū might be found. Suddenly, a policeman appeared. He marched straight up to Gen to find out who he was. He shone the lamp straight in his face and saw the round eyes, deep wrinkles and thick nose of the tough old boatman.

'You're Old Gen, aren't you?' the policeman asked in surprise.

'Yes, I am,' Gen replied hoarsely.

'What are you looking for so late at night?'

'Have you seen Kishū?'

'What do you want with him?'

'Well, it's so cold tonight, I thought I'd ask him to stay at my house.'

'All right, but not even the dogs know where Kishū sleeps. I should take care you don't catch cold, if I were you.' With this, the kindly policeman went on his way.

With a sigh, Gen went on and soon found footprints beneath the light of his lamp. They were recent, and who but Kishū would walk barefoot in the snow? Gen headed off in the direction of the footprints at a gentle run.

It soon got about that Gen wanted to take Kishū in, although the people who heard it did not at first believe it. They were surprised by the idea, and then amused. Some mocked and said it would be a real comedy to see them sitting down to dinner together, but at least it had the effect that people began to talk once more about Gen who had almost ceased to exist in their minds.

About a week after the snow had fallen, the evening sun was shining brightly and Shikoku was visible above the waves in the distance. Sails gleamed white by Tsurumi headland and plovers were flying over the sandbars at the river mouth. Gen cast off his boat which had seven passengers in all, two of whom were young men who had rushed up at the last minute. There were two girls returning to the island who seemed to be sisters; they carried small packages and wore towels tied over their hair. The remaining passengers were all bay people. Apart from the two young men who had come late, there was a child accompanied by its grandparents. All the talk was of town affairs; one of the young men talked about a play that had been performed in the town and the elder of the two sisters said that she had heard that the costumes were particularly fine, though not many of the islanders had yet seen the play. The grandmother ventured to suggest that the play was not so good as the previous year's. One of the young men asked whether it was true that the handsome actor named Kumegorō was as popular among the island girls as he had heard, whereupon the two girls blushed and the old couple laughed loudly. But Gen carried on rowing with his eyes fixed on the distant horizon, paying no heed to these laughing voices from the transient world and not joining in the conversation. Suddenly, however, one of the young men spoke directly to him:

'I heard that you took Kishū in to live with you. Is it true?'

'Yes, it is true,' Gen replied, without turning to face his questioner.

'I find it very hard to understand why you should take in a beggar child to live with you. It's very strange. Is it because you were lonely?'

'Yes.'

'But you could easily have found some child from the island or Saeki to live with you, without picking someone like Kishū, couldn't you?'

'That's so,' said the old woman looking up at Gen. He looked troubled and did not reply for a time. Grey smoke was rising from the hills in the West and glowing in the dying rays of the evening sun. But at last he spoke, as if to himself:

'Kishū has no parents, no brothers, no home. I am an old man with neither wife nor son. If I take him as my son, he will take me as his father, and isn't that best for both of us?'

The passengers, never having heard him talk this way before, were slightly taken aback. The old woman sighed.

'How quickly time passes. It seems only yesterday that I used to see your wife Yuri standing on the shore with your child in her arms. How old would Kōsuke be now, if he'd lived?'

'A couple of years older than Kishū, maybe,' Gen replied casually.

'It's so difficult to tell how old Kishū is, he's so dirty. He could be ten or eighteen!'

The laughter raised by this remark took some time to die down.

'I don't know how old he is either. He said that he was fifteen or sixteen, but I suppose only his mother really knows. Don't you feel sorry for him?' said Gen, looking at the old couple's six-year-old grandson. His voice was trembling, but out of kindness, the passengers stifled their laughter.

'If a real father-son relationship grows up between Gen and Kishū, it may be that Gen's old age will be happier. If Kishū is standing there at the gate when Gen comes home late, it won't be only Gen who cries, eh?' said the grandfather, to smooth over an awkward situation, and he was not altogether insincere.

'Yes, indeed, that would be wonderful,' said Gen, greatly pleased by the old man's words.

'Don't you want to take Kishū to see the play?' asked one of the young men, trying rather to make the girls laugh than to poke fun at Old Gen; but they only smiled slightly so as not to hurt his feelings. The old woman tapped the side of the boat with her fingers and said that it was an interesting idea. Gen, however, took it seriously.

'I don't think it would be such a good idea to take my boy to a play like *Awa no Jūrōbei*. It would most likely make him cry.'

'What do you mean, "my boy"?' said the old woman, with mock innocence, 'I heard that "your boy" drowned over there,' she added, turning round and pointing to a spot shadowed by the hills. Everyone looked where she pointed.

'I mean Kishū. He's my boy now.' Gen stopped rowing for a second and gazed towards the hills. His face was flaming, his heart filled with a confusion of anger, sadness and shame. But, most of all, he felt joy. Bracing his feet against the sides of the boat, he rowed as he had never rowed before, and then, loud and clear, he began to sing.

It had been an age since the sea and hills had heard the ring of that voice. The evening breeze seemed to waft the voice gently across the sea in an ever-widening ripple until it vanished. Then the ripples seemed to strike the shore and echoed back faintly from the mountains. So many years had passed since Gen had heard those echoes and they seemed to be calling him back from beyond the mountains, from a long, long sleep. The old couple were quick to praise his singing, saying that his voice and intonation were as good as ever, and the four youngsters listened entranced, feeling that the singing was every bit as good as they had heard it said. But Gen had ceased to be aware even that he had any passengers.

He dropped off the two girls at the island and the young men lay back then in the boat, covering themselves with a blanket because of the cold. The old couple fed cakes to their grandchild and chattered to each other in whispers about family affairs. By the time the boat got back to the bay, the sun was sinking and the evening smoke from the kitchen fires was enveloping the villages. There had been no passengers to bring back. When he came to the mouth of Daigo Bay, the hills were wreathed with storm clouds, and looking back over his shoulder, Gen could see the light of Venus fragmented on the rippling sea and the twinkling lamps of Ōnyū Island. Gen's shadow reflected black upon the water as he calmly rowed along. The bow sped lightly through the sea and it seemed as if the water lapping the bottom of the boat was whispering something to him. Gen's thoughts dwelt on many happy things as he listened unconsciously to the sound of the water which seemed to be inviting sleep. When, sometimes, sad or anxious thoughts found their way into his mind, he just shook his head and rowed even harder, almost as if he were chasing something. He thought that someone would be waiting for him at home. Perhaps Kishū would be drowsing in front of the fire or perhaps he would be looking out for the light of Gen's boat lamp, enjoying the comfort and warmth of the house and comparing it with those times when he went without. Would he have waited for Gen's return before having his dinner? When he had offered to teach Kishū how to row he had seemed quite pleased. It was natural of course that up to now he had said little and spent most of his time engrossed in thought, but surely that would change as the months went by, as he filled out and his cheeks became rosy with health.

When Gen reached the quay, he paused for a while, gazing at the lights of the storehouses flickering in the water, as if in a dream. He made fast the boat and then, having rolled up the straw matting and put it under his arm, he went ashore carrying the oars on his back. It was dusk and by then all the storehouses were shut. There was no one about. Gen walked with eyes shut until he reached the front of his house where he opened them and looked around.

'I'm home, son,' he called out, and putting the oars in their usual place, he went in. The house was in darkness.

'Hey, what's up? I'm home, my boy. Make haste and light the lamps.' There was no reply, just the faint whisper of a cricket chirruping

'Kishū, Kishū.' Disconcerted, Gen took a match from his pocket and as he struck it, the room flared suddenly into light. But there was no one there and the match quickly went out. A cold and gloomy feeling seemed to rise from the floor and lodge itself in the old man's heart. Quickly he lit a lantern and looked about him, calling hoarsely again and again until he was out of breath. The ashes in the fire were white and cold and there was no sign of Kishū's dinner. Slowly and carefully he looked everywhere and because the corners of the room were sooty and the light wouldn't reach properly, it always seemed that he could see someone. At last he buried his face in his hands and sighed deeply. Suddenly he made up his mind. He got up and without bothering to wipe away the large tear drops which were streaming down his face, he lit a boat lamp that was hanging up and hurried out of the house towards the town. The sparks were flying from the blacksmith's forge as Gen passed, so he stopped and asked if he had seen Kishū come that way. The young blacksmith looked suspicious and replied that he had not noticed anyone, then pressed on, smiling to himself that he should be disturbed at his night's work.

At last when he was about halfway along a straight road with pine trees planted along it and fields on either side, Gen saw someone walking ahead of him. Holding the lamp ahead of him to light the way, Gen hurried to catch the figure up. There was no doubt that it was Kishū, walking along with his hands in his pockets and his body bent forward.

'Is that you, Kishū?' Gen called out, catching him by his shoulder. 'Where are you going, alone like this?' he said, his heart flooded with a mixture of joy, anger, sadness and a profound despair. Kishū looked at Gen without surprise. He stood at a gate without emotion as if he were watching some stranger coming along the road. This shocked Gen and for a moment he was almost lost for words.

'Aren't you cold? Come home with me, son,' Gen took Kishū's hand and they started home. On the way Gen said that he was sorry to be back so late and that he had left dinner in the cupboard. Kishū said nothing and Gen sighed, saying yet again how sorry he was.

When they got back, Gen made up a good fire and sitting Kishū beside him, he fetched some food from the cupboard and gave it to him, taking nothing himself. Doing as Gen made him, he ate up Gen's portion as well as his own. Gen looked at Kishū occasionally as he ate, then closed his eyes and sighed. When the meal was finished, he told Kishū to move close to the fire and asked him if he had enjoyed his food. Kishū looked at him through sleepy eyes and nodded almost imperceptibly. Seeing this, Gen kindly suggested that if he were tired he should go to bed. He made up the bed and covered Kishū with a blanket. After Kishū had gone to sleep, Gen sat alone by the fire without moving, his eyes closed, while the wood burned slowly away. The faint reflections of the red flames shone on his face and it may be that the glittering thing which rolled down his cheek was a tear. The wind howled across the roof and through the pine tree at the gate.

The next morning, Gen got up early and made breakfast for Kishū, but himself drank only a cup of water for his head was heavy and his mouth dry. A little later he pressed Kishū's hand to his forehead and asked him to tell him whether he had a temperature. Deciding that he must have a cold, Gen went back to bed. It was quite unusual for Gen to be ill, for he normally enjoyed the best of health.

'I'll be all right tomorrow. Come here and I'll tell you some stories,' he said to Kishū with a smile, making him sit by the bed. Yet he spoke to Kishū just as if he were a child, asking him if he had ever seen a shark and such things. After a while he looked directly at Kishū and asked him if he ever missed his mother, but Kishū did not seem to understand, so Gen said:

'Stay here as long as you like. Think of me as your father.' Breathing painfully, he continued: 'The day after tomorrow I'll take you to the theatre. They're performing *Awa no Jūrōbei* and I think that after you've seen it you'll understand what family love is all about. Then you must think of me as your father, for that is what I shall be to you.'

Then Gen told him the plot of the play which he had seen a long time before. He sang a song from it in a faint voice and cried to himself for the sorrow of it. Yet Kishū seemed not to understand at all.

'Well, I see. It's difficult to understand when you're just hearing about it. When you see it tomorrow, you will cry too.'

By then Gen's breath was coming in painful gasps and finally he slept, exhausted by the effort of his narrative. When he awoke, Kishū was gone. But in reality he had not woken at all, he was just dreaming in his delirium. He dreamed that he was running about calling 'Kishū, my son! Kishū, my son!', but instead of Kishū an old beggar woman appeared and said that Kishū was her son. Even as he looked at her, she changed into a young woman. It was Yuri who was crying out that when she was asleep, her son Kōsuke had run away and gone. 'Come, come with me and look for him!' she cried. 'Look, my Kōsuke has dug up a piece of radish from the rubbish tip!' Then behind Yuri, stood Gen's own mother. She told him to look at a stage which was dazzlingly lit with many candles, but he only took cakes, wondering why his mother was crying and her eyes were red. At last he fell asleep with his small head on his mother's lap until he felt that Yuri and his mother were shaking him from his sleep and his dream was shattered. He looked up.

'Kishū, my son, I've had a terrible dream.' But Kishū had really gone. 'My son!' he cried hoarsely. There was no reply save the wind singing eerily through the windows. Was this dream or reality? Gen suddenly threw off his blankets and stood up, crying Kishū's name, but everything went black before his eyes and he slumped back on the bed. It felt as if he had sunk a thousand fathoms to the sea bed and the waves were crashing over his head.

That day Gen did not leave his bed, nor did he eat anything. He did not even poke his head from beneath the bedding. A wind which had risen during the morning gradually grew more violent as the day went on and the clamour of the waves beating against the shore was terrible to hear. None of the bay people left the town and there were none to cross over to the island, so there was no one to need the ferry. As evening drew on the waves grew wilder and the jetty groaned ominously making people think that it was about to be destroyed. Early next morning when the first light paled the eastern sky, many of the people, clad in raincoats and carrying lamps, came down to the jetty. It was all right after all, but even though the wind had dropped, the waves were still high and the offshore sea was crashing like thunder as the waves dashed against the shore, making a spray like heavy rain. When the people surveyed the desolate scene, they noticed the remains of a boat which had been driven onto the rocks and half broken up.

'Whose is that boat?' said one of the shopowners.

'I'm sure it's Gen's,' answered one of the younger men, and everyone looked at each other in silence.

'Someone should go and tell him.'

'I'll go,' said the same young man, and resting his lamp on the ground, he ran off.

He had not gone far when he noticed something curious hanging from the pine tree by the road. He was a courageous young man and did not hesitate to go straight up and see what it was. It was Gen. He had hanged himself.

At the foot of the hill, as close as possible to Katsura harbour, there was a grave and it was there that Gen's wife, Yuri, and his son, Kōsuke, were buried. The people erected a new gravestone there the inscription on which read: 'The grave of Ikeda Gentarō' (Old Gen's full name). Now there were three graves, with Kōsuke's in the middle and there Gen lay even as the young teacher in the capital sat musing about how he was getting along living alone by the sea shore, thinking about his wife and child.

Kishū was just the same as ever, taken by the people, as before, as a regular fixture to Saeki, and given to wandering the streets of the old castle town like a ghost escaped from the grave. When he was told that Gen had hanged himself, he just stared uncomprehendingly.

3

The Bonfire

Takibi (The Bonfire) was first published in November 1896 in vol. 19 no. 323 of the *Kokumin no Tomo* and represents one of the earliest transitional works between Doppo's poetry and fiction. It falls into the category of 'prose poetry', and, for once, is in no real sense autobiographical. As remarked in the introduction, however, it does contain many of the elements which Doppo was later to develop in his other stories — the misery of the wandering vagabond, the innocence of childhood and the cleansing imagery of water which wipes away all traces of the children's fire and thus, in a sense, the old man's misery.

With his back to the north wind, a child is sitting on the withered white grass of a sand dune, watching the evening sun as it sets beyond the Izu mountains. He waits for his father's ship which is long overdue, and his heart is lonely and sad. Dead reeds on the bank of the Saigo river rustle in the salt-laden breath of the wind as it blows and ice formed at their roots in the full of the midnight tide, unseen by the eyes of men, though shattered by the morning ebb-tide, remains unmelted throughout the day, etching white lines at the water's edge in the dusk. If a weary traveller were to stop by this stream, is it possible that he could look around him unaware and pass on unfeeling? For this is the grove of Holy Rokudai* which even after the passing of seven hundred years, still compels pity as the icy winds howl through its branches.

A boat makes its way against the gentle river current amidst the drifting fallen leaves. In other days one might have heard a jovial boatman's song come echoing from the boat to proclaim the frosty night to come, but this man — whether he is farmer or fisherman it is impossible to tell — just looks about him, saying nothing. He neither laughs nor sings, but just rows silently on in his loneliness. The shadows of a bridge and a farmer with a hoe over his shoulder reflect indistinctly in the water, but they are shattered soundlessly by the boat as it glides among the reeds. Sometimes one can see two young villagers quietly walking their horses through the shallows of the river mouth. It is just like a picture

---

* Rokudai (d. 1198). A Buddhist monk of the Taira family who was treacherously murdered on his way to Kamakura in 1198.

as they are caught in the dying rays of the evening sun. At such times the beach is empty as far as the eye can see save, perhaps, for a crow perched on the bow of a boat, flapping its wings soundlessly and flying off towards Kamakura.

December was drawing to a close, pressed hard by the New Year to come, but the seven or eight children playing on the beach were like the children of the wind, lighthearted and free. They were assembled beneath a sand dune engaged in an animated discussion, some standing and some sitting. One boy was lying down with his elbows dug deeply in the sand and his chin resting on his hands. Even as they talked the sun was sinking in the West.

Having finished their discussion, the boys all ran down to the edge of the sea where they quickly separated and ran about collecting everything that the storm of two nights before had thrown up and the tide had neglected to take back. There was a bit of rotten board, a chipped bowl, a few pieces of bamboo, slivers of wood and a ladle which was minus a handle. All the things they gathered they made into a pile in the dry sand where the tide could not reach. But everything they found was already soaked through.

What were they up to, these children running around in the chill of the evening? The setting sun had dyed gold the clouds which seemed to enshroud the peak of Mt. Ashigara, and the fishing boats were heading for harbour with their sails furled and the men applying the oars as they came closer to shore and the wind dropped.

One of the boys, handsome despite his round face and swarthy complexion, had found an old mirror with the glass missing, but to him it seemed a pity for such a thing to be burned. However, one of the older boys, just at that moment busy with a thick pole which was almost too much for him to manage, said that it would burn best of all. The round-faced discoverer of the mirror denied that it would burn, but the other turned angrily away, insisting that it would. Another boy, standing by the older boy's side, shouted out joyfully that this was the best collection they had ever made.

So this was it. The boys were going to make a bonfire of what they had collected. Just the sight of the flickering red flames would send them wild with delight and they would run and leap across the fire, just to see who was the bravest. Next they gathered dry grass from the sand dunes and the eldest boy stepped forward to put flame to the bonfire. They all stood round in a circle waiting expectantly to hear the loud report of the bamboo as it was split by the flames, but nothing happened. The grass just burned and died. There were a few puffs of smoke and that was it. The wood and bamboo failed to catch light and their only reward for their efforts was a slight charring of the mirror frame and a little steam which came hissing from the end of the thick pole. One after the other the boys got down on the sand and blew at the fire, but all they got for their pains was a gush of smoke which stung their eyes. The sea was dark now and no longer could they make out the outline of Enoshima Island. A flock of plovers flew along the beach, their sad cries first sounding near at hand and then gradually vanishing into the darkness, appearing as white shapes in the evening gloom and finally disappearing into the night. Then, with a flurry of wings, a covey of snipe flew up from the reeds.

Just then, one of the boys shouted out excitedly:

'Look! Look! The hills of Izu are on fire! If their fires burn, then so will ours!'

The boys jumped up and looked out over the sea, and there, far across Sagami Bay, two fires flickered and trembled mysteriously like will-o'-the-wisps. It must have been the mountain farmers of Izu firing their fields. And these are the fires which bring tears to the eyes of travellers in winter, for they give warning of the long, lonely road that lies ahead in the dusk.

'The hills of Izu burn! The hills of Izu burn!' the boys chanted wildly, and as they looked out across the waves, they clapped their hands and danced as if they had taken leave of their senses. Ah! How their innocent voices echoed down the desolate beach in the dusk! The murmuring waves came rushing in from the southern tip of the cove in foaming white lines, as if in accompaniment to the boys' chanting. Now the tide was beginning to rise.

'How long do you think you're going to carry on playing in the cold night air?' came a voice, calling from over the dunes, but not one of the boys heard, so entranced they were with the fires of Izu. 'Come home! Come home!' the voice called, two or three times, and at last a small boy heard.

'My mother's calling. I'm going home,' he cried. Off he ran and the others rushed after him, scrambling to be the first to reach the top of the sand dune. The eldest boy, annoyed that their fire had been such a failure, kept looking back over his shoulder as he ran and when he reached the top of the dune, he gave one last look before joining the others. At last the fire was burning.

'It's burning! It's burning!' he shouted and the other boys turned on their heels and climbed back to the top of the dune where they stood in a row and looked down. The bits of wood which hitherto had refused to catch light had been fanned into flame by the wind. Billows of thick smoke swirled up and red tongues of flame flickered in and out, with showers of sparks flying up as the bamboo joints cracked. At last, after all their trouble, the fire was burning, but the boys did not stop to enjoy it. They shouted out and clapped their hands with joy for a moment and then raced down the hill for home.

With the boys gone, it was a cheerless winter's night and the sea and the beach were in darkness apart from the fire which burned on somehow sadly, now that there was no one to tend it. And then there was a black shadow moving along by the water's edge towards the fire. It was an old man, a traveller, who had just crossed the Saigo river and come out on the beach as he headed for the road beyond. He walked faster as he noticed the fire, but his steps sounded laboured.

'What a splendid fire!' he cried, his voice cracked and feeble. He threw aside his stick and having set down his pack as fast as he could, he held out his hands to the flames, trembling all over as he did so. 'How cold the night is,' he said to himself and his teeth chattered. His face shone red in the glow of the flames which revealed a deeply wrinkled brow and sunken, somehow lifeless eyes. His beard and hair were flecked with grey and speckled with dust. The tip of his nose was red, but the rest of his face partook of the colour of earth. Who was he and where was he from, this old man? And where was he going, if indeed he knew himself?

'How cold the night is!' he said again, shivering as he spoke. Pleasurably, he pressed his warmed palms to his face. Then he pressed his cloak, which was so old that the cotton padding showed through in places, to the fire, causing steam to rise from the hem. It had been drenched in the morning rain and this was the first chance he had had to dry it.

'What a pleasant fire!' he said, picking up the stick he had thrown aside. Using it as a support, he held one leg over the flames. His leggings and socks were of a faded blue and through a hole in one of the socks peeped a small, bloodless toe. Suddenly there was a sharp crack from the splitting bamboo and the flames leaped up to his foot, but the old man made no attempt to move.

'What a truly pleasant fire! How I wish I could thank the person who lit it!' he said, changing to his other foot. 'It has been ten long, long years since I left the comfort of my own fireside and in all that time I have never found such a pleasant fire as this.' He stared into the flames as if his eyes were searching for something far away, seeing perhaps a vision of that other fire which had burned so long ago. Perhaps there were sons and grandsons too in that vision. That old fire was full of joy and this one was sad.

'But no,' he said to himself, 'what's past is past and one must think only of the present. This is a happy fire.' His voice trembled as he spoke. With a violent gesture he hurled his stick away, and with his back turned to the fire, stood up straight and looked out to sea. He pounded both fists against his hips and looked up at the sky which was black and clear. As it dipped down to meet the distant Izu headland, it seemed to enshroud the Milky Way with frost.

Now he felt warmer and his coat was dry at last. He had time to wonder again who had lit the fire and who for. His heart was filled with thankfulness and his eyes brimmed with tears. There was no wind, not even a breeze, and the sea was still. The old man closed his eyes and listened to the rippling waves of the incoming tide as it swept over the beach. Perhaps, for just a moment, he had forgotten the woes of his travelling life and his heart could dwell again on the joys of his boyhood.

Now the fire was burning itself out. The bamboo and bits of wood had burned away and there was only the thick pole which still burned happily. But the old man had no regrets. He just stood over the fire, his arms clasped firmly round him, and was lost in old memories. Then he stretched and took two or three paces before turning back to rake up the scraps of wood still burning and put them on the fire. He smiled happily as he watched the fire burn for a moment or two with renewed vigour.

Even after the old man had gone on his way, there was still a red glow from the fire as it flickered precariously in the silent blackness of the night. Later on as the night advanced, the tide came full and all traces of the boys' bonfire and the old traveller were buried beneath the waves for all eternity.

4

The Deer Hunt

Shikagari (The Deer Hunt) belongs to what is generally described as Doppo's 'Saeki period', referring to the year between 1893 and 1894 which he spent as a teacher at the Tsuruya Gakkan in the castle town of Saeki in Ōita Prefecture, Kyūshū. First published in issue number 119 of the magazine *Katei Zasshi* in August 1898, just a week after *Kawagiri* (River Mist), *Shikagari* is based on an actual experience of Doppo. His diary entry for 5 December, 1893, records the following brief description of what happened:

> 'On the evening of Saturday, 2 December, my brother and I, with ten others, were invited to take part in a deer hunt. We took a boat from Katsura harbour to a place called Uramai and spent the whole of Sunday from first light in the hunting of deer. We spent the night at Uramai, but the next morning five of us returned overland on foot to Saeki.'

Allowing for the changes in place names, this account is substantially the same as the events described in *Shikagari*, and in fact one of the men who went on the deer hunt with Doppo was actually called Nakane, as is the boy's uncle in the story. Another member of the real-life party named Ozaki was reputedly the model for 'Uncle Imai'. *Shikagari* is a pleasantly evocative story told in the first person, but in a generally detached manner. It is somewhat marred as a work of art, however, by the arbitrary inclusion of a tragic element in the form of Tetsuya's madness. This was undoubtedly an excess on Doppo's part, because the story hangs together very well just as an account of a deer hunt, and does not need this kind of forced conclusion.

'How would you like to come with me on a deer hunt?' my uncle, Mr Nakane, asked me one day, much to my surprise. 'It would be fun, you know. Well, will you come?' he insisted with a beaming smile. He was a kindly man.

'But I don't have a gun.'

'Ha, ha! That's a good one. You don't think I'd let you fire a gun, do you? No, my lad, you'd just be going along to watch.'

I suppose it was quite natural that he should laugh for I was barely eleven years old and could not have shot a sparrow, let alone a deer. But in the end I decided to go along because I had heard many times what fun it was on a hunting trip. And so on the night of 3 December I set out for my uncle's house where the hunting party had arranged to meet. My mother had tried to prevent me from going because she thought it would be dangerous, but she had been over-ruled by my father who said that it would make more of a man of me.

There was already quite a crowd when I reached my uncle's house, but I was the only child and the only one not going to take an active part in the hunt itself. By the time the whole party had assembled there were ten men altogether, not one of them under thirty years old. All came from the upper reaches of local society, including my uncle, the president of the bank, the local judge and the district governor. We lived in a small locality and all these men were very well acquainted, so their talk on this occasion was rather unrestrained. A lamp was hanging in the entrance hall and three or four wooden braziers had been put out around which the hunting party stood in small groups, laughing and bantering. Tobacco smoke hung over the room in a haze. Mr Imai, another uncle of mine, had the loudest voice of any present. He was also the most jovial, the most involved, the fattest, the oldest, and, to me, the most entertaining man there.

The eleven-strong party set out at ten o'clock. The plan was to walk the couple of miles from the town to Kanoji harbour, there to take a boat for the ten or so miles by sea to Tsunojisaki, spending the night aboard the boat, and on arrival at Sanojiura towards dawn, to begin the hunt.

'We're just like a band of brigands!' shouted my uncle Imai, laughing in that deep voice he had. And he was quite right, for we were no ordinary party if appearances should count for anything. Each man was wearing rough, sturdy western clothing, with straw sandals and leggings; each had his own gun and there was a real assortment of headgear. How could we seem other than a band of desperadoes out on a night raid? Well, we may have looked like brigands, but we certainly didn't behave like them unless it happened to be a particularly audacious band! Ten men, chattering away for all they were worth on the way to Kanoji harbour, and what a row they made! No, as I say, not at all like the usual run of brigand. I walked alone in silence a little way behind the rest, listening to their conversation. The talk was mostly of hunting, chiefly bragging of exploits and tall stories about 'the ones that got away'. In this too it was my uncle Imai who had the most amusing things to tell, making everyone laugh, and when no one else was laughing, he just laughed hugely to himself. When we arrived at the harbour, we found the boatman ready and waiting. He pushed off from the tiny jetty in the forlorn little harbour and hoisted the sail. The wind was favourable so we raced along most satisfyingly, the boat heeling a little to port.

It was a cold, dark winter's night and the stars in the sky seemed vivid enough to count and as the bows knifed through the sea, the waves were black and the island in total darkness. For me it was an unforgettable night. The men began to break out the *sake*. The talk, as ever, was of hunting, but though I listened with interest I was unable to prevent myself from falling asleep. It was a calm, innocent sleep, untroubled by dream or reality. My ear lay to the bottom of the boat and as I drifted off to sleep I could hear the sound of the water lapping against the gunwales of the boat and the gently whispering creaking of the joints which made a noise like laughter. It was a fine feeling. My uncle Imai and the others were sitting in a happy circle under the hazy beam of the dim side-light. By now some of them were jabbering drunkenly, reeling against the gunwales or catching forty winks, but my uncle's good spirits remained undiminished.

'Now, if I had your gun, my friend, if I missed with one shot, I'd nail it with the second. But with my gun, if I'm going to hit the target it has to be with the first shot, eh!' he said and laughed, 'Ha, ha, ha, ha!'

Mr Oka, the judge, apparently made some bantering remark to him, but I was dozing and did not catch it.

* * *

'Toku! Toku!' I seemed to hear a voice calling me and I felt a plump hand shaking me by the shoulder. I knew immediately that it was Uncle Imai.

'Come on, Toku. Get up. We're there. Come on now, get up!'

'I'm sleepy.'

Truthfully I was still sleepy, but as everyone was making ready to land, I got up, rubbing my eyes. A fine, crescent moon was the first thing that caught my attention. The boat was drawing up to the foot of a mountain, whether on the mainland or an island I could not tell, and the boatman was furling the sail.

On land not a light was to be seen and the only sound was that of the waves lapping the shore. It was dark and silent. The cold seemed to stab through me and it was almost as if the light of the moon over the edge of the mountain was frozen. It was indefinably macabre. Gradually the boat drew inshore and as it did so the lie of the land grew more familiar. So this was Sanojiura of which I had heard so much. We tied up the boat to a tiny jetty, hardly really worthy of the name, and made our landing. A lone fisherman's hut stood on shore. In true brigand fashion we made our way stealthily to this hut only to find that an old man of about sixty had come out to meet us, apparently thoroughly forewarned of our coming. We decided to rest at the fisherman's hut until dawn and accordingly everyone put down their guns and made themselves at home while they waited for the first light in the eastern sky. I lay down among the others by the hearth. Some of our company partook of large cups of *sake* poured out for them by the fisherman's children, but my uncle Imai, perhaps not unnaturally exhausted, stretched out his huge frame beside me and went off to sleep, snoring loudly. The flames of the hearth fire reflected red in his fleshy face.

At last it was beginning to grow light outside and everyone began to stir, everyone that is but my uncle Imai who remained dead to the world. I rushed outside and saw that where before there was only the blackness of the night, now lay a desolate stretch of beach. All round the fisherman's hut right up to the eaves sardines were hanging to dry. Some ground was under cultivation in the mountain hollows, but apart from that there was only grass and the occasional pine thrusting into the sky. I found myself wondering whether there could possibly be any deer in such a place. The hue of the sky and the rays of the dawn moon told me that we would have excellent weather that day; ah! the cleanness of the wind, the cold, the distant sparkle of the moon, the deepness of the sky! We should get our deer today. No doubt of it!

'Toku! Toku! Wake your uncle Imai, will you please,' someone called from the hut. When I went back to look I found everyone ready to depart except my uncle who was still snoring loudly.

'Come on, uncle,' I said, shaking him by the shoulder, but he did not stir. Eventually I got him up by the simple but effective expedient of grabbing his hair and pulling hard. He yawned hugely.

'This child has no heart! Well, come on then. Let's get on with it! You'll soon see who achieves the best exploits today,' he shouted, leaping up to take charge. I followed hard at his heels as if I were his man-servant.

We climbed a narrow track which wound upwards across the lower slopes of the mountain to form, at its highest point, part of the Tsuno-jisaki ridge. The sea was on both sides. Then the track forked into two, one path leading along the ridge itself and the other leading down the other side of the mountain towards Nanojiura. Where the three tracks met stood a pine tree under which we took a breather while we waited for the arrival of the professional huntsmen who were to come up from Nanojiura. The morning sun rose out of the Hiuga sea and one face of Tsunojisaki was enveloped in a crimson mist. On the distant horizon the waters of the Hiuga sea merged with the Pacific Ocean and there was not a cloud in the sky. Shikoku stood out vividly above the waves, and on all sides the view gave the impression of a vast nobility and splendour.

We made ourselves a big bonfire to ward off the cold and waited until at last ten sturdy hunting hounds came into view on the Nanojiura road, followed hard by six huntsmen all clad in strange clothes. Now these men really did look like brigands. Their guns were old-fashioned and crude, but the huntsmen were skilled in their use through many years of handling. Most important of all, they had a thorough knowledge of the Tsunojisaki terrain and they excelled in their handling of the dogs. When you take all this into consideration, you can see why it was that the relationship between them and our party was that of master and pupil, professional and amateur. Of course my uncle and the others were not too happy about it, but there was nothing they could do. Accordingly, in the planning of the hunt we were obliged to do what these professional huntsmen said.

When at last we reached it, our hunting ground turned out to be a valley, overrun with grasses and thorns, at the foot of the mountain almost at the verge of the headland. Everyone agreed that I should stay with my uncle Imai for the duration of the hunt. The hounds raced ahead and reached the hunting ground before any of the men; we could hear them baying ferociously as we walked along the ridge.

'There they go. Just look at that! They have found a deer. Quickly now!'

I followed my uncle's pointing finger and, sure enough, there was a deer bounding along the edge of the mountain with two of the baying hounds hot in pursuit. The whole scene was illuminated by the rays of the morning sun. I had seen pictures of deer before and I had seen dead ones, but this was the first time I had ever seen one for real and I clapped my hands for the sheer joy of seeing it run. Uncle Imai grinned to see my delight.

'Watch now, and you'll see them bag that deer.'

'But surely it's run away and they'll never catch it now.'

'Where can it go? The hunters have already circled round the other side of the mountain.' He was supremely elated.

By now we and the others had taken up our positions and as uncle Imai commanded the spot on the slope towards which the deer was running, he and I just had to beat aside a thicket of grass, hardly having to move in the process, to occupy a vantage point as good as we could have hoped for.

'If we wait here, the deer's bound to come this way,' he said. Again and again I gazed over the hills and valleys waiting in vain for another sight of the deer. With so many hills, fields and hollows for the deer to run into, it seemed a difficult operation to kill one with just fifteen or sixteen people and ten dogs, but of course as the hunting ground was on a headland the sea was on three sides making it almost impossible for the deer to escape that way. To add to that a high stone wall had been built over by the human dwellings to prevent their fields from being despoiled, so the deer could not go that way either. What was more, the huntsmen knew all the deer's paths. Therefore, provided the round-up was properly executed, it was not so difficult as you would imagine to kill a deer even with a small number of men and dogs. As my uncle's position lay in the path of the deer's escape it was very much to the point just to sit and wait for it to come.

My uncle gave me instructions to keep my eyes open, and with his gun at the ready and a broad smile of exultation on his fat, swarthy face, he looked around him, straining his ears for the sound of a shot. Occasionally human shapes appeared and disappeared over by the ridge and

at the foot of the headland on our side. The sun was shining brightly
and there was a gentle breeze so that every so often small thickets
rustled mysteriously. Whenever that happened my eyes widened in an-
ticipation and my uncle shifted the position of his gun.

'Hey, Toku,' he said after a while, 'I thought I heard a shot just now.
Go over to that pine and take a look. It may be they've already got one.'

I went where he indicated to a spot a little higher up the headland a
couple of hundred yards away where the crown of the mountain began
to level off a little. When I got there I saw a deer hanging in the
branches of the pine just beyond my reach. Not unnaturally, being just
a child after all, I was frightened, but when I went close up to the tree I
saw that it was not a very large deer and it had no antlers. A bullet was
lodged in its haunches. I must say I felt sorry for the animal, and how
could I feel otherwise when I saw the gentle expression in its eyes which
it still bore as in life, and when I saw it cruelly suspended from the pine
by its four legs.

Just at that moment a hunter appeared on the scene, pushing his way
through the thicket.

'Now, sonny, next time we'll get one as big as a horse.'

'You mean you're carrying on with the hunt?'

'Oh yes. We'll get ten before the day's out.'

I did not believe that for I could not see how we could take them
home with us if we killed that number. The hunter sat himself on a rock
and took two or three puffs at his pipe, but at the sound of a whistle
from the valley he disappeared into the thicket and was gone as quickly
as he had come. And I was gone too, hurrying back to my uncle.

'Well? Did they get one? Just you wait and see! We'll get a real
monster here.'

What with this and that, noon had come and there was still no sign of
my uncle and me getting a deer, but all of a sudden we heard a shot
right at the foot of the mountain and we saw a puff of white smoke. We
stiffened and looked towards where the shot had come from. Three men
came into view; one of them dropped to his knees and fired a second,
third and fourth shot. Some dogs charged on ahead, baying fiercely.

'Hey! Look! There's a deer in the sea!' my uncle shouted, leaping to
his feet in excitement. Sure enough, I caught sight of something swimming in the sea, though I could not clearly make out what it was. Even
as I watched, a small boat put out from the shore; there was the sound of
a shot from the boat and the swimming object disappeared to be seen no
more. The boat returned to the shore.

'That was a big 'un. Hmm. It was well done,' my uncle murmured to
himself elatedly. 'Are you hungry, Toku?'

'Yes, I am.'

'Well, let's have lunch then.' He took out the lunchbox and we
stretched ourselves out on the grass and began to eat. Never has a picnic

lunch tasted as good as it did that day. My uncle produced a bottle gourd and helped himself to *sake* which he drank with much relish and smacking of lips.

'I'll enjoy this *sake* much more when we've made a kill and kill a deer we will, just you wait and see! I think I'll save my *sake* until then,' he said, shaking the gourd.

We finished our lunch and my uncle stretched himself out to sleep. It was about one o'clock by now and as it was a mild region it seemed just like a balmy autumn day, for all that it was winter. The shimmering heat of the sun seemed warm enough to melt a man in heart and body. New green vegetation could be seen here and there mingled with the dried grass and it glimmered in the soft breeze as the rays of the sun beat down upon it. The rippling waves of the sea and the sky were one vast expanse of blue, the one reflecting the colour of the other. On the eastern horizon the boundless sky and sea merged and in the North the mountains of Shikoku seemed closed enough to touch. Hiuga stretched away to the right, its southern tip lost in the haze of distant spray. I gazed at this scene spellbound, but before I knew it my eyelids began to grow heavy. Beside me my uncle was already snoring loudly, doubtless because the *sake* had taken its effect. His bronzed face was turned towards the sun.

I sensed some movement in the thicket close by where we lay and when I looked casually in its direction I could see a pair of antlers which obviously belonged to a huge stag. A stag! What should I do? I tried to wake my uncle, but I quickly gave it up because I knew that if I succeeded he would surely shout out and scare it away. Without thinking what I was doing, I stealthily took my uncle's gun which was leaning against a small pine. The stag seemed totally unaware that there was any human present and it began to move towards me, walking calmly through the shade of the thicket. Then it stopped. I could have touched it with the tip of my gun barrel if only I had dared to stretch out my hands. The stag seemed very huge and already my heart was beginning to swell with a regret that I had not waited to wake my uncle; but it was too late. I just had time to reflect how odd it much have looked to see a child of eleven holding a gun to a stag the size of a small horse. Then, with trembling hands, I made the best of it and pulled the trigger. I fell over backwards with a thud from the recoil waking my uncle in the process. He leaped to his feet.

'Hey, what's going on?' He raised me to my feet, obviously thinking that I had slipped. I ran into the thicket, followed by my uncle.

'You hit him!' he shouted as caught sight of the stag and then he clutched me to him with a strange smile in his eyes which were moist with tears.

The hunt was not so successful that day as the huntsman had prophesied, but we killed six deer in all which was by no means a bad achievement. The stag I had shot was the biggest of the lot. All the way home my uncle Imai never let me out of his sight exorbitantly praising my adventure to all who would listen. For the homeward journey the party divided into two, half returning by boat and half on foot overland, and because my uncle would not suffer me to leave him I went with him by land. There were five others in our party including the judge.

As we walked along the sloping path of the Unoji ridge, the judge paused for a moment to shoot a tiny black bird which was perched on a rock in a mountain stream. I ran off and retrieved it for him. The judge whispered something to my uncle at which he looked very serious. He then took the bird from the judge with a muttered 'thank you'. This whole incident astonished me because I could not think of any reason for it.

Two months passed during which I went to play at my uncle's house every day and he always took me with him when he went out to shoot birds. However, one day my father returned home from work and astonished my mother and myself with the news:

'Tetsuya has shot himself.'

Tetsuya, you see, was my uncle Imai's only son and four or five years before he had tragically gone out of his mind. He was not violent but he was totally incapable of doing anything for himself. I think he was about twenty at the time and if he had been normal he would, of course, have been my uncle's pride and joy and hope for the future. However, with all his future hopes dashed, my uncle, almost entirely abandoned himself to despair and became addicted to just two things — *sake* and hunting. Somehow, it seemed as if he too had lost his reason, and everyone felt very sorry for him. Now, however, Tetsuya, quite contrary to expectation, had shot himself dead. A madman is a madman, but when he is your only son you will try any medicine to cure him of his madness and such it seemed had been the bird which the judge shot in the valley of the Unoji ridge. But now a cruel fate had overtaken Tetsuya and all my uncle's hopes had died with him.

It was about a month before I went again to my uncle's because it made me so sad to see him, but one day when I returned from school I found that my uncle had come to see my father and was discussing something with him in a back room. And that very same evening, my mother and father had a very earnest talk with my elder brother. The outcome of all this secretive talk was that I was adopted by my uncle — he became my father.

Thereafter I went hunting with my adoptive father many times, but whenever I saw a crow perched on a rock I quietly picked up a stone and chased it away for it always put him in a bad mood to see one.

This year is the thirteenth anniversary of his death. He was a kindly, brave, honourable, compassionate, but sad man and I have told this childhood story of a deer hunt as a memorial to him.

5

Those Unforgettable People

Wasure-enu Hitobito (Those Unforgettable People) was one of Doppo's earliest works and was first published in April 1898 in vol. 22 no. 368 of the *Kokumin no Tomo*. It is considered as being one of his Saeki period works, but in fact the actual idea for this story came to Doppo during a trip to Chiba Prefecture some four months before he went to Saeki. At an inn one night he made friends with another resident and was so impressed by the experience that he subsequently wrote it into a piece called *Shūu* (A Sudden Storm of Rain). He then decided to use it as the basis for this longer story incorporating other experiences he had at Saeki.

One of the 'unforgettable people' is a young man driving a wagon at the foot of Mt. Aso, and it is known for certain that Doppo and his brother Shūji (who is also mentioned) actually climbed Mt. Aso when they were on their way back home for a holiday. The other incidents recorded are also based on actual experiences. The story centres on a man named Ōtsu who has great difficulty in forming human relationships. He meets a young artist named Akiyama and describes to him his loneliness and bitterness. He shows him the pathetic manuscript in which he records the fleeting encounters which act for him as substitutes for friendship, but there is an inevitable irony about the conclusion. Akiyama, probably the first person Ōtsu has met for a long while actually capable of offering him the very friendship he so sorely needs, is ignored by Ōtsu who remembers only the landlord of the inn where they met.

If you cross the Tama river at Futago and go on a little way, you come to the post town of Mizunokuchi, in the middle of which stands the Kameya inn.

It was right at the beginning of March. The sky was overcast and a strong North wind was blowing, making the place seem even colder and more forlorn than usual — it was a gloomy enough place at the best of times. The snow which had fallen the previous day still lay on the ground and drops of rain, dancing in the wind, fell from the eaves on the southern side of the inn's uneven thatched roof. There were even cold ripples on the muddy water trapped in the footprints made by travellers on the road. It was dusk and most of the shops had not long put up their shutters, but for all that it was very quiet in the darkened town. Being an inn, there was still a light shining brightly through the door of Kameya's, but there seemed to be no guests that night and it was quiet inside. In fact the only sound was the occasional tapping of a pipe on the edge of the brazier.

Suddenly the door of the inn was flung open and a man lurched into the room. The landlord was sitting by the brazier, so busy concentrating on some book-work that he failed to notice the new arrival. The traveller, for traveller he was with his western style clothing, sandals, leggings, and a fowling hat on his head, crossed over to the landlord and stood before him. He was a man two or three years short of thirty. In his right hand he carried an umbrella and in his left a small bag which he clutched to his side.

'I'd like a room for the night, if you please.'

The landlord was still too busy taking in the traveller's appearance to make any reply, but at that moment there was the sound of a handclap somewhere at the back of the inn.

'Something wanted in number six!' bellowed the landlord. 'And now, sir, may I ask who you are and where you're from?' The landlord had still not moved from his place by the brazier.

The traveller shrugged his shoulders and frowned slightly, but there was a smile playing round his lips as he replied.

'Me? I'm from Tokyo.'

'And where are you heading?'

'I'm going to Hachiōji.' As he answered the traveller sat down and untied the strings of his leggings.

'Well, sir, you're taking a strange route to get from Tokyo to Hachiōji, if you don't mind my saying so.' He gazed suspiciously at the traveller's appearance as he had done before, but this time he was giving voice to his suspicions as the other immediately perceived.

'No. I'm *from* Tokyo, but I haven't come from there today. I left Kawasaki late and now it's dark. Do you think I could have some hot water, please?'

The landlord ordered some water to be brought immediately.

'Well, sir, it's pretty cold today and even worse over Hachiōji way.' The landlord spoke civilly enough, but his whole manner was very unfriendly. He was a man of sixty or so and he wore a thick cotton coat which made it appear that his head rose straight from his shoulders with no neck in between. The eyes in his broad, happy face were turned down and there was something moody about his whole countenance. For all that, however, the traveller immediately realised that he was dealing with a man of integrity.

The traveller washed his feet, but before he had time to dry them the landlord shouted out:

'Show the gentleman to number seven!' Just that, and no word to his guest. He did not even favour him with a glance as he left.

A black cat emerged from the kitchen, crawled softly into his master's lap and curled into a ball. The landlord might or might not have been aware of this for his eyes were closed. Presently the fingers of his right hand slipped into his pouch and rolled some tobacco into a ball.

'If the man in number six has finished with the bath house, show the one in number seven to it!'

Startled, the cat jumped from his lap.

'Little silly! I wasn't talking to you.'

The cat scuttled off to the kitchen in confusion and as it did so, the clock struck a leisurely eight.

'Old woman, Kichizō must be sleepy. You'd better put in the warmer and send him to bed.' His voice sounded sleepy. From the kitchen a voice which seemed to belong to an old woman replied.

'He's in here, going over a book for his homework, I think.'

'Oh he is, is he! Go to bed, now, Kichizō, and get up early tomorrow to do your work. Woman, put in the bed-warmer as quick as you can.'

'I'll do it straightaway.' In the kitchen the old woman and a maid exchanged glances and sniggered.

'I'm sleepy,' the old woman muttered from the shop where she had gone to heat the bed-warmer, yawning hugely as she did so. She was a tiny old woman who must have been five or six years past her fiftieth birthday. The door of the inn rattled in the wind, the sound made faint by the noise of the rain pattering as it was driven by the wind.

'Shut up the shop doors now,' the landlord shouted, and then he tut-tutted to himself, 'It's come on to rain again.'

Indeed the wind had grown stronger and it seemed as if the rain had started up again with the express intention of making matters worse. Although it was the beginning of spring, the wind, mingled with cold sleet, was devastating the whole Musashino region in all its fury. All night it had raged over the pitch dark town of Mizunokuchi.

In room number seven a lamp still gleamed even after midnight where the two guests, the only people in the inn still not in bed, were locked in conversation. The wind and the rain were making a dreadful din outside and the rain shutters banged unceasingly.

'It won't be any use setting out tomorrow if it keeps up like this,' said the man from number six, looking at his companion.

'Well, I've nothing special to do, so I might as well stay here all day.'

The faces of both men were red and their noses shone. Three *sake* bottles stood on a side table and some dregs were left in their glasses. They were both in a comfortably relaxed mood, sitting cross-legged round the brazier smoking. The man from number six reached out his hand to tap the ash from his cigarette, baring his arm to the elbow in the process; then he inhaled deeply. Although the two men had only met for the first time that night in the inn, they were already on very frank terms. To begin with they had just exchanged a few words from behind their respective sides of the partition, but the man in number six was prompted by his loneliness to come into the new arrival's room uninvited. They exchanged cards. *Sake* was ordered and as they found pleasure in each other's conversation, it was not long before they were talking in the mixture of politeness and frankness common to people who get on well together. On 'Number Seven's' card was written the name Ōtsu Benjirō, with no mention of rank or title and the other man's card was similarly unadorned with just the name Akiyama Matsunosuke. Ōtsu, you will remember, was the man in western clothes who had arrived at dusk. He was a pale, slender man — in fact quite unlike Akiyama who was in his mid-twenties with a round, fat, red face and attractive eyes which seemed fixed in a permanent smile. Ōtsu was a writer of no particular fame or reputation, while Akiyama was an equally unknown artist; so it was a wonderful stroke of fortune that these two similar young men had fallen in together at this country inn.

'Shall we turn in now? We seem to have quite run out of things to say.'

They had been chattering away quite freely about art, literature and religion, and in their harsh denouncements of all the giants among contemporary writers and painters, they had quite failed to notice that it was past eleven o'clock.

'It's all right for a bit. It's out of the question to do anything tomorrow so we can talk all night if you like.'

'But what's the time?' asked Akiyama.

Ōtsu glanced at his watch which he had put aside.

'It's gone eleven.'

'Well, this is going to be an all-night session then,' said Akiyama, not at all troubled by the prospect. He studied his *sake* cup.

'But aren't you tired? Wouldn't you prefer to sleep?'

'No, I'm not the slightest bit sleepy. Perhaps you are, though. You see, as I left Kawasaki late, I've only travelled about ten miles today, so I'm quite all right.'

'Well, that goes for me too, but if you do go to bed, I'd like to borrow this and have a read.'

Akiyama picked up a manuscript, about ten pages long, written on Japanese paper. On the cover was written 'Those Unforgettable People'.

'It's awful rubbish, I'm afraid. It's rather like a pencil sketch by one of your artist cronies. No one else has any idea what it's about.'

But Ōtsu made no move to retrieve his manuscript from Akiyama who flicked through a couple of pages, reading passages here and there.

'Well, sketches are interesting, you know, just for what they are. I should like to read it if I may.'

'By all means, borrow it and have a look.'

Ōtsu took back the manuscript and read a few pieces here and there.

Neither of them spoke for a while, both becoming suddenly more aware of the sound of the wind and rain outside. With his eyes fixed on the manuscript he had written, Ōtsu listened attentively to the wind and rain in a kind of trance.

'This sort of night was made for you, eh?'

Ōtsu seemed not to hear Akiyama's voice, and made no reply. Perhaps it was because he was listening to the wind and rain; perhaps it was because he was looking at his manuscript; or perhaps it was because he was thinking about someone a thousand miles away. Whatever it was, Ōtsu's face and eyes seemed to tell Akiyama that for the moment he was in a world of his own. Then Ōtsu seemed to wake from his dream and turned to look at Akiyama.

'Perhaps it would be better if you discussed the contents of this manuscript with me instead of reading it for yourself. Your see, this book is a record of something which really happened and if you read it you might not understand.'

'Well, of course, I should much prefer to have the details from your own lips.'

As Akiyama looked at Ōtsu, he could see that there were tears in his eyes and there was a strange light shining from them.

'So be it then. I'll tell you in as much detail as possible, but if it bores you, don't hesitate to say so. For my part, I shall keep nothing back and there's nothing so strange about that for I am in a mood where I must tell someone.'

Akiyama put some charcoal on the brazier and placed the cold *sake* bottles in an iron kettle.

'The people I cannot forget are not necessarily unforgettable in themselves. Look and you will see that this is the first line of my manuscript.' Ōtsu held up the book so that Akiyama could see.

'Well, perhaps I should explain that line. If I do you will be better able to understand what I'm talking about, though I'm sure you would get the general idea.'

'There's no need. Just go right ahead. I shall listen as the representative of the readers of the world, but if you don't mind I shall listen lying down.'

Akiyama lay back, a cigarette in his mouth. He supported his head with his right hand and there was a broad smile on his face as he watched Ōtsu. Ōtsu then began his narrative.

'Leaving aside parents, children, friends and acquaintances, there are older people, teachers for example, of whom it is insufficient merely to say that they are unforgettable. People who have helped you in some significant way, I mean. You have to admit that these people are worthy to be remembered. Since they have sworn no oath of duty or affection for you, they have no obligation to you. You are just a stranger to them, and even when, by the very nature of things, you have forgotten them, it does not mean that you are lacking in affection or sense of obligation. However, there are some people in this world that you can just never forget. I do not say that there are many such people, but they exist for me at any rate, and perhaps for you too.'

Akiyama nodded a silent assent.

'I remember it was about the middle of spring in my nineteenth year. I had been unwell and so to recuperate I left school for a while and went home. What I am about to tell you happened on the homeward journey. I boarded the steamer from Osaka, which, as you know, plies the Inland Sea, and sailed through the calm waters of the springtime sea. It's a long time ago now, so I can't remember what sort of people my fellow passengers were, what sort of man the captain was or what the boy who brought round the refreshments looked like. Of course there may have been passengers aboard who at some time or other poured out tea for me or with whom I exchanged a few words on deck, but I retain absolutely no memory of them. That may be because I was in poor health at the time and was consequently not the best of company, being sunk in my own thoughts most of the time. All I remember is constantly going out on the deck, dreaming of the future and contemplating the state of man in the world. But, of course, this is the habit of the young and is nothing to wonder at.

'As the tranquil spring sun scattered its rays on the oily surface of the sea and the bow of the ship cut through the almost flat calm water with a satisfying sound, I watched out for islands in the trailing mist and gazed at the scenes which presented themselves from both sides of the boat. The islands seemed to float in the mist like a brocade woven of rape blossoms and green shoots of wheat. We passed by one small island about a thousand yards off on the starboard side and I went up to the railings to survey the scene. Here and there at the foot of the hilly coastline, there were groves of small pines, but as far as I could see there were no fields and no sign of human dwellings. The quiet and lonely beach, left bare by the ebb tide, shone in the sun. Tiny waves seemed to be almost playing with the shoreline and occasionally long rivulets of water glittered like naked swords before they disappeared.

'I could tell that the island was not uninhabited by the faint sound of the the songs of skylarks high in the sky above the hills. "If you see an ascending skylark, you know that the island has fields." That was a saying of my father's and it was the memory of that saying that made me realise that beyond doubt there were human dwellings on the other side of the hills. As I watched, I noticed a man walking along the shining beach where the tide had ebbed, repeatedly stooping to pick things up and put them in a basket — I had no idea what they were. I say it was a man because although I could not see clearly I was sure that it was a male and certainly not a child. Every two or three paces he bent down and picked something up. I stared intently at this man as he foraged about on the tiny beach in the shadow of the lonely island. As the boat moved forward his figure became a black speck and, eventually, man, beach and hills disappeared into the mist. For almost ten years now I have thought of this man in the shadow of the lonely island and whose face I never saw. He is one of those unforgettable people.

'About five years ago, I celebrated New Year's Day with my parents and then immediately set out on a journey in Kyushu, striking across the island from Kumamoto to Oita. Early one morning my younger brother and I, clad in straw sandals and gaiters, set out from Kumamoto in fine spirits. While the sun was still high in the sky we had walked as far as a post town called Tateno where we decided to put up for the night. Before sunrise next day we left Tateno heading in the direction of the white smoke of Mt. Aso which we both wished to climb. We trod through the frost across the bridge and eventually, after missing our way once or twice, climbed almost to the peak of the mountain by about midday. It must have been one o'clock by the time we reached the crater.

'Kumamoto is a warm region and as it was a fine, clear, windless day it didn't feel all that cold even on that lofty peak which towers some six thousand feet into the sky. It's true that the vapour belching from the crater was turning white as it froze in the air, but I couldn't see much snow anywhere on the mountain; only withered vegetation rustling in the slight breeze and here and there red or black patches of scorched earth formed into precipices, remnants of the older of the two craters on the mountain. It was a desolate scene, one where both the written and spoken word fail. I should think that the depiction of such a scene lies more in your province, Akiyama.

'We climbed right up to the lip of the crater, peering for a while into its awful depths and taking our fill of the glorious views all around us. Naturally, however, we couldn't put up with the chill of the breeze right on the peak, so we descended a little from the crater and ordered some rather inferior tea at a small hut which stands by the Aso shrine. We ate some rice-balls at this welcome refuge and then returned to the crater, our spirits restored. By this time the sun was sinking fast and a burning red haze hung over the Higo plain tinging it the same colour as the mountain cliffs. The many miles of withered vegetation at the foot of Kokonoetōge, which soared conically and surpassed in height all the surrounding mountains, was bathed in the evening sunlight and so clear was the air that we could see the passage of men and horses on the plain beneath us. The vast expanse of heaven vanished from our sight where it skimmed the lofty peak which groaned dreadfully beneath our feet and shot dense spirals of cloud into the sky above our heads. Perhaps because we were young; perhaps because it was so beautiful; or perhaps because this mountain was so merciless and cruel, we stood there for a while in total silence, like statues carved out of the rock. It seemed only natural to me at a time like this when heaven and earth were so calm, that an awareness of the miracle of man's existence should fill my heart.

'However, what attracted us most was a great depression situated between Kokonoetōge and Aso. We had previously been told that this was the remains of the world's largest volcanic crater, and we could clearly see where the Kokonoetōge plateau suddenly sloped away and the cliffs, extending over several miles, enclosed the western side of this depression. The Nantai Sanroku crater has become the picturesque and secluded Lake Chūzenji, but this great crater at Aso has been transformed into thousands of terraced fields which produce the five staple cereals. Now the villages, trees and wheat fields of the crater were glowing in the quiet of the evening sun. That night we would walk on tir̃ed feet until we reached the post town of Miyaji, which also lies in the crater, where we would sleep peacefully, enjoying our innocent dreams.

'We had discussed the idea of spending the night in the little mountain hut in order to see the activity of the volcano at night, but we had a long way to go and no time to spare, so in the end we decided to ease our way down the mountain, with Miyaji as our objective. The descent slope was much gentler than that of the ascent and we were able to hurry along the path which twists and turns like a snake through the withered vegetation between the ravines and the skirt of the mountain. As we approached a village we overtook some horses which were laden with this withered vegetation. Around us we could see several men and horses wending their way home, to the accompaniment of bells, along the tracks which wound about the lower slopes of the mountain, bathed in the evening sunlight. All the horses were loaded with the dead vegetation. Although we could see the foot of the mountain quite clearly it was no easy matter to reach the village and as dusk was almost upon us, we hurried down the mountain at a run. By the time we reached the village dusk had fallen and it was almost completely dark.

'The village was exceptionally busy with all the young men and women hurrying to finish their day's work and the children in groups, laughing, singing and crying in the shadows of the gloomy hedgerows or in front of the houses in sight of the hearth fires. It's the same everywhere in the countryside of course, but I have never been so struck by such a scene as I was then, having rushed down the desolate, grassy slopes of Mt. Aso to be suddenly hurled once more into the world of humanity. We dragged our weary legs, the coming of dusk having made us more conscious of how long a road lay ahead of us until we should come to our yearned-for destination at Miyaji.

'Leaving the village, we walked for a while through the woods and fields until the sun had completely disappeared and we could see our shadows clearly stamped on the ground ahead of us. We looked back at the western sky where we saw the new moon at the shoulder of one of the peaks in the Aso group, shining in lordly splendour over the villages in the great depression with a light like that of blue water. We looked up at the sky and saw that the volcano's smoke, white at noon, but now grey under the light of the moon, was thrusting into the emerald sky, even more beautiful and dreadful. When we came to a bridge we were happy to lean against its railings for a while to rest our weary feet and gaze at the various transformations in the volcano's smoke. Although we were not listening for it, we could hear the sound of human voices from the village, and after a bit we heard the sound of a waggon, seemingly empty, echoing through the woods, gradually drawing nearer until it seemed as if we could have reached out and touched it. Soon afterwards we were aware of another sound to accompany that of the waggon — the song of a pack-horse man, sung in a clear voice. As I gazed at the smoke from the mountain I strained my ears and, perhaps not quite consciously, waited for the owner of the voice to reach us.

'Miyaji is a fine place; it's a-at the foot of Aso.' At last he came into view, drawling the line from the popular song, until he reached the bridge on which we were standing. How deeply I was moved by that song and the tragic voice in which it was sung! He just flicked on the reins and passed by without even noticing us, but I had time to have a good look at him. He was a sturdy young man in his early twenties, but as his back was to the light of the early evening moon I could not make out his profile clearly. Even so, the dark outline of his brawny figure remains before my eyes to this very day. I followed him for a while with my gaze and then turned my attention back to the volcano's smoke. This young man is another example of 'those unforgettable people'.

'The next incident occurred during a stay at Mitsugahama where I spent a night while waiting for the steam packet. It was the beginning of summer, as I remember. Hearing that the steamer would be arriving in the afternoon, I left my inn early in the morning to take a stroll along the beach and through the harbour town. Mt. Matsuyama stands in the hinterland and the town is a very prosperous one.

Most noteworthy to me was the morning fish market all around which was a great hustle and bustle. The morning sun was shining serenely in an unblemished sky reflecting from shiny objects and giving light to coloured ones which had the effect of making the whole bustling scene even gayer. Everywhere was the sound of laughing and shouting voices; a mingled cacophony of sellers shouting their wares and the voices of the buyers. And everywhere old and young, men and women, bustling about, completely taken up with the sheer joy of rushing and pushing. The street stalls stood in lines ready and waiting for people to come and buy and eat. I won't bother to go into details about the goods that are sold in the market, but customers are usually of the ship's captain type. Sea bream, halibut, conger eels and octopuses lay scattered about and discarded everywhere and pungent smells assailed my nostrils fanned in the breeze made by sleeves and hems as people rushed hither and thither.

'I was a traveller and had no real affinity with the locality, so I did not recognise any of the faces. As a matter of fact there aren't even any bald heads which stand out in my memory! The scene before my eyes gave me a strange feeling as if I were seeing the world somehow more vividly than usual. I almost forgot myself as I strolled leisurely through the hustle and bustle round about me until eventually I came out at the end of a street which was somewhat quieter. It was then that out of nowhere I suddenly heard the sound of music, and there, in front of a shop, was a monk playing the lute (*biwa*). He was a short, fat man with a broad, square face, probably in his mid-forties. It seemed to me that the expression on his face and the light in his eyes perfectly matched the sad strains of the lute, and the sound of his voice as he sang to its seemingly choking accompaniment sank low. None of the harbour people so much as gave him a glance and I could see no sign of the people in the houses being very intent on listening to him. The transient world in the morning sun was too busy to listen.

'I, at least, gave my undivided attention both to his music and to his appearance. Somehow he seemed incongruous as he stood by the house fronts in the narrow street and the very idea of a monk playing the lute, the music itself even, did not harmonise with the bustle of the harbour town. It seemed to me that he was playing under the force of some profoundly important promise he had given. The sobbing music of the lute wafted from house to house, mingling with the clamourous shouts of the stall-keepers crying their wares. As I listened to this pure crystal spring flowing through the muddied waves as it were, I began to feel that the heart strings of these joyful, interested and busy harbour people were playing one of nature's tunes. The lute-playing monk is another example of what I mean by "Those unforgettable people".'

At this point in his story, Ōtsu laid down his manuscript and thought deeply for a while. The clamour of the wind and rain had not abated.

'What happened after that?' asked Akiyama, sitting up.

'Let's call it a day. It's late and there's so much more to tell. Among others there was the miner in Hokkaido, the young fisherman at the head of Tairen Bay, and the boatman with the wen on the Bansho river. If I were to go into detail about all the people who appear in my manuscript it would take all night. They are all people I cannot forget. Why do I remember them? That's really what I should like to tell you.

'All my life I have tortured myself with the problems of humanity and because of that I have become disillusioned with any hopes I may once have had for a great future for myself. Suffering has made me an unhappy man and on nights like this when I sit up late under the lamp light, I find it difficult to bear the isolation, and so I seek sympathy. My ego becomes twisted and I long for human company. It is then that I recall things that happened a long time ago, and I remember my friends. At such times it is often these people I have described who come to mind usually without any conscious thought on my part. Well, perhaps not so much the people themselves, but the people as they stand in the scenes in which I first saw them if you see what I mean. Perhaps I am different from other men. Others walk along the quiet road balanced between heaven and earth and in the end they return hand-in-hand to a truly eternal heaven. At least perhaps they do. This is what I feel at such times and always cry. I cannot help myself. And when I feel this way, I have no existence of my own, so neither does anyone else. I just have a secret longing for this or that person. It is only then that I experience true tranquillity and freedom. Never at other times do I feel such freedom from the struggle for wealth and fame. Never do I feel such a profound sympathy for all things. I know somehow or other that I must write down what I feel for I believe that somewhere in the world there must be someone who will be sympathetic to me.'

Two years passed. Ōtsu was living in a part of Tōhoku. He never again saw or had any communication with Akiyama whom he had met for the first and only time in the Mizunokuchi inn. One rainy evening in the same season of the year as when he had stayed at that inn, Ōtsu was sitting alone at a table, deep in thought. He had in front of him the manuscript 'Those Unforgettable People' which he had shown to Akiyama those two years ago. The latest entry was under the heading 'The Kameya innkeeper'.

Of Akiyama there was no mention.

6

The Stars

Hoshi (The Stars) is another prose poetry work which falls very much into the same category as *Takibi*. In fact it was published only a month later than *Takibi* in vol. 19 no. 328 of the *Kokumin no Tomo* in December 1896. More than any other of Doppo's stories it has the atmosphere of a fairy tale and presents the image of a world where everything is fresh, beautiful and entrancing. It has a lyrical beauty, the overtones of which are still manifest in *Gen Oji* written about six months later. The poet is presented as the very incarnation of the spirit of love and freedom and the whole work has an optimistic spirit seldom found in other of Doppo's works.

There was once a young poet who lived in a cottage at the foot of a small hill in the countryside near the capital. His chief delight was his garden which, if the truth be told, was far too large for such a humble dwelling. It was threaded through by a crystal stream which ran down from a thicket of trees on the hill and because he allowed all of his trees to grow wild, his garden presented an ever changing scene as season followed season. In spring it was a riot of cherry and plum blossom and in summer the waters of the stream were darkened by the thick green foliage. As summer passed into fall the garden became a beautiful brocade of autumn colours and when at last the season grew old and the wild geese wailed mournfully as they flew overhead, an infinite sadness lay over all until the coming of winter. Then when all the leaves had fallen only the bare surface of the soil remained apart from a few pine and cedar which here and there still vaunted their greenery. This garden was the poet's delight from morning to night all the year through.

Early one winter, the poet and his old servant did as they did every year and went out morning after morning to sweep up the fallen leaves which they made into seven separate piles and left by the banks of the stream. For twenty days the leaves remained untouched until one Sunday evening when the frost lay white on the ground and it seemed that before long the waters of the stream would be frozen. The poet spent some time that evening wandering in his garden and singing songs of love in his pure, clear voice. Young blood ran in his veins and in the chill of the winter night sorrow and joy seemed to mingle in all things

47

the poet beheld. Calling on the very depths of his soul, he sang and composed poems. He wept in his happiness. The night sky was high and clear and the starlight was remarkably vivid causing him to linger by the stream despite the intense cold. At last he decided to go in, but before he did so he summoned his servant and ordered him to set fire to one of the piles of leaves. Even in the depths of the night when everyone was fast asleep, this fire still burned brightly sending its smoke straight up into the heavens and its flames reflecting in the waters of the stream. A pall of blue smoke hung over the clump of cedars like a fog.

As night advanced, the sky and the earth seemed to draw gradually closer together and one by one the stars came down to the treetops where the clinging dew sought to return to the heavens from which it had come. Silence reigned over all and there was only the smoke from the poet's bonfire rising steadily into the sky.

In the heavens above there were two stars who were lovers. Though they were far apart their love made nothing of the light years separating them and together they entered a dream of love. Each night they descended to earth and were happy for a while in each other's company. Sometimes they came to the rocky crags on mountain peaks; sometimes to the waves of the great sea plain; and sometimes they came beside the mountain streams. All night through they exchanged their sweet nothings until at last, taken unawares by the light of the sun in the eastern sky, they fled back to the heavens.

The female star was quick to notice the smoke rising from the poet's garden. The night was intensely cold and there was a frost even on the river of heaven, so she suggested to her lover that they should go down to the garden, rake up the fire and talk awhile. The male star smiled and locked in an embrace they descended noiselessly into the poet's garden. On her brow the female star wore a jewel which shone with a red light while her lover wore one which emitted a light of the palest blue. Helplessly she leaned on her lover's shoulder, drunk with the fragrance of her celestial love. And so they remained until the pile of leaves had burned away, whispering sweet nothings until dawn drew nigh when they had to return into the distant western sky. The next night the poet fired the second pile of leaves and again the stars came down from the sky to talk the night away. And thus it happened every night that the pale blue light and the red light would come down side by side to the smoke of the fire in the poet's garden. But the poet himself had no idea at all of what was happening.

By Saturday six of the seven piles of leaves had been consumed and only one remained. When she saw the slender spiral of smoke rising from the last fire, the female star stood forth on the edge of the galaxy enveloped in a crimson mist and silently descended into the garden for the last time. That night the stars talked regretfully that no more would they be able to come to the garden and, deciding that they should say some words of thanks to its owner, they went together into the poet's room. For a while they watched his face as innocently he slept; it was a young face which had a nobility all too uncommon in this transient world. Scattered in confusion by his bed lay collections of poetry from many lands. One of these was open at the poem *My Heart's in the Highlands* by Robert Burns. A line from this poem had been underscored in red:

'Farewell to the mountains, high-cover'd with snow'

The female star read this and as she did so tears sprang to her eyes. To her companion she said:

'This young poet's heart is noble indeed.' Then she bent down and whispered something in the young man's ear after which she and her lover looked at each other and smiled. Then they each kissed his tender cheek and bade him sleep in peace. At last they left.

When Sunday morning dawned the poet awoke and remembered a dream he had had that night. In the dream a celestial maiden wearing a ruby star on her brow had appeared and beckoned him to climb a hill with her. At the top she had drawn close and asked him in a whisper whether he desired love or freedom. He had replied that love was the lifeblood of freedom and freedom the wings of love, so he did not desire one without the other. Then she smiled and told him that there was something she wished to show him. She pointed far off into the western sky and told him to concentrate on what he saw there. Then the maiden had departed, whither he knew not.

Remembering this dream, the poet sprang up and climbed alone to the top of the hill outside his cottage just as the eastern sky was beginning to grow light. When he looked into the western sky he saw two small stars hanging low over the earth and shining faintly. Presently the eastern sky was tinged with gold and the stars vanished. He could see the eyebrow-like outlines of the mountain range just above the horizon, but the whiteness of the snow which enshrouded the peaks was fainter than in his dream. The poet's heart melted into ecstasy at this sight and his eyes were brimming with tears. These were tears which only the mature can cry and those who drink such tears yearn for a freedom where their desires for earthly things are of no consequence to them. Among those things which have the power to summon tears from such people, there is probably nothing to compare with the snow on the mountain peaks soaring into heaven as it traces faintly in its image the dream path of love.

The poet raised up his voice and declaimed the poem which the star had seen by his bed that night, and when he reached the line which had been marked in red his voice grew higher still. He gazed at the distant mountains and love and anger stirred within him. His black hair hanging to his shoulders waved in the breeze and glittered in the morning sun, and as he stood facing the vast blue sky it was as if he were the very incarnation of freedom.

7
Third Party

Daisansha (Third Party) is interesting for several reasons. It is an unusual (and by and large successful) attempt to construct a story on the basis of the correspondence between two men (the third parties in a divorce case). This style is used in order to obtain the effect of a detached account of the tragic affair between two lovers. Perhaps it would be best, however, to describe this affair as tragi-comic because there is little doubt from the commentaries of the third parties that Doppo intended his readers to see the humourous side of the relationship between two ostensibly rather silly people.

It is one of the most successful uses of humour in all Doppo's fiction. The genuinely tragic aspect of the story can be seen against the background of Doppo's own diary entries for the period of 1896 after the break-up of his marriage with Sasaki Nobuko. The feelings recorded in the diary appear time and again in *Daisansha* and there can be no question that Doppo wrote this story from bitter experience. The suicide, however, is perhaps somewhat contrived. *Daisansha* was published in October 1903, vol. 9 no. 13 of the magazine *Bungei Kurabu*.

'Dear Mr Ōi,

'You and I are both third parties in this affair — men who are supposed to be able to make cool and impartial judgements. It is my belief that the role of the third parties is of the utmost importance in the emotional problems of marriage and divorce and you and I had best resign ourselves and get on with the job in hand. My duty is to represent O-tsuru and yours is to represent Ema. I can't help feeling that "represent" is perhaps not quite a fitting word, but I am O-tsuru's elder brother and you are Ema's friend, so I suppose we had better regard ourselves as 'representatives'.

'To get straight to the point, there's no hope as far as O-tsuru is concerned. It's absolutely useless I'm afraid, for no longer do love and passion for Ema run hot in her veins. In fact she is quite indifferent towards him and I should be most grateful if you would make him aware of that fact. The female of the species is rather like that other animal "opportunity" — the more you try to take it the further it runs away. Please tell Ema that and make him realise that divorce is the only path open to him.'

'Dear Mr Takeshima,

'I can't tell you how much I agree with your analogy about "opportunity". However, Ema is not so resolved for he believes that he still has a firm grasp on his opportunity and he is making himself ill with the effort not to let go. I did as you said and told him of O-tsuru's indifference, but he just said pathetically:

"Yes, of course I believe what you say. I know her love for me cooled long ago."

'But I am sure he was not truly convinced, for he added:

"Ōi, she may not love me, but I love her, so divorce is out of the question." He sounded close to tears. Well, Mr Takeshima, it's up to you. Please explain to O-tsuru the way things are. Try at any rate to get her to come home even if it's only for a visit, because if that could be arranged, Ema might be able to prevail upon her himself. I'd like to say, though, that in my opinion divorce is preferable.'

'Dear Mr Ōi,

'I've said this before, I know, but it really is hopeless as far as O-tsuru is concerned. She told me yesterday:

"If I ever marry again, I should prefer a very gentle man, because, being such a selfish person, I find it hard to be tolerant. I should despair of the marriage lasting if he were not very gentle."

'In other words, she has had enough of Ema and you can see that if she can talk about the prospects for a second marriage, there is nothing to be gained from asking her to return to him.

'For all that, I saw her yesterday evening standing on the veranda, obviously turning something over in her mind. She was crying, probably because she was saddened by old memories. However, it was as if she were making her mouth water at the memory of an excellent dish of eels. The eel she eats next time will be different, I'll be bound! I too think that divorce is the only answer.'

'Dear Mr Takeshima,

'I saw what you mean about the eel. What has happened is that O-tsuru has eaten her fill of Ema and in the process he has been quite eaten away. The tragedy is that Ema has not had his fill of O-tsuru. We must let him pick the bones, for he has become very thin! I went to see him this morning and found him still in bed.

"What's up with you?" I said. "It's past nine o'clock."

"I don't care what time it is," he said, burying his face in the bed clothes. By the bed lay two or three letters O-tsuru had written to him at a time when they were still in love.

"Why, you're crying!" I exclaimed thoughtlessly.

"Don't talk nonsense!" he said, thrusting his face up from beneath the bed clothes. Indeed I could see that he was telling the truth for there was no sign of tears, but his face was deathly pale and his cheeks were hollow.

"Ah, you do not know the joys of having a wife." I said.

"You mock me!"

"Indeed I do!"

"Well, it's very ill-mannered of you. It does you no credit."

"That doesn't bother me. I mock you nonetheless. I, Ōi Tokugorō, mock you. I cannot help myself."

"You can't help yourself, eh? Be so good as to tell me why. It doesn't seem any laughing matter to me!" He sat up as he spoke. You'd have found it very amusing if you'd been here, Takeshima. I could hardly prevent myself from laughing aloud, but Ema looked so threatening that I forced myself to be serious.

"Go back to sleep. You'd better not get up. You're a sick man, you know," I said. He lay back, staring at the ceiling.

"Look here, Ema, just listen to what I have to say without getting worked up. I'm your friend after all, but I despise you. I can't help myself."

"Well go ahead and despise me then. See if I care."

"Be quiet and listen. For a marriage to work there must be love on both sides. You ought to know that. You have always said that I was just a Philistine who gave myself airs, so it seems a little embarrassing for me to have to give you a talk on love. But I know this much — a marriage with love on just one side is no marriage at all. And what of O-tsuru? Did she not run away and leave you? If she did that how can you possibly think that she loves you? And if she does not love you, she cannot be your wife. She is a stranger to you and surely you don't want such a person for a wife, do you? You have to be a man about it. I admit that when I first saw your pale face I felt sorry for you, but now I just want to despise you."

"You are a Philistine. You talk about manhood, eh? People like you are always talking about enduring things that cannot be cured, but I shall not so degrade myself."

"Well that's fine. What a splendid fellow you are! But however much you love O-tsuru, face facts. She does not love you."

"It can't be helped."

"I'm glad you realise it."

"Yes, but it may turn out that my love reawakens hers."

"Don't talk such nonsense. Divorce her."

"I can't do that for I shall love her for ever."

"You are most odd. Would a woman whom you loved so much run away and leave you?"

"Well, I am suffering for it."

"So you may be, but let's be logical about it. You may be consumed with love for her, but your woman has run away and you do not have the power to make her come back. Nor can your love reawaken hers. It's just common sense if you'll only look at it dispassionately."

"No, you're wrong. Up to now O-tsuru hasn't realised how much I love her. I have loved her with all my heart, but she hasn't been aware of it. It's a tragedy for me and what I don't understand is why she hasn't realised the depths of my love for her?"

"Well, I don't know, but if I were you I'd divorce a woman like that."

'That's how things stand, Takeshima, and I'm at my wits' end. He's so slow to make up his mind to the facts. My pathetic friend is still head over heels in love with O-tsuru. There must be something remarkable about her. Women are strange creatures, aren't they? I think it's best now if we just wait and see what happens. We must maintain our dignity as third parties, don't you agree?'

'My Dear Ōi,
'I read your letter with great interest. You are quite an artist with the pen. You should resign your present job and make a career as a writer, taking the pen-name of "Philistine" of course! Thanks to you I now know how things are with Ema, and I am much moved by his plight. I cannot accept what you suggest that there is anything good about O-tsuru. It may just be that love has made Ema blind to all her faults and he cannot bear to see them. I showed your letter to O-tsuru and she cried so that I just had to ask her whether her tears meant that she wanted to go back to Ema.

"What do you mean?" she said.

"It's just that it seems a crime to discard a husband who thinks so well of you."

"I tell you, brother, I just couldn't bear to go back to him."

"You don't hate him, do you?"

"No, of course not. But I couldn't bear a repetition of how things have been up to now."

"If you want my opinion, I think that if you go home to him now, Ema will never offer you any violence again."

"Do you really think so?"

"A man's character doesn't change overnight and there are some who would say that basic character never changes, but I reckon there will be some improvement. You shouldn't expect too much, though, especially after running away as you did."

"No, it's no good. I've thought about it a lot and I don't think he will ever change. If he were going to change there would have been some sign of it before now. It's not as if our troubles have just begun. Don't you remember I came to you at the beginning of last month and you said then that ours was a tragic love? You were absolutely right. Ema and I are very unhappy."

'She burst into tears. O-tsuru does not deny Ema's love and she even seems sorry for his unhappiness, but she no longer loves him. When she ran away Ema's love turned to violence, as it always will do, his character being what it is, and she felt the full fury of his anger. Now she cannot find the strength to accept his love again. When the trouble began about a month ago and O-tsuru called on me for help, I realised that Ema's love was not a shallow thing, but I felt that the root of all their unhappiness was that their temperaments were just not compatible. Then I told Ema that his was a tragic love. I advised him that he should be calmer and not so irritable. Would it not be much better, I suggested, if he could bring himself to the frame of mind where he could see himself and O-tsuru strolling hand-in-hand together through life as if they were walking over the fields where the spring breezes blow.

'However, a clash of personalities cannot ever be truly resolved, least of all by someone else's advice. A month ago I felt sure that sooner or later the marriage would explode. In fact they have been neglectful of one another this four or five months past, or perhaps it would be better to say mistrustful. Oh yes, they have lived together as man and wife under one roof, but treating each other as enemies. From time to time they have ceased hostilities under the magic power of love, but it seems to me that each has been tackling their mutual problems as an isolated individual. Is it logical to expect a relationship to continue harmoniously under such conditions? Their tragedy is not that they love each other but that they are both mistaken about the best method of demonstrating their love. This is because of their different natures. I am forced, therefore, to the conclusion that they will never be happy together. O-tsuru has begun to feel this way also and therefore cannot return to Ema, but he is endowed with a deeper love and cannot see the end results as dispassionately as she can. We third parties are in total agreement and before long Ema as well will come to our way of thinking because his emotions will calm down and when he is quite cool he will feel as O-tsuru does.

'My Dear Takeshima,

'You and I intended to look on and see what happened, but the two parties in our little drama are much more involved than we third parties. I received this letter or little essay, call it what you will, from Ema and I enclose it for your reference.

"O-tsuru does not love me now, but once she did. I used to love her and I still do — even now. My love is real. She ran away and left me but that does not diminish my love for her. I never knew before how deep my love could be. Now that she has left me it is as if a chill wind is blowing through my heart and mind, tormenting me. My grief is unbearable. Ah! The pain of love! What is there that compares with the pain of chasing a dream of love grown cold? I shall love her for ever and I cannot let her out of my heart for even a moment. Perhaps O-tsuru is the grave of love where I am to bury myself. You and Takeshima urge me to have done with her, but that is like telling me to kill myself. I know the depth of my grief is such that death would come easily to me."

'He goes on and on in that vein saying that we who are third parties should understand the depth of his grief. Of course we do know, but knowing and feeling are two different things. A doctor knows a patient's pain, but he does not feel it. He just administers the medicine and waits for the fever to abate, but it doesn't look as if our patient's fever will abate very easily. His mother and sisters are distraught to see his pain and consequently they have no respect for O-tsuru's position. That they should harbour so much ill-feeling towards her is a result of her own character, but it does seem that all around Ema are urging him to divorce her. Of course they are not the most dispassionate of third parties and their help with Ema's and O-tsuru's suffering is, to be blunt about it, embarrassing.'

'My Dear Ōi,

'What Ema has written is a full and perfect statement of the sufferings of love and when I read it I could not help but feel sympathetic. However, although it may be gratifying to the listener to hear expressions of sympathy it has little positive value for him, for he knows that in the final analysis his audience does not feel the smallest fraction of what he feels. In other words, we and O-tsuru must resign ourselves to Ema's unhappiness. He has experienced the joys of love more than most people are capable of doing and occasionally he has been able to impart a fraction of that feeling to others, so accounts can be said to have balanced out.

'As I said, I felt sympathetic when I had read Ema's letter, as no doubt would anyone, and I thought that if I read it to O-tsuru it might prompt her to more than just sympathy. Thus I exercised the discretion of a third party and showed it to her, a course of which I think you will approve. After all O-tsuru is a woman and therefore a slave to passion. The failing of people who are ruled by their passions is that they often deceive themselves. It is logical therefore that women deceive themselves far more than men and as they do so they are convinced that they are acting for the best. Therefore it seemed to me that when she read Ema's letter, O-tsuru would be dreadfully upset and would immediately become a dutiful wife (thus deceiving herself), thinking that she had better be dutiful to a man who loves her so much. If she were to quickly become used to the idea of being a dutiful wife, she would not then persist in her efforts to leave a man with whom she had lived for more than a year. O-tsuru is the most passionate of women and because, in addition to that, she has little natural courage, she tends to burst into tears even when addressed with gentle words. It is in this respect, I think, that she has done most to wear away Ema's love for her. She makes a great fuss about everything which is almost inhuman, as if, indeed, she were mad. She cries, she turns pale, she glares at people, her eyes brimming with venom. She hates, bites, scratches and is groundlessly suspicious. In fact she is scarcely controllable and I deem that she is responsible for most of the clashes with Ema.

'O-tsuru is not suitable material for a wife, but her character is very much disposed towards love. It seems that she thinks this herself for yesterday I talked with her about it as we strolled along the beach.

"My dear brother, you know that I could never make a good wife," she sighed.

"You may be right."

"Of course I am. No one could put up with someone as selfish as me. It's only because Ema's the sort of man he is that it lasted for more than a year."

"If that's the case, surely you'd have done better not to run away."

"No, you don't understand. It was me who couldn't put up with the situation."

"Well, that is selfishness."

"Maybe, but that's the way I'm made so if I got married again, I'd prefer a middle-aged man who would think of me as a child and find my wilfulness charming."

"Well, in that case, how about Furukawa Ichibei? I can't think of anyone else who fits the bill. Oh, wait a bit; there's Hiranuma Senzō!"

"Don't be wicked! I'd probably be better off to remain single."

"You want love without marriage, eh?"

"Don't be ridiculous!" she laughed, blushing a little. Then she seemed to remember something else she had meant to say, and went on:

"Marriage is really a waste of time. My life seems to have been decided for me and I have no hopes left. People are happiest when they are in love, not when they are married."

"You really are absurd. You're saying that if Ema hadn't married you, the present state of affairs would never have arisen and you'd be perfectly happy together."

'About nine o'clock last night I went along to my wife's room and found her doing her needlework, with O-tsuru sitting beside her. O-tsuru was resting her chin on her hands and was busy reading a book. She looked very serious, full of pent-up emotion.

"Brother," she said, "have you ever known any Christian missionaries?"

"Several. Why?"

"That's what I'd like to be."

"And what about marriage?"

"No, I'd like to do some good in the world. It's all very well just living here in the country, but ..."

"What are you trying to say?"

"I'm saying that I want to preach the Gospel. Country people are so unsophisticated and I'd like to save the souls of the villagers and lead them in God's path. Even one soul saved would be something."

'Well, when I heard that I just wanted to laugh and I daresay you'd have had a job to hold yourself back as well. It just had to be a passing fancy. "The Country Missionary". How about that for the subject of a novel?! Still, there must be many people like O-tsuru among the ranks of the young Christians. That's women for you! When they have no lover, they quickly become sad, serious and full of emotion, planning great undertakings like the saving of souls.'

'My Dear Takeshima,

'I think you are too hard on O-tsuru, but I must admit I couldn't help but laugh at the idea of her becoming a missionary. However, here is something you will not laugh at. This morning I had a visit from a very pale-faced Ema. He spoke with much anguish.

"I just can't resign myself to losing O-tsuru. You have seen what I've written. I just can't bear the pain. I need your help."

"Well, I've been doing my best," I said, somewhat at a loss.

"All your efforts have been directed towards breaking up the marriage. You've never wanted to see us together again. I think you're very cruel."

"But that's the duty of the third party. If I were as unbalanced as you, I'd be no use at all."

"That's not the sort of duty I want."

"Thanks a lot. I didn't want to get involved at all."

"Are you serious?" He looked dreadful.

"Are you, for that matter?" I countered.

"How can you doubt my seriousness when you see me suffering, perhaps to death?"

"You're sick. You're fevered."

"You're right, but you are just watching me die."

"No, I'm waiting for the fever to cool. When you're unreasonable like this, you're having a relapse!"

"Don't make a joke of it," said the sufferer, recovering his spirits a little. "My fever will never cool. Once it's up it cannot be cooled, but O-tsuru will get colder and colder if you carry on acting as you have been."

"You're still taking that line, are you? It was precisely because she had grown cold towards you that she ran away."

"Maybe, but O-tsuru is human, isn't she? When she hears that I am suffering so much, she will be moved. She doesn't hate me. Well, that's enough for me, so talk it over with Takeshima and do your best to make her come back. I'm relying on you to help."

"I ask you, do you think you will be happy when she is back at your side? You're overrating her value. You refuse to attack the woman who was once your wife, but after all she is just a woman and she is unmanageable. Remember what Takeshima said in his letter; O-tsuru is fit for love, but not fit for a wife. You should have had enough of her by now."

"I know her character well enough by now and she is more than I can manage, but my love for her has not changed. I may be unhappy if she comes back, but I don't care."

"You're like a fisherman yearning after the one that got away."

"Never."

"Well, I must say, you are a kind-hearted man! O-tsuru ran away and you feel all the more grateful to her. Fish for her if you like, but you'll find she's just a tiddler. Moreover, she's a dangerous little fish who will bite you. As they say, there are plenty more fish in the sea. Try for one of them instead."

"She may be of small value. She may bite me. But the fish that got away is the one I want."

"Unfortunately, she wants to escape and is swimming joyfully away."

"Those are cruel words," Ema said despondently, and was silent. Then I showed him your letter which arrived yesterday, thinking it would be kind to let him read your criticism of O-tsuru so that he could get a better idea of what she was feeling. After some show of reluctance, he read the letter enthusiastically and when he had finished, he closed his eyes and sighed.

"You third parties are cold indeed."

"That's an odd thing to say."

"O-tsuru may well be the sort of person Takeshima suggests. That's all well and good, but there's no justification whatever for trying to make me turn away from her. You say that she has grown cold towards me, but in reality it is you and Takeshima who are making her so. What I want is to see her face to face and let her hear of my sufferings from my own lips."

"You want to meet her? The wife who ran away from you?"

"That doesn't matter. I cannot leave it to you third parties. I thank you for your consideration of my future, but it's cruel of you both to make my wife cold towards me when her love is not necessarily so. I shall write and tell Takeshima that I want to see her."

"Well, that's your prerogative of course. But O-tsuru may not want to see you," I said, feeling a little foolish.

"No, that will not happen. I am determined to see her," he said, and left for home.

'You may, then, be getting a letter from Ema. I can give you no advice about what to do and I leave it to your discretion. I'll just watch and see what happens.'

'My Dear Ōi,

'The letter has come! It's a long, rambling piece, but the general drift is that he wants to see O-tsuru. I'm sure that no good will come from such a meeting for either of them, but as I was determined to maintain the "coldness" (as Ema puts it) of the third party, I decided to ask O-tsuru what she thought of the idea.

"What do you think is for the best?" she asked.

"Well, I think it's better not to see him. Do you think that you will go back to him if you do see him and talk to him?"

"No, I've no desire to go back to him, but I'd like to see how he's getting on."

"If that's all there is to it, you'd do better not to see him."

"Yes, you're right. I won't see him."

'Well, that's women for you! I just said again that I thought there was nothing to be gained from such a meeting and left it at that. I'd appreciate it if you would go to see him and tell him how things are.'

'My Dear Takeshima,

'Ema has gone. I went to see him the very night your letter came, but he had left by the time I got there. I called in on his mother and learned from her that he had seen your letter somehow. He told his mother that he was going along to Zushi and she had been unable to prevent him from leaving. Apparently I only missed him by a few minutes. I must say that he has gone down in my estimation, but I never thought he would leave after your efforts to stop him.'

'My Dear Ōi,

'Our drama is approaching its climax. About ten o'clock this evening Ema turned up out of the blue. Cool I may be, but I couldn't help but be surprised. Even when I had rubbed the sleep from my bleary eyes, it was still the same deathly pale Ema. His eyes were terrible to behold.

"Why have you come?" I asked.

"I want to see O-tsuru."

"She's asleep," I said, feeling the humour of the situation despite myself. "But I did say in my letter that it would be better if you two didn't meet."

"Yes, I saw your letter, but I haven't come to gain any advantage for myself. I just want to see her and hear for myself what she really feels."

"You're angry."

"No, not angry. I couldn't be angry even if I wanted to. Please let me see her. I ... I want to say something to her."

When I saw his face and heard him speak I had to give way.

"Very well, then. See her," I said. Then I woke O-tsuru and told her what had happened. She was surprised and frightened.

"Please come with me. I'm scared to see him alone." She was trembling. When it comes to the point where a woman is afraid of a man, I feel that any love or passion she once felt for him has disappeared for good.

'Well, anyway, I sat beside O-tsuru, with Ema opposite us. Not surprisingly, she could not bring herself to look up, while Ema, for his part, gazed at us defiantly. Ema was doing his best to look contemptuous of O-tsuru, for there is always an element of "show" in such cases.

"I'll ask you just one more time. Won't you consider coming back to me?" he asked.

'O-tsuru raised her head for a moment and then looked down again without saying a word. Ema persisted.

"Do you doubt my love?"

"Of course not." She shivered like a sparrow under the gaze of a hawk and her spirit seemed to wander. I saw what was happening and guessed the likely outcome of the meeting. Even if they were frank with one another it was unlikely that Ema would get what he wanted. It was as if they were locked in diplomatic negotiations where yet no fruitful discussions were possible. The woman was retreating ever further from the man's outstretched heart.

"If you don't doubt my love, why did you abandon me?"

"Because it seemed we were both unhappy."

"That's odd. If I love you and you love me, how could we be unhappy? Is it then that you no longer love me?"

'Quite naturally O-tsuru found no reply to this question.

"Well, if you don't love me, say so. Make no bones about it!" Ema's voice was shrill.

'I became aware then that this very scene must have been re-enacted many times as Ema and O-tsuru sat by their own fireside. Ema was furious.

"Am I to have no reply?!" In their own home this question would have been the signal for the fists to start flying. O-tsuru, with tears in her eyes, looked at me for help.

"You are distressing her, Ema. She never said that she didn't love you, only that she thought that you would never be happy staying together, because your natures are incompatible."

"I wasn't asking you. I want a clear answer from O-tsuru!"

"You want a politician's excuses?" I wanted to interject. My dear Ōi, I have become more convinced than ever that Ema just cannot manage a woman.

"I agree with everything my brother has said," said O-tsuru.

"If that's the case, please tell me in what respect we are incompatible. If we are, we could surely put it right. It's just an excuse, isn't it? You don't really love me."

"If that's what you think, there's nothing I can do about it," O-tsuru replied, with a touch of irony.

"I realise that, but I shall always love you."

"Do you call what you feel love?"

"Of course it's love."

"You have a strange way of showing it then."

"What on earth do you mean?"

"Well, isn't it strange? Do you call it love when you beat me? If that's love, then I ask your pardon."

'At this point I had to butt in.

"I suppose you two can't help talking this way, but you, Ema, are missing the main point at issue."

'My dear Ōi, I congratulate you on missing this foolishness. They were making far too much of this thing we call love, making it into a dumpling which Ema was trying to force down a protesting O-tsuru's throat. It's the sort of dumpling any woman would spit out no sooner than it had been put in her mouth!

"Pray tell me, then. What is the main issue?"

"Divorce."

"I'll never consent to it. O-tsuru may have pushed me aside, but I love her, so divorce is out of the question."

"But you can see how it is with her. You will never be happy if you don't divorce her. If you love her as much as you say you do, surely you should put her desire for a divorce above your own love? Think about it. For you this is a matter of honour."

"I care nothing for honour or happiness. Divorce her while I still love her? No, I do not desire to be such a saint."

"Well, what do you suggest then?"

"That O-tsuru comes back to me."

"She will never consent to it."

"O-tsuru. Is there nothing I can say to make you come back to me? Will you perisist in leaving me despite my pleadings?" Ema said, fixing O-tsuru in his gaze.

"Please pay heed to what my brother says. I am in his hands entirely."

"Don't give me that! I want a straight answer."

"Please speak for me, brother. I'm frightened and I can't stay here any longer," she said in a small voice, and fled. Ema was taken by surprise and couldn't stop her. He gazed after her and for a while remained silent.

"I understand!" he said at length. "I'll ask Mr Ōi to get in touch with you about the divorce. Goodbye."

"You are welcome to stay the night."

"No, I have a room at the inn. Farewell."

'He left with no more ado. This is the result of the meeting — not what Ema expected I imagine.'

'My Dear Takeshima,

'When I went to visit Ema this morning he still had not returned. His mother was in a real state and hadn't slept all night. Well, in the end he did come back, and when I saw his face I wanted to cry. He went to bed without a word to either of us and fell asleep straightaway. Thinking it better to leave him to rest, I went off to work, but when I got home about four o'clock there was a letter waiting for me — from Ema. As far as I can judge from what he wrote he is resigned to a divorce, but does not want it to happen just yet, for he says that if they remove O-tsuru's name from the register he will feel that they no longer have any connection and that would be unbearable. He asks me to see about the question of the register in a little while, but he is obviously an unhappy man. In the letter he goes on and on about being so much in love with a woman who did not love him and how he was unable to demonstrate the reality of his love. Although I've heard from you what happened at their meeting, I thought you would like to know about this. I, at least, can do no more. O-tsuru shows no sign of wanting to marry again so I think we should do as Ema suggests over the matter of the register.

'Today I received orders that I was to go to the Hokkaido branch of my company and I shall have to leave in three or four days. I would like to have seen you before I go, but I'm so busy that it will not be possible. If you could get up to Tokyo, I'd be delighted, for I should indeed like to meet you.'

'My dear Ōi,

'Since you went away we have had two weeks of great calm. O-tsuru is much the same as usual. She paces about singing hymns in a doleful voice and striking poses. Surprisingly high spirits alternate with fits of depression when the smallest thing displeases her. When she is in one of those moods she snaps at my wife and says things which are naive enough to have come from a thirteen-year-old. In short, she is her usual self! At the same time, however, there is some thing about her which makes me feel rather uneasy, a sort of fretfulness I think. One day she asked me right out of the blue:

"Brother, do you know how Ema is?"

"He's all right, I believe. I think his illness is getting better."

"Oh, I'm glad to hear that, but ..."

"Are you worried about him?"

"Well, I was his wife for more than a year. Of course I'm a little worried."

"That's splendid. I believe his sickness would be completely cured if only you'd go back to him."

"I hate it when you say such things. Please listen seriously to what I have to say and don't make fun of me. I had a dreadful dream last night."

"Did you dream that you were pursued by Ema?"

"I dreamed of a lovers' suicide! It gives me the shivers just to think about it. I dreamed of the time Ema and I went to Omiya before we were married."

"That's strange. Go on, I'm listening."

"I think it's something I should tell you. As I said, I dreamed that I was at Omiya. I was peeping out from the trees in a wood at a man who was pacing to and fro round a pond. Under the moonlight it seemed as if it was Ema, and when I went out to see if I was right, it was him. 'What are you doing here?' I asked. 'I heard that your illness was much better, but you look so sad.' He replied: 'I can't resign myself to losing you, so I am going to kill myself. But I do not hate you, O-tsuru. I'm grateful that you put up with a madman like myself for a husband for as long as you did.' Then he looked into my face and burst into tears. Of course this made me sad too. 'Oh, Ema', I said, 'I've been completely in the wrong. Please forgive me and I'll never leave your side again.' Then we embraced and cried with all our hearts. But then Ema said that you and Ōi were right in thinking that if we went back to Tokyo as man and wife we should never be happy. He said that as our characters and natures would never improve, it would be better if we were to die in each other's arms even as we were at that moment. I said that I thought so too and together we jumped into the pond. I won't tell you any more because you'll laugh."

"Try me and see."

"Well, it was so strange. At the moment of death there was no pain. I asked Ema whether we were dead yet and he said that we were. Then we joined hands and walked together through a meadow, and our hearts were light. Ema was very gentle as I had never known him before and it seemed that at last our characters were transformed and we were as angels. I tried to sing my favourite hymn, but the words would not come. And then as I struggled to sing, I suddenly woke."

'When I had heard the tale of O-tsuru's dream, I just smiled slightly and said nothing. To tell the truth the dream did not seem to have disturbed O-tsuru herself all that much. However, two or three days later an unexpected letter arrived from Ema. He said that his illness was no better and that although he thanked me for all my attentions, he did not want ever to recover. He went on:

"I am no real man. Indeed I feel that you can no longer have any feelings towards me, be it love or hate. I do not understand my own heart. When I paid you that surprise visit in the middle of the night, it was my intention to reveal what I felt and appeal to you and O-tsuru. However, things turned out differently. There is no tranquillity in my nature. I am not a bowl to be filled with love. I am not a pool from which O-tsuru can calmly extract water without any reaction from me. I bewail my fate, but I shall never hate O-tsuru — indeed I am thankful that she put up with such a monstrosity as myself for so long. It makes me sad to think of her, for like me she is spiritually deformed. Her heart is pure and righteous, but her nature is deep and turbulent. She has scorched her pure heart with her burning love. Indeed I pity her. We were both born under unlucky stars. Like anyone else we knew what it was to love, but because one of us burned with a love so much fiercer than that of other mortals, we have both been plunged into a tragic unhappiness such as befalls only one in a million.

"I no longer have any hopes of this world. Even if my health recovers, my soul will be in ashes. Over and over again I have tried to bring myself back into the world through concepts such as honour, truth, justice and enterprise. But these concepts have proved unexpectedly brittle and give no strength to my heart, broken as a reed by love. I feel an unendurable loneliness as if I were standing alone in the vast expanse of heaven and earth. How much I love you, O-tsuru! Come and save me. Save me from my unhappy loneliness. How many times have I cried out these things? But now I am resigned or so I seem. I have come to feel the unnatural calm of a man decided on death. I shall divorce O-tsuru. Please tell her that. It is one year and fifteen days to the very day since we were married."

'We may think ourselves dispassionate third parties, but it is impossible not to cry after reading such a letter. What is really peculiar about it is that there is the same feeling in the words of Ema's letter as those spoken by him in O-tsuru's dream. It may be that there is still a mysterious empathy between their two hearts. Nothing is quite so strange as love and certainly there is nothing quite like a woman for peculiar behaviour. It almost seems as if the impartiality of the third party is quite out of place in such circumstances.

'Well, at least Ema had finally agreed to the divorce, so four days after I received his letter I went up to Tokyo early in the morning. About four o'clock the same day I paid a call on Ema, but when I came through the garden and called to him from outside his study, there was no reply. Thinking that he might be away, I asked his mother whether he was in or not and she told me that he was as far as she knew.

However, there was no sign of him. Suspecting that he must have gone out for a walk, I passed the time of day with his mother for a while and learned from her that Ema had received a letter from O-tsuru that very morning. There was no sender's name on the envelope Ema's mother showed me, but there was no mistaking O-tsuru's hand. I was deeply shocked.

"There must be some mistake. She couldn't have written," I said, but there was the handwriting to confound me. Well, if they had had a fight there was nothing I could do about it, so I just remarked how strange it all seemed and went home.

'As I left home next morning to call again on Ema, a telegram arrived from my wife telling me to go straight to Zushi. Nothing specific was said, but my first thought was that it must concern O-tsuru and, sure enough, I was right, as I found when I got there.

'The bodies of Ema and O-tsuru had already been brought into a room. I was told that about eight o'clock the previous evening O-tsuru had gone for a stroll on the beach to look at a particularly fine moon, and she had not come back. My wife had sat up all night anxiously waiting for her. When morning came there was a rumour going around that there had been a lovers' suicide beneath a cliff and on eliciting the woman's description, my wife hurried along there, dreading what she might find. By the time she arrived the bodies were already laid out on the beach.

'I must confess that I could never have foreseen that such a bizarre thing would happen. It was too much like a novel, too fantastic for a mind like mine to grasp. Neither of them had left any sort of farewell note, but in Ema's pocket we found the letter from O-tsuru and from this I gathered she had read Ema's last letter to me. I had left it in the drawer of my desk. Until this time, O-tsuru had never seen any letter without my permission, but either deliberately or by chance she had discovered and read the letter I had hidden away. This was very serious to me and I felt like crying as I read the letter O-tsuru had written. It contained an account of her dream, but there was not the faintest suggestion of turning the dream into reality, nor were there any words calculated to put the idea into Ema's head.

'I could guess what had happened the previous night. Ema had had no thought of a lovers' suicide and O-tsuru had not set out with the deliberate intention of meeting Ema. Beyond that, third parties like ourselves can make no judgements. I can only imagine, my dear Ōi, that this tragic couple stood on the cliff looking out at the moon across the vast expanse of Sagami Bay and as they did so they conceived a desire to consign their ill-starred bodies to unfeeling nature and preserve at that instant a burning love which would last for all eternity. They must have been in each other's arms, crying.

'The suicide received the usual sort of write-up in the Tokyo newspapers about "foolish passion" and so forth. "Foolish passion"? What does that mean? If a would-be suicide were to ask whether there were any meaning in life, who could give him a satisfactory answer? Of what use were our explanations and excuses as third parties? I think that now Ema and O-tsuru are walking hand-in-hand through the grassy meadows she saw in her dream, and she is singing her favourite songs to her heart's content.'

8
Woman Trouble

Jonan (Woman Trouble) was first published in vol. 2 no. 7 of the famous literary journal *Bungakkai* in December 1903, just two months after *Daisansha*. It is yet another story about a man buffeted by the callous hand of fate, but in this case it is quite apparent that although we are meant to sympathise with the blind flute (*shakuhachi*) player, we are equally meant to realise that what has happened to him is largely his own fault.

The hero of the story is a culmination of a succession of rather weak and womanish characters (such as Toyokichi in *Kawagiri* and Ema in *Daisansha*) who seek to escape from their misfortunes, rather than confront them. And yet like Toyokichi who seeks oblivion in the river mist, and the lovers of *Daisansha* who find happiness together after death, the hero of *Jonan* also escapes through the thoughts of his dead mother and the music of his flute.

Again, this rather long and very effective story is not altogether a tragedy, but in terms of its inevitability it is approaching the quality of *Gen Oji*.

Four years ago (a man once told me), I was walking along the Ginza where I had some business, when at one of the intersections I saw a man playing the *shakuhachi**. There was already a group of some seven or eight people standing around listening to him play and I joined them for a moment to hear for myself. It was the end of May and the setting sun was causing the shadows of the buildings on the western side of the street to fall on the houses opposite so that from the waist up the *shakuhachi* player was bathed in the evening light. It was almost dusk — a time when the Ginza is at its busiest. The sound of horse-drawn carriages going to and fro, of the wheels of rickshaws passing along from East to West, and the noise of people's footsteps as they hurried on their various ways made everything noisy and confused. And yet, here in this clamorous place at this clamorous time, was a man calmly playing the *shakuhachi*. How calm and tranquil he seemed in the evening sun and it was as if his playing had created a haven of peace for as far as his notes carried. As I listened to the mournful tune he was playing, the notes high and low, fading but never ceasing, I studied the man attentively.

---

* A bamboo flute resembling a recorder in the way it is played.

He was blind, perhaps thirty-one or thirty-two years old, but it was not easy to tell his age because his face was blackened by the sun and begrimed with dust. I could see that he was not only dirty, but haggard. I imagine the dust of the streets was blown in his face by day, and by night he slept beneath filthy bedding in a corner of some cheap lodging-house. His face was long, his nose high and his eyebrows bushy. His forehead was half obscured by a thick tangle of hair which he obviously never combed, but I could see that it was well-developed and not the bony, flatly protruberant sort such as one sees so often in low-bred people. The power of music in an awesome thing and however low-bred the person playing the instrument, he still compels respect. This blind man had a nobility of character reflecting through his squalid appearance and this moved me all the more. I suspect the others who were listening felt the same. It seemed as if the sad tune he played bespoke the former appearance and present tragedy of this wretched man. Few people passed by without listening and most slipped a few coins into his hand before leaving.

★ ★ ★

In the summer of the same year, I rented a small cabin near the mountains at Kamakura and took my family there to escape from the heat of Tokyo. One evening when the moon was particularly clear, I took a stroll on the beach where, despite the moon's splendour, there were few people — a marked contrast to the usual daytime bustle. I stood at the water's edge where a stream ran out into the sea and gazed at the moon's silver light being shattered by the waves. I heard the faint notes of a *shakuhachi* and when I looked about me I saw that the music must have been coming from a spot quite close by where several fishing boats were moored. As I approached I saw a group of about ten people whose attention was focused on a small boat which was moored about 24 feet above the water line. Some were perched on the gunwales of surrounding boats, some were crouching on the beach and others were standing. All were looking at a man who was leaning against the boat and playing the *shakuhachi*.

I did not join the audience myself, but stood a little apart to listen. The moonlight reflected on the group who were listening in a breathless hush. Just when the music seemed to have finished, three or four of the group got to their feet and left, and although the majority waited to hear the next piece, the player put the *shakuhachi* in his lap and remained motionless, his head bowed. A few minutes passed thus until three or four of the others decided to go, leaving only one beach urchin and two young villagers. I went right up to the man and stood waiting. He looked up and, much to my surprise, I realised that it was the very same blind man whom I had seen in the Ginza that spring. He, however, would not have recognised me, even if he had been able to see. His

sightless eyes were turned towards me for a moment and then he began
to play again, trilling his fingers and producing some low, thready
notes. Then abruptly he stopped and stepped off the boat.

'Wait a moment, blind man,' I said. 'Would you do me the honour of
coming to my house and playing a piece or two?'

'Yes, yes!' he said, looking at me sharply as if surprised at such a request. Then he hung his head again and nodded slightly. 'Yes, I will
come, wherever it is.'

'Shall we go, then,' I said, leading the way.

I walked on a few paces and then a thought occurred to me and I turned back.

'Are you totally blind?'

'Not quite. I can see a little from my right eye.'

'Well, that's splendid, then, if you can see even a little.'

'Ha, ha,' he laughed lightly. 'No, to see a little is not good. It makes
you greedy for more.'

'Mind out. There's a bridge ahead,' I said, drawing his attention to a
small bridge over a ditch. 'If you're not totally blind, why do you have
to come to such a place to earn your living?'

'I prefer to work, and singing from door to door is my trade.'

'Where were you born?'

'In western Japan.'

'The reason I ask is that I saw you this spring in the Ginza, and for
some reason I've thought about you from time to time. I recognised you
as soon as I saw you.'

'Really? That's because I travel wherever my feet take me, all over
Japan sooner or later. I think someone is coming.'

Two or three young people were coming along the road towards us.
Light cloud was shading the moon a little, so it was rather dark. As we
walked along we could hear the light strains of a concertina echoing
from a window high above us. Presently we reached my house.

★ ★ ★

We took our seats on the veranda and after a cup of barley tea, I asked
him to play something for myself and my family. Now, I am a novice
when it comes to the *shakuhachi* and I could not understand the finer
points of the piece he played, nor the skill of his technique, but the insistent tone of the music got to me somehow and subconsciously I was
awed. Should I cry? The grief I felt was too profound for tears. Did the
player feel nothing as he played? Usually when a piece finishes, the
player smiles and says a few self-deprecatory words, but this man drew
back in silence and his spirit seemed to be straining to follow the notes
he had played as they vanished into thin air. From the way the man
spoke, I had realised from the beginning that his appearance and manner must conceal some worthwhile story and I could not help but put

my thoughts into words.

'Excuse me asking, but you must surely have taken formal lessons in the *shakuhachi*?'

'No, that's not so. I'm completely self-taught. It's just that when I was a boy, I was very fond of this instrument and learned to play it. I never told anyone about it.'

'I cannot believe it. Your skill is too great. Anyway, I should have thought that even if you had no formal tuition, you would have a much more comfortable life if you were to take pupils yourself. Are you alone in the world?'

'Yes, I have neither parent, wife, nor child. I am a carefree soul,' he said, with a touch of irony.

'You can't really be carefree. How could you be when you are roasted by the sun, beaten by the rain and wander all over Japan with nowhere fixed to live? But I suppose there is some freedom in such an existence. I wish you'd tell me about yourself,' I asked with decided honesty. I agree that it can never be right to pry into the secrets of a man's run of tragedy, but I must confess that my two or three meetings with him had moved me not a little and this seemed to give me justification.

'I'd be quite happy to. For some reason I've been thinking about my childhood today. A while ago I heard some children in a villa garden singing and it almost brought me to tears.

'When I was eight or nine, my mother often took me to visit an aunt who lived in the mountains a few miles from my native castle town. We used to stop there for two or three nights, and, funnily enough, it was about that very thing I have been thinking today, for the first time in a long while. Memories of that time grip my heart with just the same emotions as I felt when I first heard someone play the *shakuhachi*. I lost my father when I was only five years old and I was raised by my mother and grandmother. I can see the house now. There was about a quarter of an acre of grounds which were filled with sasanquas, crape myrtles and golden litchi fruit hanging from trees over the fence. The house and grounds were extensive all right, but for all that we were a poor family who often had trouble in finding enough to eat. My days were carefree, but my mother had to take in work. She was a lonely woman and her occasional trips back home into the mountains were her greatest pleasure. The ten miles or so along the mountain path to my aunt's home were difficult for a child to manage, and although at the outset I would dance bravely ahead of my mother, tossing stones at the carp in the ditches, I had always lost heart by the time we had got half way. To encourage me, my mother would rest at the tea house which stood at the top of the mountain pass and the old woman who ran the place used to derive great pleasure from seeing me eat the speciality of the house. Once we had crossed the pass and come to the half-way mark, we could see my aunt's village beneath our feet. It was like a picture in the early

spring with the trailing mists hanging over the narrow ravines. As soon
as the village came into sight, we used to sit on a stone by the wayside,
feeling we were as good as there. My mother would have a smoke and I
would drink the clear water which tumbled down from the mountain
peak.

'My aunt's house was an old *samurai* mansion, and, although by this
time most of the family wealth had disappeared, it still seemed a very
opulent place to me. I felt warm inside at the sight of the great, thick
pillars, the gloomy granary, the ivy-covered plaster walls and the deep
well, and it pleased me that the servants spoke of me as the "young
master". However, what made me happiest of all and is most painful for
me to recall now is the hours I spent playing with my young cousin who
was about the same age as myself. Together we often went to the mountain stream in the narrow gorge to fish for dace. On the opposite side of
the mountain this stream was formed into a deep, blue pool, but on our
side it was swift and shallow. We used to stand in the shallows and drop
our lines into the pool. When we looked up we could see the mountains
on both sides thrusting jaggedly into the sky, their flanks dense with
vegetation and red pine trees, so that from below the sky took on the appearance of a narrow belt of blue. The mountains echoed our voices
when we spoke, but we never used to speak when we were fishing so
that the silence was almost deafening.

'One day we were concentrating on our fishing, when, before we
realised it, the sky changed and suddenly it began to rain. However, as
the fishing was particularly good that day, we decided not to go home.
Thick raindrops struck against our rods and danced on the surface of
the water, sending up tiny jets of spray. When we looked up, we could
see the rain falling from the peaks in bars like white threads. Our
clothes were soon wet through, but just as we were about to give it up as
a bad job, there was a vigorous tug on the line. We had caught a purple
and red-scaled dace almost a foot long. It struggled fearfully and by the
time we had got it into the fishing basket, it was soaked with rain and
twice as bright as at other times. It seemed like a new thing.

' "Let's go home now," one or the other of us said, but as we half
turned to go, we were struck again by the appearance of the rain on the
water in the stream.

' "Yes, let's." But this time neither of us made any move to go. In
fact we were in a dream and oblivious to what the other was saying.
Thunder cracked overhead and began to echo round the mountains
with such a terrible din that it seemed as if they would split asunder.
We wound in our lines in silence and picking up the fishing basket, fled
for our very lives. On the way back we met a servant who had been sent
to fetch us, and when we got home we received the expected scolding
from my mother and aunt. Flinging the basket by the well, we changed
our clothes and went up to the first floor storeroom where we made

ourselves as small as possible and passed the time in looking through the illustrations in an old edition of the *Tales of the Taira and Minamoto*.

'Even when they were together my mother and my aunt never used to laugh. They were a sallow, taciturn and anxious-faced couple who used to talk to one another in whispers. On one occasion I saw my aunt with tears in her eyes, standing beside my mother who was also crying, but I didn't take much notice at the time. I just felt a little angry for some reason and ran straight off to the sitting room.

'Well, I should like to have stayed at my aunt's place for a week or ten days, but when four days at the most had passed, my mother would say that we had to go home and, as there was nothing else for it, I went home. Once I stubbornly insisted on staying on alone, so my mother set out by herself. When dusk fell, I stood out on the veranda. As my aunt's house was built high up on a mountain, I was able to look down and watch the dusk as it swept over the village. The western sky was clear as water with traces of the evening sun still remaining, and the mountains were a faded grey, with palls of blue smoke floating over the woods and valleys. It made me feel sad somehow and even the knell of the temple bell sounded different from usual as its long drawn-out notes trailed across the valleys and vanished. As I listened, I suddenly felt a surge of love for my mother and wondered why I had not gone home with her. Just now she would be arriving at our house and talking with my grandmother. It was so unbearable, this feeling, that I told my aunt I wanted to go straight home, but she laughed and took no notice. The lamps were lit indoors and soon I was diverted from my thoughts by a game of chess with my cousin. Next day, however, I was sent home with a servant.

'Looking back at those times, I recall that the unhappiest moments were when my mother and I set out for home together. She used to rest several times as we crossed the pass and I can well remember how she looked at those times. She used to sit on a stone, sighing and looking miserable, so that even a child like myself could not help but share her misery. I used to sit by her in blank silence. Then she would always say:

"Are you hungry? If you are, have a cake. Would you like one?"

'If I said that I wasn't hungry, she used to say:

"Of course you are. Do have a cake. I'm going to have one as well." And I would be obliged to eat a cake I didn't want. This used to make me more miserable than ever and as I clung to her knee, I felt I wanted to cry. Even now, I still feel that same, painful love for her.'

Unable any longer to endure these memories of days gone by, the blind man suddenly stopped speaking and hung his head. After a few moments, however, he continued with such enthusiasm as to suggest that he had completely forgotten who was listening.

'There is nothing very strange about my relationship with my mother. She lived for me and loved me with a love that was blind. She seldom scolded me and even when she did, she always propitiated me as if it were she who had been in the wrong. It would not be quite true to say that I grew up obstinate and self-willed, but while being generally naughty there was always something weak and womanish about me. This did not please my old-fashioned grandmother who often used to rebuke my mother about it.

"You're too gentle with Shūzō," she would say, "and he has ended up a weakling. You must be firmer and bring him up as befits a man."

'But my mother did not have the temperament to apply the strict up-bringing necessary to achieve this. She loved me blindly and thought of nothing but what the future might bring to me. This irritated me, because she always thought of my future in terms of disaster rather than good fortune. On one occasion when she was worrying more than usual about my future prospects, she took me along to a strange fortune-teller who had a booth beside the Zenkōji temple. I well remember him. He was a little old man with deep-set eyes, round face and weird countenance, belying this somewhat sinister appearance with the very gentle and polite manner in which he spoke to my mother.

"Ah yes, I see. It must be a worry for you. Quite natural. I'll see what I can do," he said, when she had explained her fears.

'He looked at my face through a magnifying glass and made a clatter with his divining rods, for he was a man who practised both physiognomy and divination. Presently he said:

"No, there's no need to worry. This child will certainly get on in the world, for he has a fine physiognomy. But he will have one trouble and that will be with women. If, throughout his life, he pays careful attention to his dealings with women, he will do splendidly. Yes, he's a fine child." He patted my head and stared into my face.

'My mother was overjoyed at this and lost no time in telling my grandmother what had happened as soon as we got home. My grandmother laughed.

"It would have been more manly if he had said the boy would die by the sword. He is a pale, weak child and that's why the diviner said he would have trouble with women. Still, there's no need to worry about woman trouble as yet. Soon enough when he's sixteen or seventeen."

'However, I, who was only eleven at the time, already had my share of woman trouble. I'll tell you now about two or three cases of the trouble I had with women, for, needless to say, the diviner was entirely accurate with his prophecy.

'At this time there was a family by the name of Iizuka, living about three blocks from us and they had a fourteen-year-old daughter named O-sayo, who was a slender, pretty creature. Whenever I met her, she used to ask me to come in to her house and play. I didn't go at first, but she was so insistent that in the end I gave in. She wouldn't let me go for an hour or two which she spent hugging me, putting her arms round my neck, combing my hair and pressing my face to her soft cheek. This all made me feel very happy and thereafter I went to her house again and again and grew to feel dissatisfied if I didn't see her. Meanwhile, of course, I had been told by the fortune-teller that I would have trouble with women and had received several lectures on the subject from my mother. Being a child, I grew angry at the thought that what was happening at present might be classed as such, but I didn't show my anger to my mother, and although suffering secret pangs of guilt, I continued to visit O-sayo at frequent intervals. When I think of it now I am sure that I must have been in love with her, for although on the surface I hated the way she hugged me and treated me like a child, in my heart it delighted me and even now I remember the feelings it gave me when she pressed my face against her soft, warm skin. If this were woman trouble, then it would do me just fine. Every day my mother lectured me on the terrors of womankind, giving me examples of what she meant both from the tales of antiquity and, more pertinently, from the youngsters of the castle town. She was always telling me that on the surface women appeared saints, but underneath were really demons and that I had better regard any woman I met as a demon or a snake. She said that all women who spoke kind words were deceivers and that if I spoke unguardedly, I would find myself in big trouble.

'Well, I trusted my mother and didn't doubt a word she said. Therefore I was angry that perhaps O-sayo too was a secret demon and I thought of confessing what was going on. After all O-sayo was still a child and I was a child myself, so perhaps my mother would not be too angry. It also occurred to me that O-sayo's love for me might be real and thus she was no deceiver at all. At any rate this is how I rationalised it to myself. However, one day at dusk when I was passing by the Iizuka's, O-sayo came running out, and dragged me inside. She asked me why I had not been to see her for the past four or five days, and when I replied that I had had a cold, she peered into my face and said what a pity it was and was I better. Staring into my eyes, she told me that I still looked ill and should take care of myself, because if I got ill, she would die. Weakling that I was, I felt joy and sadness at being so spoken to and involuntarily I burst into tears. She hugged me to her and I saw that there were tears in her eyes as well. She told me to stay the night, because then she could hold me and sleep with me instead of my mother. I said that it wouldn't do because I should be scolded, but she overruled my protests by saying that it would be all right if I went and got her approval. I told her quietly that if I went and asked my mother, I should be scolded for it was a secret that I came to see her. O-sayo thrust me away from her. She glared at me and asked why was it a secret and was it such a bad thing for the two of us to play together, because if it were, I'd better not come any more. Trembling, I jumped down from the veranda and ran away as fast as I could. I never went to the Iizuka home again. If I happened to meet O-sayo, I ran away, and as she watched me, she just laughed so that in the end I came to believe that she was a deceiver.

★ ★ ★

'My next woman trouble did not occur until I was eighteen, by which time both my mother and grandmother were dead. Through the offices of my aunt I got a job at the village school for a salary of five yen a month. It was during the spring of my fourteenth year that my grandmother died, my mother following her the same autumn so that I had been orphaned very suddenly. I was taken in by my aunt. Until the age of seventeen I lived in the lonely mountain village and did not go much on scholarship. My only modern reading matter was the young people's magazines sent me by my cousin who was by then a boarder at the middle school in town. Apart from that I just read the old war tales which had been in my aunt's family for years. That being the case, I was a doubtful proposition even for a primary school teacher, but my aunt's family was one of the oldest in the village and secured me this quite unwarrantable position through their influence. When my mother was ill, she admonished me over and over again to be careful with women and continued to do so right up to her death. She urged me to get on in the world and said that she would pray for me from the grave. And so she died. But how was I to get on in the world? My mother had no ideas as to that. She had tried to get my aunt's family to pay my way through school, but when this failed, she had nothing else to suggest and just clung rigidly to the belief that I would get on in the world. Of course, this was all rather vague and caused her no end of worry. As for myself, I had no spirit and did not take much thought of how I was going to do. The sadness of being so suddenly parted from my mother was such that, even after I had been staying with my aunt for a month or two, I still used to cry when no one was looking.

'As the months passed, my grief was slowly assuaged until in the end I only thought of her occasionally and otherwise came to regard my aunt as a mother because she was so kind to me. After my seventeenth birthday, I came to find more interest and pleasure in life, as I went back and forth to the primary school where I and three or four others of the same age had charge of the village children. In the evenings I practised the *shakuhachi*. As a matter of fact there was in the village at this time an old man who was self-taught on the *shakuhachi* and who was regarded as a great master by the young people. Eventually, I became his pupil, but because he was self-taught, all the pupils had their own styles and just played as they pleased. As they became more used to playing, they grew arrogant, each with his own idea of who was skilful and who not. Perhaps because of my temperament, I was the only one to give myself wholeheartedly to the instrument, and whenever I played I felt all sense of greed and desire for advantage leave me. Early each morning before the sun was up, I used to go into the mountains and sit on a rock, bathed in the dawn mist, and play. Indeed it sometimes seemed to me that the music of my *shakuhachi* itself dispelled the morning mist and that the sun rose to its accompaniment. It came about quite naturally, therefore, that I was the most skilled of all the master's pupils and the old teacher even went so far as to say that, with practice, I could become the best player in Japan.

'Meanwhile, I had attained my eighteenth birthday. One evening right at the beginning of spring, I was sitting by the bank of the village stream playing my *shakuhachi*, when I heard someone call my name. Looking round, I saw a young man whose home lay on the slope leading to the next village. He had the somewhat pretentious name of Takenojō which had been given him by a temple priest. He grinned.

"Say, Shūzō, you're pretty good on the *shakuhachi*."

'He was rather an odd young man, a sly individual who liked to make fun of people, so I just brandished my *shakuhachi* and made as if to hit him, whereupon he suddenly turned serious.

"Shūzō, there's something I should like you to have a look at."

'Thinking this a rather odd request, I replied:

"Something you want me to see? What is it?"

"It's nothing much really, but I'd like you to see it all the same."

"Is it some sort of object?"

'Take smiled mysteriously.

"It's something you'll really enjoy seeing."

"You're having me on!"

"No, really I'm not. I'd really like you to see it. Please do as I ask."

'This time he was very earnest.

"All right, let's see it then."

"Oh no. It's not here. I'd like you to come to my house."

"Is it one of your household treasures then? A sword or something?"

'He laughed strangely. "Something like that. It's certainly a treasure, a real treasure."

'By now, I could hardly contain my curiosity. I really wanted to see this thing.

"All right then. Let's go."

'We set out together and came to Take's house. As I have said before, this house stood at the top of a gentle rise, perhaps seven or eight blocks from my aunt's house. The *shakuhachi* master's house stood at the bottom end of the rise, so I was used to coming in this general direction, but I had only been to the top end three or four times. Beyond this rise there was a dell where stood less than ten houses, so consequently there was seldom occasion for any of the villagers to venture so far. Take's house consisted of a main building and a storeroom outhouse, the door of which was always closed. On the cliff above it there stood an old oak tree overshadowing the place so that it seemed rather gloomy. Under the cliffs opposite the house was a shallow, square well which was always brimful with pure water. The whole place gave an impression of weirdness and as I came along the rise and passed in front of the house itself, I brought to mind several disturbing novels I had read. I had come full of curiosity, having been told something strange by this Take whom I hardly knew. It was all very weird and wonderful. Time and again on the way I had asked Take what he had to show me, but he would say nothing and just laughed rather ill-naturedly, as I thought.

'The sun had disappeared by now and the moon was shining brightly, but as the rise was surrounded by trees not much light filtered through. It was only about two hundred yards to the top and it was not long before we reached the house. Its frontage was wide and the trees cast no shadow so that the moonbeams were clearly visible on the ground. A faint light gleamed through the door and the house was quiet. Take entered the garden in silence, but I hesitated outside.

"Come in!" Take invited darkly. His voice was soft, but it had power and seemed to compel me. But I stayed where I was.

"Bring it out here, whatever it is you want to show me."

"I said, come in!"

'This time he spoke more forcefully, and, unable to help myself, I reluctantly entered the garden. Take went ahead into the sitting room and didn't emerge for some time. He seemed to be talking to someone. Presently, however, he came out and this time his tone was milder.

"Come in. I apologise for the mess."

'A little reassured, I went in and Take led me to a back room which was surprisingly neat, with a lamp glimmering in the corner. What struck me most forcibly, however, was that there was a girl sitting there. As I entered she made as if to get up and sitting quite erect, she looked across at me. So strange it was that I was unable to bring myself to sit down. Suddenly Take spoke up.

"This is what I brought you to see."

'The girl bowed low. I said nothing, not knowing quite what was for the best, and just stared at Take in blank amazement. He blushed a little, but said, with dark significance:

"Sit down, won't you. I have to pop out for a minute." He made as if to leave.

"Here, hang on," I said, "you can't leave me here alone."

"Please sit down," he said, glaring at me angrily.

'I knew that if I said I was going home, he would threaten me and refuse to allow me to leave, so I made the best of it and sat down without another word. By now the girl was crying her heart out and when he saw this, Take's face was indescribable. The blue veins stood out on his forehead and he gnashed his teeth. There were tears in his eyes and he appeared to be on the point of saying something, but he rubbed his mouth with the back of his hand instead.

"What's going on?" I asked.

'He stammered something about me being able to guess. In fact, he said, this girl was his sister and she had asked him to arrange a meeting between myself and her, but he had refused. Apparently she had been so persistent in her requests that eventually Take had agreed to bring me to the house by a ruse. He held out his hands beseechingly and asked me to have pity on her. This all sounded so ridiculous to me that I wanted to laugh, but nevertheless it was obviously the truth and the conclusion forced on me was that I had in some way become the Don Juan of the village. Now you are not to think that I had completely forgotten my mother's warnings about women, but when all is said and done, it was just a small mountain village and whenever two or three young men were together, the conversation inevitably turned to girls. My colleagues at school were always discussing the beauty of some girl or another and their affairs — in fact it seemed their only pleasure. Occasionally, therefore, I felt like trying my luck with such girls. I never actually did anything, because I remembered what my mother had said, but to tell the truth I was not afraid of girls and if a suitable opportunity had presented itself, I make no doubt that I would have had an affair.

'To return to Take's sister. Her name was O-kō, she was sixteen, and by local reputation she was the sweetest girl in the village. Of course, I knew her by sight, but I had never exchanged any conversation with her, although on account of my family's distinguished position and the fact that I was a teacher, she always made some polite greeting whenever we happened to meet. She had clear eyes and a whiteness of skin uncommon in country girls. Her figure was slender, not unlike O-sayo's. It was the villagers' proud boast that there were few girls to match her even in the castle town and from the times I had seen her I was compelled to the same judgement. Now that her brother had thrust her before my eyes and she had made advances to me, any consideration of "woman trouble" was cast to the winds. Weakling that I was, even though I was aware of the possible dangers of such a liaison, I could not find it within myself to turn my back on her and run for home.

'From that time on, I visited O-kō every two or three days, but I took great pains to keep it a secret, so none knew of it. We were helped in this desire for secrecy by Take and his wife who was in on it from the very beginning and did her best to ensure that things between us went smoothly. This meant that we could be open in the house at least, and in fact so good was the relationship between us that Take and his wife sometimes bantered us about it. What with one thing and another, two or three months passed by until the evening of 7 June — an evening permanently ingrained on my memory. I reached O-kō's house at about eight o'clock as usual, and about ten o'clock the rain which had

HOOK/BEN

15066

TERMS: PAYMENT DUE UPON PRESENTATION

TICKET NO. 7562:601:628

ORIGINAL INVOICE

— FLIGHT NO. —	DATE —	DEPART—	ARRIVE —	STATUS —
93B	28JAN	820A	1217P	OK
BREAKFAST				
93B	1FEB	125P	446P	OK
SNACK				
78B	5FEB	340P	519P	OK
SNACK				
78B	5FEB	640P	841P	OK
DINNER				

TX   11.85 TTL   499.35

INVOICE TOTAL   499.35

KIWI TRAVEL, INC.

OUR BUSINESS"

CS ☐ C-C

RE-CONFIRM ALL FLIGHTS AND TIMES
-CONFIRMED AT LEAST 72 HOURS PRIOR TO DEPARTURE OR THEY
URE.

1. Please check your documents when you receive them. Cal

2. For international flights, reconfirm the return or continuing
   tions will result in automatic cancellation of all continuing a
   enroute.

3. Hotels are usually confirmed on a guaranteed payment bas
   datory payment.

4. **PROMOTIONAL FARES**—Most discount fares involve certa
   could result in a carrier demanding a full fare. Your ticket
   reservations, advise the airline or travel agent of the special
   do so may result in an increase in fare and/or penalty.

5. **AIR FARES**—Fares change frequently and information may
   reference sources or from airline quotations may turn ou
   ASSURED THAT WE LOOK FOR THE MOST ADVANTAGEO

6. **SERVICE CHARGES**—We reserve the right to charge a proce
   imposed by airlines, hotels, tours, cruise companies, etc.

7. **TICKETS**—Cancelled or unused tickets must be returned fo
   paid for until refund is received from the issuing carrier; s
   schedules, most tickets are interchangeable between airlin
   higher fare, you need pay only the difference between fares

8. **RESPONSIBILITY**—This travel agency represents, and is
   operators, hotels, wholesalers and service companies; all of
   not responsible for any negligent act or omission by any o

9. **IMPORTANT**—In the unusual event that you arrive at the cu
   reservation for you, DO NOT LEAVE THE COUNTER. Check y
   must accommodate you on that flight, or if that is impossib
   compensation. If necessary, ask to speak with the supervis

ıve any questions.

st 72 hours prior to departure time. Failure to reconfirm reserva-
servations. Please advise the airlines if your travel plans change

ncel or change plans, please notify your hotel(s) to avoid man-

ns. A change in carrier(s), flight(s), time(s), date(s), or routings
"Special Fare" travel regulations. When booking or changing
he may assist you in complying with the regulations. Failure to

in a short time. Also, information given in good faith from quick
ırrect. The fare printed on the ticket is the binding price. BE

the event of a refund or cancellation in addition to any charges

redit to your account. Lost, stolen or destroyed tickets must be
ı airline imposed service charge. In the event of revised flight
. no need to purchase new tickets. If your itinerary calls for a

ır, carefully selected carriers, transportation companies, tour
ısclosed principals and independent contractors. This agency is
nizations.

ıck in counter with your ticket to find that the airline shows no
ıf the status box shows OK for the flight in question, the airline
ıt either find you a substitute flight or pay you denied boarding
ıer . . . . if your ticket reads OK . . . . you are OK.

KIWI TRAVEL, INC.

12339 SO. HARLEM AVE. • PALOS HEIGHTS, IL 60463

PHONE: 312-361-1133

	JAN 14 1985	11272

FROM	TO	CARRIER
CHICAGO/OHARE	MIAMI	EAST
MIAMI	SAN JUAN PR	EAST
SAN JUAN PR	MIAMI	EAST
MIAMI	CHICAGO/OHARE	EAST

AIR TRANSPORTATION FARE

"WE THANK YO

☒ A/R ☐

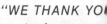

BECAUSE OF FREQUENT SCHEDULE CHANGES, WE RECOMMEND
INTERNATIONAL FLIGHTS: ALL ONGOING OR RETURN FLIGHTS M
WILL BE CANCELLED — **CHECK IN AT LEAST ONE HOUR PRIOR T**

threatened all evening began to fall. I said that I would go home before
it got any worse, but O-kō and Take's wife stopped me. Take was away
at the time, but he was due back any moment, they said, so that he
could go with me as far as the bridge on my way home. So I waited until
he came in, obviously the worse for drink. I was lying down in an inner
room with O-kō seated beside me when he unceremoniously burst in
and plumped himself down beside us.

"Why don't you stay the night? There's a dreadful storm outside," he
invited mysteriously. I say mysteriously, because I had often wanted to
stay in the past, but Take had always packed me off home, saying that it
would be awkward if the fact of my staying became known.

"I'd better not," I said, but Take waved aside my refusal.

"To tell the truth, there's something I want to discuss with you. I
have asked you to stay and you'd better do as I tell you." This time his
tone had become angry and I was terrified.

"Out with it then. What do you want to discuss?"

"Haven't you noticed?" he said suddenly.

"Noticed what?" I couldn't guess what he was talking about.

"Ah, then you haven't. Take a look at O-kō," he said, putting his
hand on her stomach, significantly, much to my surprise. O-kō got up
and left the room.

"Is it true? Really?" I asked in a small voice, not really thinking what
I was saying.

"It's true all right. You ought to have known, but you didn't.
Anyway, that's about the strength of it, so now you do know, what do
you intend to do about it?"

"I don't know. What's the best thing to do?" I asked nervously, losing all presence of mind. Take looked angry.

"What sort of question is that? Isn't it manifestly obvious? You
should have been prepared for this to happen."

'When put like that, it was indeed quite obvious, but I hadn't been at
all prepared. I had just come to O-kō almost as if in a dream and when
thus confronted by Take, I had nothing to say. Noting my silence, Take
clicked his tongue vexedly.

"You must marry her."

"Marry her?"

"Well, is it such a hateful idea?"

"No, of course not, but I don't know whether my aunt will give her
consent."

"Whatever she says won't matter if it's what you want. You've but to
say the word and tomorrow I'll publicly announce that you are to be
man and wife. After all this village is not the whole world, and if your
aunt and the villagers make a fuss, you can go away together. Life will
go on."

'At this I suddenly took heart.

"Right, I'll do it. I'll discuss it with my aunt and if she approves, all well and good. But if she objects, I'll do as you say and take her away to Tokyo or Osaka. But does O-kō agree to this course of action?"

"Yes! Need you ask? She would come with you were it into the heart of the fire or the depths of the ocean."

'Take poked my cheek with his finger, now in good spirits.

'Well, when I got home that evening, I just couldn't bring myself to tell my aunt. The point was that my aunt had heard from my mother about the diviner's prophecy and before she died, my mother had asked her over and over again to keep an eye on me as far as this was concerned. I suspected that she would be both surprised and worried if I told her about O-kō and me. For the next three days, I was in and out of my aunt's room, trying to raise the subject, but I could never bring myself to speak. Failing in this, I resolved that there was nothing for it but to elope with O-kō, and I went to Take's house to make plans accordingly. However, at the last moment I could not go through with that either. The dreadful thought haunted me increasingly that this was "Woman Trouble" with capital letters, and when I went over in my mind how up to then I had behaved with O-kō, it occurred to me that it had all been a terrible mistake. I thought that if I ran off with O-kō, I would be letting myself in for all sorts of trouble in the future. I would fall irretrievably into the pit of "woman trouble". I just couldn't go through with the elopement, but after much anguished thought, I resolved to run away all the same, but alone. I shall never forget the night of 15 June — just a week after I had first learned of O-kō's pregnancy. I really wanted to see her one more time, but the affair in hand was too important and so, muttering my mother's name like an incantation, I fled into the darkness — away from the village. Doubtless an unsuspecting O-kō was waiting in vain for me to come to her. I, who had been taught never to be deceived by a woman, was myself deceiving an innocent girl. However, did I but know it, by abandoning one woman in an attempt to free myself from "woman trouble", I was running into even bigger trouble of exactly the same kind.

'I had brought very little money with me from my aunt's, so as soon as I reached Tokyo, I was obliged to go from door to door playing the *shakuhachi* to earn my living. I'll skip the next ten years of my life until I reached the age of twenty-seven. During that time I had no news from home and I had no family or close friends in Tokyo. I did many things, but always, inevitably, I blundered over anything important to do with women. By the time I was twenty-seven I had been married once, but had run away from my wife after only six months. Now I had my last ever entanglement with the female sex and since that time I have left well enough alone. So I'll cut a long story short and tell you about this final incident.

* * *

'It was the summer of my twenty-seventh year and at last fortune had smiled on me a little. I had secured a post with the Tokyo Railway Bureau at the reasonable salary of eighteen yen a month. I had learned by my bitter experiences with women and so I rented a small room in a tenement house where I lived alone with neither wife nor woman to look after me. I cooked for myself and commuted to the Bureau. My tenement was situated in a narrow lane in downtown Atago, surrounded by other similar buildings. Right in front of me there lived a carpenter and his wife. As doubtless you know, tenement dwellers are different from those who live in the better parts of town in that they are very friendly. Soon after I moved in I was on terms of nodding acquaintance with most of the other residents. The carpenter was about the same age as myself and went off to work and came home at the same time as I did. Seeing each other so often, we were soon on good terms and eventually took to going to each other's homes. His name was Tōkichi and he was a very interesting man to know, having all the characteristics of a real Edo artisan, a snappy dresser and a glib talker. His looks, however, were not so prepossessing as he suffered from particularly round eyes and a narrow forehead. When he laughed he seemed a fine fellow, but when he had occasion to speak sharply there was something rather odd about him, which was, however, part of his charm. Whenever he came round to my place, he always smelled of drink and it was his habit to sit cross-legged, with bare thighs. He was constantly chaffing me about my not drinking, mixed with unceasing admonishment of me for not being married. Sometimes he used to say:

"People like you have never been caused any suffering by a woman, but as a result, neither have you any idea of a woman's blessings."

'I used to reply that as far as I could see he hadn't suffered very much and his wife and parents looked after him very well.

'Of course he did not know it, but I had suffered in many ways during the ten years since I had come to Tokyo. I must have seemed anything but a man of the world to Tōkichi, because I had nothing to do with women and because my character was such that I was unable to do or say anything violent. It was not unreasonable, therefore, that he should think me something of a dullard and suggest that I knew nothing about the opposite sex. I have sometimes thought that the reason I have had so much trouble with women during my life is not so much my basic nature as the fact that I am naive and gentle.

'One evening Tōkichi came in and told me that if I had any washing to give it to him for his wife to do. I did not hesitate to give him some undershirts. Well, towards evening the next day, his wife brought back the washing herself. She threw the bundle onto my lap, saying that I should hurry up and find myself a wife so that I would realise the blessings of being married. Then she went home. Her name was O-shun and she was in her early twenties. I suppose I felt from the very beginning that she was no ordinary woman, because the other women in the tenements were always singing her praises, sometimes even in front of her.

'In time it became so that Tōkichi was coming round to my room every night, one reason being that he was keen for me to teach him how to play the *shakuhachi*. However, an instrument like the *shakuhachi* requires a natural talent and although Tōkichi was very nimble-fingered, he never made much progress. That did not stop him trying, however. O-shun used to come with him, unasked, but subsequently on Sundays and other times when Tōkichi was not around, she took to coming alone for a chat, even during the day. Later I used to go over to them and quite often we would talk together, the three of us, until after midnight. Frequently O-shun would cook for me and bring vegetables around when she could get them. Sometimes I found she had prepared my evening meal for me, even before I got home from the office. On one occasion Tōkichi saw fit to banter her about it.

"You must be very busy, having two masters as you do!" he told her.

'And yet Tōkichi never entertained any suspicions of me and what began as a next-door-neighbour relationship soon developed into him taking me into his confidence and discussing his private affairs with me. I was equally friendly and became a great help to the fellow, even, on occasion, lending him money so that he came to believe that I was an indispensable friend. When I was laid up with a cold for a couple of days, he even took a day off work to be with me. It was not only Tōkichi. Everyone in the tenements made a great fuss of me, praising me as being gentle, good and trustworthy. Thus, not only O-shun, but all the women did jobs for me entirely unsolicited. However, what was odd was that O-shun was very jealous of me and would frown at the other women whenever she thought that they were doing too much for me. This led to the women poking their noses into my affairs just for the fun of seeing her reaction. But they never showed any suspicion regarding the relationship between O-shun and me and trusted me as if I had been made of wood and metal instead of flesh and blood. They were not quite so trusting of O-shun, however, and to tell the truth their slight suspicions were not unfounded. One evening she came rushing in just as I was making my bed and snatched the bedding from me to arrange it herself.

"Sleep well, young sir. You're a very troublesome master!" she said, and there was unfeigned seduction in her eyes as she stared hard at me. My feelings were strangely stirred, for contrary to what the people of the tenement believed, I was not made of wood. Once I spoke to Tōkichi about her.

"I hope you don't mind me saying so, but it seems to me perhaps that O-shun is not the normal run of housewife."

'Tōkichi grinned and said:

"That's a good piece of judgement! In fact she made quite a name for herself as a maid in a tea-house, where my foreman first found her, but when she was sounded out about it, she said she would like to be the wife of an honest craftsmen. My good fortune that she came to look after me!" he told me elatedly.

'Well, from that time on I began to feel a strange fascination in watching her manner and the way she carried herself.

'At any rate, the days passed peacefully enough until one terribly hot evening in the middle of August. All the residents of the tenement had gone out to escape from the heat and keep cool, but I had caught a chill the previous evening and as I was not feeling too good, I went to bed early. About ten o'clock I heard whispering outside my room. This gradually subsided and I realised from what I heard that O-shun must have stayed in as well. The atmosphere was very oppressive and I couldn't sleep, so I got out of bed and sat awhile by the brazier, smoking a cigarette. I was suddenly seized with a desire to go out, and without thinking about the fact that I was dressed only in my nightclothes, I rushed into the main street where I paused to look up at the moon which was setting over Mt. Atago. There was a slight breeze that night and as I was strolling along, my attention was caught by the figure of a man on the opposite side of the street who was muttering something to himself. As he appeared to be drunk, I avoided him, but he staggered over to me and I was able to recognise his face. It was Tōkichi.

"My dear fellow, am I glad to see you! Do say you'll come home with me. You must excuse my condition, but there's something I want to ask you about." He took me by the hand and pulled me towards the alleyway.

'I realised he was drunk but thought it best to humour him so I went with him and told him I would be happy to listen to anything he had to say. His face was pallid enough to be frozen and there was a set expression to his eyes, as he began to tell me a long, rambling narrative, slurring his words because of his drunkenness. He had been having a drink that day with four or five other men when one of them, on some pretext or other, had started a quarrel with him. Apparently there had been some exchange of insults and one of the men had said that Tōkichi must be a real milksop to be so grateful for the foreman's cast-offs (meaning O-shun) and told him that he would do better, therefore, to keep his mouth shut. It appeared that Tōkichi's exasperation stemmed from the fact that his workmates had two or three times made fun of him by insinuating that O-shun had embarrassed him by carrying on with the foreman. Although he never said anything about it, this was a point which had caused Tōkichi some considerable suffering, and now having it raised in the form of an insult was more than he could stand. The unwarrantable injustice flared up inside him.

"Who asked your opinion?" he had shouted. "If she's the foreman's cast-off, what of it? I suppose you wouldn't be glad to accept such a cast-off, eh?!"

'Then the man had laughed at him and remarked maliciously:

"Oh yes, I daresay. It would be all right if it were all in the past. But it's not, see. She's still carrying on with him even now, two or three times a month."

"We'll see about that!"

'When he had heard the man's remark, Tōkichi left hurriedly and had been on his way home to have it out with O-shun and find the truth when he had met me.

'He told me that he intended to kick her out of the house and asked if I thought that was the right thing to do, so I have him an honest opinion and said that although I had no idea whether she was the sort of woman who would behave so badly with the foreman, it would not be a good idea to throw her out, because she was obviously fond of him and had made him a good wife. As far as I could tell, I said, there were no suspicious signs of such a relationship between O-shun and the foreman. Despite my reassurance, he said:

"If there's anything funny going on, I'll kill her. I've heard that there was something between them at one time, but it's unacceptable now. I'll kick her out and give him a good thrashing into the bargain."

'I tried to placate him, but he wouldn't listen to anything I said and in the end he went back to his house. Not willing to leave the matter at that, I tried to follow him, but he wouldn't let me in, saying that it was nothing for me to be concerned about, and so there was nothing for it, but to stay outside and listen for developments. Apparently O-shun was already in bed, but Tōkichi dragged her out and began to shout at her. She seemed to be listening in silence, but a few moments later she suddenly came running out where she saw me.

"He's talking a load of nonsense in there. He's drunk and there's nothing I can do about it, so I thought it best to leave him to himself," she said, walking into my room without ceremony. I followed her in.

"Who put such nonsense into his head, that's what I'd like to know? He's really stupid to believe it." She sat down beside the brazier and lit herself a cigarette which I had left there. I tried to console her.

"It'll be all right in the morning," I said and as she showed no sign of going back to her room, I added:

"He seems to have quietened down now. I think it would be a good idea if you went back to him."

'Silently, O-shun got to her feet and left my room, whereupon I clambered under the mosquito net with the intention of going to sleep. However, a few moments later she was back again.

"He's fast asleep, so I've locked the door from the outside," she said.

"But what about you?" I asked.

"I'll go without sleep until morning."

"Wouldn't it be better to go back to your place and sleep, if you can manage it?"

"Please let the subject drop. He's drunk and there's no telling what he may do if he wakes up in the night. I'm frightened," she said, calmly smoking a cigarette.

'As I had no answer to this, I held my peace and it was then that it struck me that O-shun was not her usual voluble self. Peering from under the mosquito net, I was able to see her silhouette, complete with her luxuriant hair, in the dim rays of the lamp. Because the atmosphere was so close, she seemed languid and this made her bewitching to me more than ever before.

'About twenty minutes passed during which I was aware that O-shun was repeatedly driving off the mosquitoes with her fan until at last she sprang to her feet.

"These horrible insects!" she cried. The she came over to where I was lying under the mosquito net. "Are you asleep yet?" she enquired.

"Almost," I replied, feigning a drowsy voice. I'm not quite sure why.

"I'd be very grateful if you'd let me come under the net with you. I can't stand these mosquitoes any more."

'And so at last, she crept under the net with me and that was that.

'Early next morning, she went back to her house and perhaps because she had been able to restore his humour or perhaps because when he sobered up, he had thought better or the previous night's actions, Tōkichi went quietly off to work as usual. On his way out he poked his head round my door and said good morning. Then he laughed strangely and scratched his head.

"I'll apologise properly when I get home," he said and, with that, went on his way.

'A terrible shocked awareness of the wrong I had done him ran through me, but I didn't follow after him. Well, after that O-shun did indeed have two masters, as Tōkichi had once jokingly remarked.

'Before another month had passed, Tōkichi came home in great anger one evening after having had more words with his foreman, but on this occasion he had not been drinking. This time he had made the dreadful resolution that he would leave O-shun and go off to Yokohama to find work, and I was unable to stop him. When I said that I would then look after things for a while and that instead of divorcing O-shun, he should go away for six months or so and then come back to her, he wept tears of joy. He said that as I was going to see all was well I should give up my house and move in with O-shun who could then look after me. When these arrangements had been made, he duly went away to Yokohama.

'This of course settled things nicely and O-shun and I were able to live as husband and wife. However, a month later I got something wrong with my eyes. Thinking that it was nothing of importance, I did not bother with the doctor at first and just carried on with my work as normal, but it gradually grew worse until in the end I had to stay at home. The doctor told me that it would take a long time to clear up, but although I took the quickest possible steps to get treatment, as time went by, there was no sign of improvement. O-shun nursed me very attentively and in the meantime there was still no news from Tōkichi. Whenever I thought of him, I was filled with guilt at the great wrong I was doing him, but my resolve never reached the point where I did anything concrete about it like going after him to tell him the truth. I just thought over and over again how wrong it was, but was content to let O-shun console me.

'As time went by my eyes got worse and after I had been away from work for about a month I was completely disconsolate. I was given much anguish by the thought that perhaps I was going blind. And then O-shun began to change. She was not so attentive in her nursing as before and even the smallest trifle began to arouse her anger towards me. She sometimes took to going out for almost half a day without telling me where. I never said anything about it, but I was uneasy in my heart. One day a man came to see her.

"Excuse me," he said.

"Come in," she said.

'There was a whispered conversation between them for a few moments and then she came over to the bed where I lay.

"It's the foreman to see you. There's something he wants to discuss with you."

'Just as I was wondering what foreman this could be, he came straight up to the bed.

"I'm pleased to meet you," he said, "I am the master carpenter Sukejirō, and on behalf of Tōkichi, I can never thank you enough for all you have done for O-shun. On his behalf I should like to thank you formally for all the kindnesses she has received at your hands. I have decided, however, from now on it is proper that I should look after her and to that end I shall be taking her away as soon as possible. I beg you to understand the position and give your consent."

'His tone was pompous and effusive at the same time, and I just couldn't think of anything to say. Continuing their grand charade, the foreman and O-shun packed up her things, but just before the two of them left, O-shun came over to me.

"I have my reasons for doing this, so don't think badly of me. Goodbye and take care of yourself."

'It was beyond me either to cry or to scream in rage. So this was what my sins had come to. Clearly before my eyes came the images of my haggard mother and O-kō whom I had left behind me at home, pregnant.

'Well, there I was. No job; blind in one eye and my vision in the other so badly impaired as to be of little use; and without any savings. From that time forward I descended to the state in which you see me now, but

I do not feel any regret for that. I just play my *shakuhachi* and when I do, I think always of my beloved mother. When I think of her I wish I could die, but I cannot.'

Wishing to be on his way, the blind man played one more piece, but I could heardly bear to listen to the sad, pathos-filled notes, now that I had heard his story. They seemed to embody all the eternal bitterness of yearning for days gone beyond recall and the sorrows of the wandering vagabond. The moon was sinking in the west when he left. The next day I saw him again at Kamakura.

9
Poetic Images

Shisō (Poetic Images) is the third of Doppo's prose poetry works represented in this anthology, although it postdates *Takibi* and *Hoshi* by some eighteen months and is infinitely less complete as a work of art. It was published in April 1898 in issue no. 115 of the *Katei Zasshi*, and is substantially no more than a well expressed collection of thoughts, suitable perhaps either for working into a poem as the title implies or into short stories. The philosophical feeling underlying the four passages is Buddhist, emphasising the transience of human life.

The white cloud over the hill

One autumn day a boy climbed to the top of a hill and lay down in the shade of a pine, gazing intently at a single white cloud which floated in the vast expanse of heaven. After a while he drifted off to sleep and dreamed a pleasant dream; he dreamed that the cloud had borne him up and away into the limitless blue of the sky. Never had he known such peace. Such was his joy that before he knew it he had forgotten all about the earth beneath him.

When he awoke, the autumn sun was sinking in the west. The leaves of the maple trees on the hill shone like fire and the sound of the breeze wafting through the pine tops was like the murmur of waves pounding on a distant island shore. Such was the tranquillity that he fell asleep once more, entering again into his dream.

Before long the boy forgot about the cloud. Later he grew into a man of the world, embroiled in all its unhappy affairs with so many things to trouble him. It was then that he sometimes remembered that sunny autumn day and the white cloud over the hill. And with that memory came tears.

* * *

The two travellers

Once a traveller was walking alone along a little-used pathway in the heart of the mountains where the snow lay thick on the ground. The snow grew deeper and deeper, the path more and more dangerous until at last, unable any longer to endure the cold, the traveller collapsed. As luck would have it a second traveller came along the same path and was much disturbed to see the plight of the other man. He raised him up and gave him something to revive him. The first traveller thereupon took the hand of the kindly newcomer and swore that as long as he lived he would never forget what he owed him. The other smiled faintly and said nothing. The first traveller then said that when he got home he would tell everyone what had happened. He would proclaim this kindly deed far and wide, setting it down in prose, composing a famous poem for posterity. Again the other smiled and said nothing.

Together they hurried on their way only to find that the path grew still more dangerous and the snow deeper and deeper until one of the travellers stumbled. With a cry he grasped his companion's hand and they both plummeted into a bottomless ravine and were lost. Ten thousand years might pass and none would know of their fate — still less would they know of the second traveller's great kindness.

* * *

Barren ground

Once there were two seeds. One was the seed of the beautiful violet and the other the seed of the tender camomile. The camomile seed fell on barren ground where there were many stones, little water and a strong wind, but the violet seed fell on the rich soil of a field where the spring breezes blew, where the mists trailed, a fresh stream ran and the birds sang. The camomile seed withered and turned to dust while the violet seed produced young shoots and blossomed so that in less than a hundred years the whole field was a carpet of violets.

There was once a wise man who sought to open the hearts of his people by teaching them this parable of the seeds. But the people's hearts were barren ground, strewn with many stones, where the winds blew strong and there was too little water so that his wise words never took root. They bore no blossoms, neither did they bear any fruit. The country became a wasteland.

* * *

The wayside plum

One day a young girl was given a plum to eat at a friend's house. Finding the taste of it sweet she decided to take the plum stone home with her to plant by the hedge. Her father owned a small tea shop which was frequented by travellers on the road.

The years passed and the house crumbled into decay. The place where it once had stood became a field of tall grass, and only the old plum tree continued to prosper, bearing blossom and fruit year after year. Travellers on the road ate the fruit to quench their thirst, but none of them knew of the young girl who had planted the tree for them so many years before.

10
Phantoms

Maboroshi (Phantoms), although published as early as May 1898 in vol. 22 no. 369 of the *Kokumin no Tomo*, has distinct overtones of works which were to come. It is divided into two parts sub-titled 'despair' and 'the man' (literally just 'he') and apparently the only connection between the parts is the idea of 'phantoms' from which the story is named. The girl comes into Bunzō's life only to vanish like a phantom, and the mysterious Mr X (named Tanaka for convenience in the translation) also vanishes like a phantom into the night.

It may be that this connection of ideas is the whole story, but there is just a suspicion that the disillusioned Bunzō at the end of the first part becomes the cynical, drunken failure of the second. Certainly the idea that the man of the second part of the story sowed the seeds of his own ruin is an early departure from the genuinely tragic figure of Old Gen. This is one of the few stories which contain no readily identifiable autobiographical element.

Faithful to his promise, Bunzō did not call on her that evening, but waited until noon the next day. Being a friend of the family, he was able to go through to the drawing room unannounced, but there he found only Ayako and Haruko. He patted their heads and then asked if their sister were any better and if he might see her. It was Ayako who replied:

'I'm afraid she's gone out with mother.'

'Gone out?' Bunzō felt vaguely uneasy. 'But surely she ought to be in about now to give you your music lessons?'

'Oh no. She doesn't teach us any more.'

'Not any more,' echoed Haruko.

'Is your father in then?'

'No, he's out as well. Sister's very ill, you know. She was crying all last night.'

'Crying?'

'Yes, O-mine told us so, and her eyes were all red and swollen.'

Bunzō brooded for a while, trembling as if taken with a chill. Then he left abruptly and made his way home, heedless of all that was going on around him. He felt as if he were standing on a giddy precipice looking down into a deep chasm and everything began to spin before his eyes. A multitude of thoughts revolved round and round in his mind as on a wheel. He felt as if he were wandering in a trackless wood and hearing the sudden echo of a distant gunshot. His throat was dry and he wanted to cry, but the tears would not come. A bitter smile hovered on his cheeks and a disembodied cry sprang from his lips. Over and over again he cried out:

'I'll never see Umeko again. But why, why? What has happened to make her change so suddenly? Why won't she see me? Why won't she confide in me if something is troubling her?'

At last he reached his house.

* * *

'Excuse me, sir.'

Bunzō whirled round in surprise to see a messenger boy with a letter in his hand. It was from Umeko. He knew that without even breaking the seal and he shrank back, his head hung low, almost as if he were expecting to be attacked. Finally he summoned the courage to open the letter which was written on a half-sheet and read:

'Forgive me if you can. Our love has become as meaningless as air bubbles on the surface of water. I must go to Tokyo. Sadness and misery tear my heart, but it is the only thing I can do and I am resigned to my fate. I won't offer you any excuses. It's just that what I feared before might happen has become a reality. Forgive me and try to forget me. Think kindly on one who was never any good for you, if you can, but never try to see me again. Umeko.'

Bunzō fell gently backwards as if pushed by some invisible force and the letter slipped from between his fingers. He picked it up and read it once more. 'She's gone to Tokyo,' he whispered faintly and dropped the letter again. As he raised his hands to adjust his collar he began to feel a leaden despair settling on his heart. He thought:

'A man who has received a mortal wound must feel just this same calm as I feel now. Like a phantom she came to me, and like a phantom she has gone. It's quite natural. I was expecting it.' But in this Bunzō was deceiving himself for it was the last thing he had expected to happen. 'Of course, she never really loved me. Oh yes, I understand her perfectly. How right she was to say that she was no good for me!' He smiled bitterly. 'She just never realised my true worth, but what I do not understand is how she could discard a simple student like me just because of one incident. Oh yes, I understand her!' He laughed ironically.

But when Bunzō thought of Umeko's kind words, her smile, her loving eyes, and when he remembered those same eyes brimming with love and happiness whenever she looked at him, an unbearable grief stabbed his heart. In his agony he beat his head violently against the wall. Burying his face in the bedclothes, he sobbed himself to sleep.

* * *

It was the end of autumn and I was hurrying back to my home in Akasaka late one night after visiting a friend in Surugadai. There was a thick fog and particles of vapour shone in beautiful halos round the gas and electric street lamps. Pedestrians and rickshaws emerged like phantoms from the fog and like phantoms disappeared as quickly as they came. I have always enjoyed walking along the main streets on nights such as this when I can see people walking along enshrouded in mist, wrapped up in their thoughts, both merry and sad. Like them I walked along in my own particular reverie. When I reached the bottom of Kudansaka, I heard a voice in the fog right in front of me:

'Drunk am I?! Nonsense! It takes more than a few cups of *sake* to get me drunk.' The owner of the voice staggered past me.

'I don't carry this sword for nothing, you know. Any more cheek and I'll have your head off! Ha, ha, ha!' He appeared to be talking to himself. Looking over my shoulder in surprise I caught a glimpse of him in the hazy, slanting beam of the fog-enshrouded street light, just like a phantom. But almost immediately the fog swallowed him up, leaving me with a thought that flashed through my mind. Could this be Mr ...?

'Ridiculous,' I muttered, dismissing the thought from my mind. 'And yet Tokyo is a bottomless pit in which all manner of men collect, so it's not impossible that he could have come here.'

By this time I had reached the top of Kudunsaka where I commanded a good view of downtown Tokyo. The night was dark and the fog was thick so that it seemed just like a fathomless pool with just the occasional lamp flickering mysteriously like burning phosphorus.

Who was this man I have just referred to? Well, I do not want to reveal his real name, so let's just call him Mr Tanaka. This Mr Tanaka was something of an enigma, a figure of tragedy. There is a saying that the times produce the man and the man makes the times and Mr Tanaka had done everything he could to help create this present age in which we live. However, the tragedy was that in the final analysis he was untouched by the spirit of the times he had helped to create and while breathing the very air of the age, he came to delight in abusing the present, praising the days gone by, belitting the heroes of his own time. I had first met him some seven years before at a private school in a village in my home province where he had gathered about him four or five young people to whom he was teaching the Chinese classics. To see him at that time gave me great pain. It would not be enough to say that he embodied the spirit of the past, nor that he was a fossilised remnant of the feudal age. He was like a mountain stream which, instead of pouring into other streams and flowing out into the ocean, meanders away to form a stagnant and putrefying swamp. In hot weather the mud of such a stream boils and in cold weather the water freezes until eventually it dries up and disappears. When I sat opposite him, looking into his eyes and listening to his words, it seemed that even this analogy does not suffice and that the secret of some sad and bitter fate lay hidden within him.

His eyes glowed with a mysterious blend of pride, envy and injustice. Self control and desperation warred in the smile which played about his lips and he laughed like a man who had long since ceased to hope. To hear that laugh brought tears to my eyes. This is how he used to talk:

'The National Diet? Don't talk to me about that! Just a collection of peasants. What can people like that achieve? Come to that, what about the Tokyo Council. The people of Tokyo are dirt and you can tell Shunsuke from me not to think so much of himself.'

This sort of talk was all he seemed to live for. Doubting my own intuition and wanting to confirm it, I later asked a friend of mine why on earth Mr Tanaka had ever come to Tokyo if he felt like that about it. My friend just shook his head.

One day about two weeks later found me lying in my garden drowsily watching the autumn sun climb steadily over the pine trees until at last it disappeared from my view. I had been talking business with a client of mine for about three hours and after he left I felt completely exhausted. Well anyway, I was lying there when suddenly there was a voice from the doorway:

'Hello, anyone home?'

'Drat!' I thought, 'it's him.' And sure enough, it turned out to be my Mr Tanaka

'How are things with you?' he asked by way of greeting. I was about to make some polite reply when he forestalled me:

'Don't bother. I do so hate formality.' He stank of drink. 'Here's a present for you. I haven't anything else. Here, take it.'

He tossed me a dagger. I was completely taken aback by his abrupt manner which was totally out of character as far as I knew him, and it did not take long for me to realise that this was not the man I had known those seven years before. He picked up the knife and thrust it into his waistband.

'This is how you hold it. Here, like this. When you grapple with an enemy, you push him to the floor with the left hand and take the knife in your right, like this.' He assumed a suitably fierce expression. 'And then you stab him, like this.'

He plunged the dagger into an imaginary body and laughed long and loud. He was obviously in an excitable mood.

I tried to talk about one thing and another, but he was so wrapped up in some personal preoccupation that he was quite incapable of holding a coherent conversation. He was very fidgety and unsettled, refusing to look me in the face. Occasionally he laughed out loud, but it was not the same laugh as I had know all those years before.

'No thanks,' he said when the *sake* I had ordered arrived, 'I've had too much to drink already.' But he was fooling no one but himself. I offered him the cup.

'Go on. Have one at least.'

'Thanks, I will.' He was unable to conceal his joy. When he returned the cup for me to drink, I declined and merely refilled it for him. I watched intently as he emptied it with obvious relish. He looked at me, but when he saw that I had noticed the look of boorish pleasure on his face, he averted his eyes. I could see that he was trying, but he was totally unable to look me in the face and in the end I myself could no longer bear to look at him.

'You're getting old,' I said before I could check myself, and although I had meant the words sympathetically, somehow they did not come out that way.

'What me? I'm as healthy as you any day. This is excellent *sake*.'

'Better than the rubbish you're used to, I'll be bound! Ha, ha, ha!'

The words just slipped out and even as I said them I knew that they were cruel. Now I regret what I said, but I cannot deny that at the time I could feel no sympathy for the changes time had wrought in him, and that subconsciously I held him in contempt. He was laughing too. Once those eyes of his had glowed with injustice, envy and pride, but now the pride was half shattered, the injustice drowned in *sake*. Only the envy, fused with boorishness, remained strangely and indistinctly apparent in his bloodshot eyes and the shadows of ruin hovered dark over his features.

I wanted to ask why and when he had come to Tokyo; how was he living and so on, but there was no need to, for it seemed to me that I understood his secret even better than he did himself. As he drank, he talked in the same grand manner of old, but this was merely a kind of compensation for the miserable failure he in reality was. Once or twice he said in a whisper: 'It's all up with me. I'm a failure.' And it was in these words that the real truth lay, even though he was not quite aware of what he was saying. It was only then that I began to feel a semblance of pity for what he was going through. No doubt he was scared of what the future held in store for him and is there any fear as tragic as that? To me it was unbearable that he should be tormented by the regrets which haunted him like an old wound. Some of his friends were now in the Tokyo Council; some were worshipped almost as gods, glorified by their contemporaries. And here he was, untouched by the spirit of the age in which he lived, abusing the present and fallen so low.

I offered him the *sake* cup.

'Let's drink to our friendship. Long may it continue!' He took the cup without a word and gulped down the *sake*. He hung his head mournfully. Then, without any warning, he put down the cup and got to his feet.

'I'm drunk. I'd better go. I'll be seeing you.'

Alarmed, I tried to stop him, but it was no good.

'Please come again,' I said, but whether or not he heard me I do not know, for he had vanished into the dark of the night. Like a phantom …

11

Musashino

Ask any Japanese to name his favourite Doppo short story and the chances are that he will say *Musashino*, which is probably more of a commentary on the Japanese education system than it is on the quality of the story itself. Doppo wrote *Musashino* either in late 1897 or early 1898 and it was published in *Kokumin no Tomo* vol. 22 no. 365 in February 1898 under the title *Ima no Musashino* (Musashino As It Is Today).

After his tragic affair with Sasaki Nobuko, Doppo fled with his brother Shūji to the village of Shibuya on the plain of Musashino, probably in order to recapture memories of the holiday he and Nobuko spent there in August 1895. He stayed at Shibuya throughout the autumn and winter of 1896 and the spring of 1897, spending his days wandering around the woods and fields of the plain which occupies a very special place in Japanese literary and military history.

The quotations from Doppo's diary, the *Azamuzakaru no ki*, and Futabatei Shimei's translation of Turgenev's story, the *Rendez-vous*, give a rather disjointed effect to a narrative which is very much in the tradition of Japanese *zuihitsu* (random jottings) writing, and contains no fictional element at all. The overall effect of *Musashino* is enhanced by some fine descriptive writing, but it is probable that its uniquely Japanese flavour prevents it from being truly appreciated by the Westerner.

'The only traces of the Musashino region remaining today are to be found in the Iruma district.' I once read this statement on an early nineteenth-century map, which went on to describe Iruma as follows: 'On the 11th day of the 5th month of 1333, the Taira and Minamoto fought a day-long battle involving many skirmishes at Kotesashihara near the Kume river. At dusk, the Taira retreated about six miles and took up a defensive position on the banks of the river. Next dawn the Minamoto advanced and succcessfully stormed the Taira defences.' Thinking that this battle site might be one of the surviving relics of Musashino referred to on the map, I thought of going to see for myself, but at the time I did not go, as I was worried about what I might find. The desire to see what remains of the Musashino we visualise through pictures and poems is not exclusive to me by any means and I think it was about a year ago that I conceived the strong wish to see in detail, for my own satisfaction, how much of that ancient Musashino survives today. As the days passed, the wish grew ever stronger. Is it possible to satisfy such a desire? I do not say it is impossible, but I do not believe it is easy. I confess at any rate that I found considerable charm in modern Musashino and I suspect that there are many who would feel about it as I do.

To begin with, I should like to fulfil a small part of my desire by recording my feelings during the autumn and winter I spent there. I found the first part of my answer in the fact that Musashino is every bit as beautiful as it must have been in ancient times. Doubtless it is not really possible to visualise its former beauty, but the beauty of modern Musashino moves me to reach an exaggerated conclusion. I have just said that modern Musashino has beauty, but perhaps, all things considered, it would be more appropriate to say that it has charm.

* * *

For lack of any other material I should like to call on the notes I made in my diary covering the period from autumn 1896 to spring 1897, during which I lived in a tiny, ramshackle cottage in the village of Shibuya. It was during the winter that my reasons for making the trip, stated above, were fulfilled, but to present a complete picture, let me begin with the autumn.

7 SEPTEMBER   'Yesterday and today a strong southerly wind blew up clouds, sweeping them away again as quickly as they came. It rained intermittently and when the sun filtered through the clouds, for a time there was a glittering sheen over the trees of the woods and forests.'

This describes a typical autumn day in modern Musashino. The trees are as green as they are in summer, but the skies are completely different, for the driving south wind brings low cloud and frequent rain. In the clear intervals, the sunlight beats down on the forests sending up clouds of vapour and making the trees sparkle. I often thought how beautiful it would look if one could get a bird's eye view of the whole of Musashino on such a day. Two days later, on September 9, I wrote in my diary as follows:

'The wind was strong and the voices of autumn filled the fields. The cloud formations were constantly changing.

The weather at this period continued broken as I have described and the skies and fields were a picture of incessant change. The sun when it was out was like summer, but the colour of the clouds and the sound of the winds belonged to autumn. It was profoundly charming. This describes the beginning of autumn in modern Musashino and until the end of winter I continued to make a record in my diary of the changes in the scene. The following entries, I think, may indicate essentials of all the various transformations.

19 SEPTEMBER   'Morning; the sky was cloudy and the wind died away. There was a cold mist and a chilly dew.

Everywhere I could hear the chirruping of insects and it was almost as if the very heart of heaven and earth had woken from a dream.'

21 SEPTEMBER   'The autumn sky was cloudless and the leaves on the trees shone like fire.'

19 OCTOBER   'The moon was bright, casting black shadows over the forests.'

25 OCTOBER   'In the morning there was a heavy mist which cleared during the afternoon. At night the moon shone through gaps in the clouds. In the morning before the mist had cleared, I went out for a walk in the fields and I visited a part of the forest.'

26 OCTOBER   'In the afternoon I went again to the woods. I sat in the heart of the trees, looking around me, straining my ears, and silently contemplating.'

4 NOVEMBER   'The sky was high and the air was clear. In the evening I went for a solitary walk in the fields where the wind was blowing. The mountain chain surrounding the province, close to Mt. Fuji, was black against the sky and the stars were little pinpoints of light. At last twilight came and the black shadows of the trees receded into the night.'

18 NOVEMBER   'I went for a moonlit stroll. Palls of blue smoke crept over the earth and the moonlight was shattered against the trees.'

19 NOVEMBER   'The sky was clear, the wind pure and the dew chill. As far as the eye could see, the yellow autumn leaves mingled with the rich greenery of the trees. Birds flew from branch to branch. There was no sign of any other human as I walked along in silent thought, letting my feet take me wherever they would through the countryside.'

22 NOVEMBER   'Late at night the wind moaned through the trees rustling the leaves with a sound like rain, though the rain had actually stopped some time before.'

23 NOVEMBER   'Almost all the leaves have been brought down by last night's storm. The rice harvest is almost completely gathered in. The whole scene begins to take on the look of the withering decay of winter.'

24 NOVEMBER   'Not all the leaves have fallen yet. When I look at the distant mountains, my heart is filled with yearning and longs to vanish into them.'

26 NOVEMBER   'Ten o'clock. Outside the wind and rain moan forlornly, answered by the steady dripping of water. It was misty all day, as if the fields and woods were

wrapped in an eternal dream. In the afternoon I took my dog for a walk. I went into the woods and sat in silence while he slept. There was a stream wending its way through the trees, carrying with it the fallen leaves. Occasionally the autumn rains pattered dismally on the treetops and branches and it was so peaceful when the drops fell through onto the fallen leaves.'

27 NOVEMBER 'It is clear today and there is no sign of last night's storm. The sun rose gloriously in the sky and when I stood on the hill at the back of my cottage, I could see the pure whiteness of Fuji towering above its neighbouring peaks. It was truly a morning appropriate to the dawning of winter. The irrigation ditches had overflowed into the fields and the inverted images of the trees reflected from the water.'

2 DECEMBER 'This morning the frost glittered beautifully under the morning sun, like snow. After a while it clouded over slightly and it was cold despite the sun.'

22 DECEMBER 'The first snows of winter fell today.'

13 JANUARY 'Late at night the wind died away and the woods were
1897 silent. There were frequent snow showers and once when I went out with a lamp, the falling snow danced and glittered under its light. Ah! The silence of Musashino. Straining my ears, I could hear the distant sound of the wind in the trees — the voice of the wind perhaps!'

14 JANUARY 'A very heavy snowfall this morning and the grapevine trellis collapsed. Late at night I could hear the wind in the treetops. Ah! The cold wintry blast sweeping from wood to wood in the land of Musashino! I could hear the sound of thawing snow round the eaves.'

20 JANUARY 'A beautiful morning. Not a cloud in the sky. The ice needles formed by the frost glittered like silver on the ground. Little birds wheeled in the treetops and the tips of the branches were needle-sharp to touch.'

8 FEBRUARY 'The plum trees are in bloom and at last we are getting some really beautiful moons.'

13 MARCH 'Midnight. The moon waned and a wind sprang up, stirring the frost and making the woods sing.'

21 MARCH 'Eleven o'clock at night. I listened to the wind now distant and now close. Spring was on the attack and winter was flying before it.'

* * *

According to long tradition, Musashino in ancient times was incomparably beautiful on account of the endless vistas of miscanthus reeds all over the plain, but nowadays it is covered with woods. In fact you might even say that these woods form the distinctive feature of modern Musashino, being composed mostly of varieties of deciduous oak which lose all their leaves in winter. In spring the fresh greenery almost gushes from the trees. This annual transformation from bare trees to fresh greenery can be seen all over the plain which extends about thirty miles to the east of the Chichibu ridge.

Throughout the year, in mist, in rain, in moonlight, in wind, in fog, in the early winter snows, in the shade of the trees and in the colours of autumn, Musashino offers an ever-changing variety of scenes. Its wonder is such that it is not understandable to the people of western and north-eastern Japan, for it seems that in the beginning the Japanese did not comprehend the beauty of the deciduous oak. When a Japanese writer wrote of woods, he was thinking principally of pines so that the very idea of listening to the early autumn rains in an oak forest does not figure at all in our literature, not even in poetry. I myself come from western Japan and ten years have passed since I first went up to Tokyo as a student. It is only recently that I have come to understand the beauty of deciduous woods, something I first learned in reading this following passage from a short story:

'One day about the middle of September, I went into a birch wood. There had been a steady drizzle since morning, but in the clear intervals a warm sun shone. The sky was truly capricious. One moment fleecy white clouds were trailing across the sky, covering it, and the next, without any warning, there would be a rift in the clouds revealing patches of blue sky which shone forth like the eyes of a man shining with wisdom.

'I just sat there, looking and listening. The leaves of the trees above my head were engaged in faint combat, and just by listening to the sound they made, I could tell the season. It was not the cheerful, laughing sound of early spring; it was not the gentle wafting sound of summer; nor was it the long conversational sound or the nervous chatter of late autumn. No, it was a melancholy whispering which sometimes you could catch and sometimes not. It was almost as if the gentle breeze was stealing its way into the treetops. The appearance of the sodden wood under alternating sun and cloud was constantly changing.

'Sometimes it was as if everything in the wood smiled for a moment, with red tinges everywhere and the scarcely living birches would suddenly seem like white silk, taking on a gentle lustre. The tiny leaves scattered on the ground would shine like gold, taking fire under the rays of the sun. The graceful stems of the fern and bracken would take on the colour of over-ripe grapes, tangling and entwining with each other infinitely, so that there was suddenly a clear space before my eyes.

'Sometimes it would become gloomy equally suddenly and in a single instant everything would lose its colour. The drizzle would come pattering down weirdly as in a whisper, leaving the clusters of birch trees in a white mist such as one sometimes sees when the sun shines on snow as it falls from the skies. Although the lustre of the leaves of the birch trees would fade, they would still be greener than those of the young oaks which were all coloured red and gold. And sometimes the sun managed to seep through the rain onto the dense branches now soaking wet, making them glitter.

This passage is taken from Futabatei Shimei's translation of the short story *The Rendez-vous* by Ivan Turgenev. It was the power of his description which first led me to an appreciation of the beauty of deciduous woods. Of course he is describing a Russian scene and talks of birch trees rather than the oaks of Musashino, but plains covered with deciduous trees are all alike. It occurred to me that if the trees of the Musashino plain were pines instead of oaks, it would be very uniform and singularly lacking in such brilliant transformations. It would not be something to prize in the same way. Being oaks, the leaves take on the colours of autumn and in due course fall from the trees. The early autumn rains whisper and the winter winds scream and howl so that when gusts strike the hilltops, thousands of leaves flutter into the sky like distant flocks of tiny birds. When all the leaves have fallen, you are left with mile upon mile of bare trees, and with the blue winter sky hanging high over all, there is an air of tranquillity pervading the plain. The air is perfectly still so that even distant sounds can clearly be heard. My diary entry for December 26 reads:

'I sat in the wood and looked and listened and contemplated.'
Just like the man in Turgenev's story.

How did the sounds of autumn through winter match up to my expectations of modern Musashino? In the autumn there were sounds from within the woods, and in winter from beyond them. The sound of birds' wings and their twittering voices. The soughing of the wind. There were singing, howling, screaming voices. The chirrupings of insects in chorus beneath clumps of grass in the woods. The echoes of carts as they wound their way between the trees, down the slopes and along the paths through the fields. Horses' hooves scuffing through the fallen leaves — perhaps a cavalry patrol out on manoeuvres or a foreigner and his wife out for a long ride. The harsh voices of the villagers as they make their way along — gone almost before you realise they are there. The footsteps of a woman hurrying along a lonely path. A gun fired in the distance or a sudden shot from a nearby wood. Once I visited a wood with my dog and I was sitting on a tree stump reading a book when suddenly I heard the sound of something falling. The dog who had been lying at my feet pricked up his ears and gazed in the direction of the noise. That's all there is to tell about that incident. Perhaps a chestnut had fallen, for there are many chestnut trees in Musashino.

Nothing is so quieting as the sound of the early autumn rains. Even in Japan, the theme of the autumn rains on the mountain hut has found its way into poetry, but how quiet it is when, instead of a hut, you hear the rain falling all over the wide expanse of wood and field. It gives a feeling of generosity, of gentleness and sweetness which is the special feature of the rains in Musashino. I had encountered the same type of rain previously in the dense forests of Hokkaido where the effect is that much greater because of total absence of humanity. By contrast, the Musashino rains are somehow more human and have a kind of whispering charm.

During the period of my stay on Musashino, I visited several woods in the Nakano area at Shibuya, Setagaya and Koganei. Every so often I would grow tired and sit down just to listen to the noises of the woods. These sounds came and then vanished as quickly as they had come, now approaching, now receding. There was the sound of leaves falling on a windless day. When this finished, I always felt the tranquillity of nature and was somehow aware that the breath of eternity was pressing upon me. Late in the Musashino winter nights when the stars were out, I frequently wrote in my diary of the sound you get when the winter winds blow chill across the woods as if they were striving even to sweep the stars from the sky. The noise of the wind summons a man's thoughts into the beyond and as I listened to that forlorn sound, now near, now far, I sometimes thought of life in ancient Musashino and of Kumagai Naoyoshi's poem:*
> 'In the night I listen to the sound of the leaves of the trees, and hear the wind come softly creeping.'

I knew what it was like to live in a mountain hut, but you need to have lived in a village through a Musashino winter to really appreciate this poem.

It is from the end of spring to early summer that one most feels the warming beauty of the sun's rays when sitting in the woods, but I shall not write about that here, for I want to treat of the season when the leaves are tinged with autumn colours. When you walk in the woods just as the leaves are turning colour, the clear sky peeps through gaps between the branches and the rays of the sun splinter on the leaves as they sway in the breeze. It is indescribably beautiful when a broad plain

---

* Kumagai Naoyoshi (1782-1862): Edo period *waka* poet.

such as Musashino has its trees bathed in tongues of flame as the sun sinks in the West. If you climb high enough you can command an overall view of the plain, but even if you cannot get that high, there is no need to worry for as the scenery of a plain is the same everywhere you only need to see a small part to be able to imagine the whole. How splendid it is when, moved by this vision, you walk as far as you can amidst the autumn leaves under the setting sun until at last there are no more trees and you come out into the fields.

* * *

On 25 December I wrote in my diary:
    'I walked over the fields and visited the woods.'
And on 4 November I wrote:
    'I stood alone in the fields at dusk with the winds blowing about me.'
  Let me quote from Turgenev again:
    'I stood still and picked a posy. Then I left the woods and went out into the fields where the sun was low in the blue sky. Its light was pale and cold, and everything was a uniform pale green in colour. There was still half an hour to sunset, but already the heavens were stained a faint red by the evening glow. Tiny leaves were being swept by the strong wind across the yellow stubble in the fields, along the path through the woods and past me in flurries. The whole wood, standing like a wall against the fields, was rustling feverishly and the leaves were not shining, but flickering like a scattering of tiny jewels. I did not mind the withered grass, the tares and the straw; somehow they were not disagreeable. The spiders' webs were waving and billowing in the wind.
    'I stopped, suddenly depressed. All the images that assailed my eyes were there all right, but they roused no interest or curiosity in me any more and it seemed that I was aware only of the coldness of impending winter. A timid crow flapped its wings heavily and cut through the wind with its head held high. Suddenly it turned its head and glared at me before flying quickly up into the sky, and crowing as if it would tear its voice, it flew for the shelter of the woods. A flock of doves flew vigorously from a granary, but suddenly danced upwards, almost as if forming themselves into a pillar, and scattered rapidly over the fields. Ah, autumn! Someone seems to pass over by the bare mountain and the sound of an empty cart echoes across the sky.'
This passage describes the scene in the fields of Russia, but what Turgenev says is equally applicable to Japanese fields from autumn through winter. There are of course no bare mountains in Musashino,

but the countryside undulates like the surge of the ocean. At first glance, Musashino looks like a level plain, but it is set high and here and there are shallow depressions and valleys. At the bottom of these valleys you usually find paddy fields whereas the higher spots which are normally divided between field and wood are given over to dry fields. The plain is so constructed that you might get mile upon mile of woods or fields or perhaps just a little of each so that a wood is surrounded by fields and sometimes the fields are surrounded on three sides by woods. The farmers have their dwellings scattered about over the plain and divide the fields among them. Fields and woods are so confusedly scattered that sometimes you enter a wood and come straight out into fields again. This is a special feature of Musashino. Here there is nature and life with a flavour all its own, completely different from the great plains and forests of Hokkaido.

When the rice ripens, the paddy fields in the valleys turn yellow. After the rice has been harvested and the shadows of the trees reflect in the fields, it is the turn of the radishes. When the last radish has been plucked from the ground, they are washed in streams or small pools of water. Then at last the fields turn green with the new shoots of wheat. Sometimes the fields where wheat is growing are left untouched at one end and you can see miscanthus and wild camomile waving in the breeze. The miscanthus plain stretches up and away to the horizon. If you climb a hill, you can see the black peaks of Chichibu, which form the boundaries of the province, stretching away through gaps in the trees and it seems as if these mountains run along the horizon and then dip below it. Shall I go down to the fields again? Or shall I lie down on the miscanthus, make a wind barrier for myself from dead grass, expose my face to the warm rays of the sun in the southern sky, and watch the woods as the leaves rustle and glitter in the wind? Or should I go my way among the trees again? This is a problem which has often confronted me. But it is no real problem to me now, for I know all the paths which criss-cross Musashino and whichever I choose I know I shall not be disappointed.

★ ★ ★

A friend of mine once wrote me the following letter:
> 'The other day I was walking over a miscanthus plain deep in thought. It occurred to me that so many people must have walked over paths through fields in the dim and distant past, thinking to themselves, according to the season, how beautiful was the morning dew or marvelling at the colours of the evening snow. Perhaps even enemies may have become the best of friends in such beauty and walked their way home hand in hand.'

If you walk through ordinary fields, you may have such beautiful notions, but the paths of Musashino inspire a very different feeling. If you go to meet someone by the paths of Musashino, you may miss him and meet instead someone you wished to avoid. This is because all the paths twist and turn through the woods, across the fields and there are so many forks that it is easy to go round in circles. The paths vanish constantly into woods, emerge into fields and vanish again, so that you can never keep track of anyone as he walks along. But for all that, the paths of Musashino are much more rewarding than any others, and people should not distress themselves at getting lost, for wherever you go, there is something worthwhile to see, hear and feel.

The beauty of Musashino can first be appreciated simply by walking the length and breadth of the plain. It does not matter when you go — whether spring, summer, autumn, winter, morning or evening, in the night under the moon, in snow, wind, frost, fog or rain. Just by walking you come across a multitude of things to delight you everywhere you go, and this, to me, is Musashino's most special feature. Where else in Japan is there such a place, leaving aside the obvious choice of Hokkaido? Is there anywhere else where you meet such a satisfactory mingling of wood and field, and where life and nature maintain so close a harmony?

If you are walking along a path and come to a fork, there is no need to trouble yourself. Just go wherever your stick points the way. The path you choose may lead you into a small wood and if there it divides further, choose the smaller track for it may lead you to some delightful spot, such as the site of an old grave. You may find four or five such graves in a line, covered with moss, and with a small open space before them and flowers blooming at the side. And to complete your happiness, perhaps some small birds singing in the treetops. Now go back and take the other fork. Immediately the trees thin out and a broad field stretches before you. You walk down a gentle slope and everywhere there is miscanthus, its tips glittering under the sun.

Beyond the miscanthus, the fields, and beyond them a clump of low trees. In the distance you will see, perhaps, a small grove of cedars. Fleecy clouds gathered on the horizon and perhaps a chain of mountains, deceptively taking on the colour of clouds themselves. On a warm October day, the sun shines balmily and a pleasant breeze sighs through the trees. When you go down towards the miscanthus plain, you come out to the bottom of a small valley and the great vista which stretched before your eyes just a moment before is completely hidden. Suddenly amidst the miscanthus and woods, you discover a long, narrow pond where you would least expect it. The water is pure and clear, vividly reflecting the white clouds in the heavens.

By the pond there are just a few withered reeds, perhaps. As you walk along the path, presently it forks with a wood to your right, and to your left a slope, which, of course, you climb, because wherever you walk on

Musashino you are searching for a spot high enough to provide a panoramic view. This is not easily attained, for there are hardly any places where you can look down and see over the whole plain. You must resign yourself to that disappointment from the very beginning.

If you need to find some particular path for a special reason, ask the way of a labourer working in the fields. If he be a man of forty or more, you must raise your voice to attract his attention whereupon he will give you your directions in equally loud tones. If it should be a young girl, however, you must go right up to her and speak softly. Then again, if it be a youth, you should doff your hat and ask politely for he will then tell you freely what you need to know.

On no account, should you speak angrily for that is the bad habit adopted by youths who come from Tokyo. When you go on your way, you will almost certainly find that the path forks again, but always follow the way you have been directed, no matter how insignificant or odd it looks, and you will soon reach the garden of some farmer. It will always come when you least expect it, but you should try not to be surprised. Just ask at the house and go on your way. Shortly you will smile to yourself in recognition of the familiar path you first wanted to find and you will be grateful to the man who told you the way.

Sometimes, as you walk along a straight path, you will come to places where woods in beautiful autumn colours extend unbroken on both sides for half a mile or more. What a pleasure it is to walk along such a path in calm solitude with the tops of the trees gleaming brightly in the evening sun. All will be quiet save for the sound of the occasional falling leaf, quiet and delightfully melancholy. No one for miles around. If you go when all the trees are finally bare, the path will be buried with leaves and with every step you take, there will be a pleasant rustling sound. You will be able to see right into the hearts of the woods where the treetops point like slender needles into the blue sky. Still there will be no one around and it will be ever more melancholy. There will be just the occasional surprise of a dove flying from a tree with a flurry of wings.

It would be nothing short of folly to trace your way home by the same path along which you came for it is impossible to get lost on modern Musashino and there is much to be gained from heading in your homeward direction by a totally new path. The sun on its downward track over the shoulder of Mt. Fuji has not yet completely disappeared and the clouds gathered round the mountain's slopes are dyed gold, changing their shapes even as you watch. The surrounding peaks, covered in snow like a silver chain, run far away into the distant North, finally disappearing into banks of dark clouds.

When the sun has set, a strong wind blows up and the trees moan. Then Musashino seems to come to life and you should hurry on your way as quickly as possible because the cold pierces through you. Looking back over your shoulder, you will see the new moon sending forth its cold light over the bare treetops. It seems that, any minute, the wind will sweep the moon down from the sky until at last you suddenly come out into the fields once more.

* * *

One summer about three years ago, I and a friend of mine left our temporary dwelling in the city and boarded a train which took us as far as Sakai. There we alighted from the train and walked about half a mile to the North until we came to a small bridge known as Sakura-bashi. Just across the bridge, we stopped at a teahouse. The old woman asked us why we had come that way whereupon my friend and I looked at each other and laughed.

'We've come for a stroll. Just for pleasure,' we said. Then it was her turn to laugh, for she seemed to regard us as fools.

'Don't you know that the cherry blooms in the spring?' she said. Of course it was quite useless for us to attempt to explain to her the pleasures of just strolling in the outlying districts of Tokyo in the summer as well as in the spring. Tokyo people just do not understand such a mentality. So we just wiped the sweat from our brows and ate the melon the old woman prepared for us. Then we washed our faces in the waters of a small stream which flowed past the teahouse and left. This stream probably was part of the Koganei system and its waters were very clear as it threaded its delightful way amidst the green vegetation on its banks. From time to time tiny, chirruping birds flew up, flapping their wings as if waiting for an opportunity to quench their thirsts in the stream. To this, however, the old woman gave no heed, seeming to regard the stream as there morning and night for her convenience to wash her pots and pans in.

After leaving the teahouse, we began to walk leisurely upstream. Ah, the pleasure of that day! Of course Koganei *is* famous for its cherry blossoms and, to the casual observer, it seems foolish to walk nonchalantly along the banks of its streams in the height of summer, but to take that view implies a total lack of knowledge of the rays of the summer sun on Musasino. The atmosphere was sultry that day and there were layer upon layer of clouds in the sky with here and there a patch of blue. Where the clouds met the blue sky there were bands of translucent, pure white light like the colour of silver or snow. There is nothing very summery about that in itself, but there was also a kind of muddy mist intermingled with the clouds, making the sky seem somehow uneven and hazy. There was a criss-crossing of shadows released by rays of light piercing through the clouds and the whole sky seemed to be atremble with a spirit of unrestrained motion. The trees in the woods seemed to melt in the light and heat and became drowsy and limp, almost as if drunk. The trees were set out in straight lines so that it was possible to see the wide fields through them, but a shimmering heat haze hung over them, making it impossible to look for very long. As we walked along, we panted and wiped the sweat from our faces, pausing at times to look up at the sky, or into the woods or to stare at the point where trees met sky. Suffering? Not on your life! We were brimming with health and vitality.

We walked about six miles without seeing anyone apart from the occasional dog which came unexpectedly rushing from some farmer's garden or wayside thicket. These dogs would look at us in wonder, yawn, and then disappear again. There was also the noise of the occasional rooster, proclaiming the time of day with a great flapping of wings. These were kept by their owners on the walls of rice granaries, in cedar woods or thickets and their calls could be heard loud and clear. We also came across groups of chickens scratching around in the shade of cherry trees. When we gazed far into the distance where the stream ran ahead of us, we could see its waters flowing in a straight line until disappearing into a shadow like a scattering of silver powder. Nearer at hand it glittered under the sun like a silver arrow. My friend and I stood on a bridge judging and making observations on these two different appearances of the waters of the stream as it shimmered and unceasingly transformed itself under the rays of the sun.

Sometimes we could see a shadow on the water in the distance — the shadow of a cloud which reached where we were standing in an instant, stopped for a second and, as quickly as it had come passed beyond us. A moment later the stream glitered brilliantly again and the trees in the woods and the cherry trees on the banks rejoiced in bright greenery again, just the colour of spring grass after rainfall. Under the bridge there was the gentle murmur of the water — not the sound made by water as it dashes against the river banks, nor yet that of shallow water. It was a full, rich sound, a warm human sound! We thought how fortunate the farmers were to walk by the banks of such a stream every day, to say nothing of ourselves as we strolled along with straw hats on our heads and sticks in our hands.

★ ★ ★

The friend with whom I made that trip has now become a magistrate and has moved to the provinces, but I showed him what you have just read and he made the following remarks about Musashino:

    'The plain of Musashino does not belong to what we popularly call the eight provinces of Kanto and I have worked out my own definition of it, using natural boundaries such as mountains and rivers. To begin with, I consider that Tokyo lies at the heart of Musashino, but that we must leave out, because it is impossible to imagine what it must have been like in the days of old when, now, it is filled with busy streets and soaring government offices. A German woman of my acquaintance once described Tokyo as a "new metropolis" and you can see what she means, nothwithstanding what it was like in the days of the Tokugawa Shoguns.

'However, though we exclude Tokyo itself from the definition of Musashino, we must be careful not to exclude the city's suburbs and outlying districts which, in my view, are part of the poetic beauty of the plain. Take for example Shibuya where you lived, Meguro, Waseda where you and I have enjoyed so many walks, Shinjuku, Shirokane — the list is endless. In other words, if you want to savour the real flavour of Musashino, you must not think only of Mt. Fuji and the Chichibu range, but also the central, city area they surround.

'In your piece you speak of the close harmony existing between life and nature and depict several scenes which have delighted you. With all that you say, I wholeheartedly agree. Once I took my brother on a long excursion in the area surrounding the Tama river. During a five ór six mile walk, we became aware of the different delights of so many different types of life we encountered. For the first half mile there were houses all the way; then they gave out only to be replaced by more houses a little further along. In one short walk there were trees, grass, men and animals for us to see — such a variety. Of course, we must include the Tama river itself in our definition. There are six rivers in Japan to which our ancestors gave the name "Tama", but where else is there such a one as this? It connects flat fields and low-lying woodlands with just the same charm as that with which the outlying districts of Tokyo are connected with the city itself. Let us consider the fields on the east of the plain. There are many paddy fields and despite the low horizon, this is unmistakably Musashino, and from Kinshibori to the area round the Kinu river, the paddy fields, trees and thatched cottages provide all the charm one associates with the plain. It is only in this region that Mt. Fuji stands high against the sky almost as if it is gazing down over our town of Zushi. Consider also Mt. Tsukuba. When we see the shadow of this mountain low in the distant horizon, we understand what is meant when it is said that Musashino somehow lives and breathes in its corner of the eight provinces of Kanto.

'However, the boundaries of Musashino extending to the North and South of Tokyo are extremely narrow, almost nonexistent one might say. This is because the railways run straight across it, somehow carrying Tokyo itself across Musashino to the regions beyond.'

* * *

I am in complete agreement with my friend's opinions, particularly with regard to the Tokyo suburbs. It may sound odd to include a city's suburbs in Musashino proper, but this is not really so, because it is no more than mentioning the beach when you describe the sea. I shall postpone further discussion of this, however, as I should like to treat of the waterways which cross Musashino.

Of course there are the Tama and Sumida rivers, but I shall concentrate on the less important streams, of which the Koganei is one. The Koganei system flows into the Tokyo suburbs at Shinjuku, by way of such villages as Yoyogi and Tsunohazu, to form part of the Shiya network and others. There are many other nameless streams which run into it, and to the casual observer it offers very little to marvel at, but its charm as it twists and twines its way through woods and fields, appearing and disappearing, offers something for everyone at all seasons of the year. I was brought up in a mountainous district and the rivers I was used to were clear whatever their size. Therefore when I first saw the streams of Musashino, excluding the Tama river, I was disagreeably impressed by their muddiness, but as time went by and I got used to them I felt that this muddiness was somehow appropriate to the plain as a whole.

I remember one summer evening four or five years ago when that same friend and I went for a stroll in the Tokyo suburbs. At about eight o'clock we crossed a bridge over the upper reaches of the Kanda stream. It was one of those almost indescribable nights when the moon was bright, the wind pure and woods and fields enveloped in white gossamer. On the bridge was a group of four or five villagers, leaning against the railings, talking, laughing and singing. But there was one old man with them who kept interrupting their talk and songs. The moon shone clear, describing the scene in a hazy oval of light which floated before our eyes like a stanza from an idyll. We joined them against the railings to gaze at the moon and watch its reflection in the gently flowing waters of the stream. Every time an insect struck the surface of the water, it set up ripples and for a moment there were wrinkles on the face of the moon. The stream wound its way in among the trees disappearing in a semi-circle. The light of the moon as it shattered on the treetops fell, glittering, onto the dark surface of the water. Vapour enshrouded the stream to a height of four feet or more. During the radish season you can see farm labourers everywhere on the banks of these little streams washing the soil from the radishes.

* * *

Why do such places delight us so? I can answer in a few words. It is because these suburban scenes somehow manage to let people see society in miniature. The reason for this is that one feels behind the facades of the houses are concealed stories to arouse the interest of all men, whether from town or country — small stories, sad stories, funny stories. City and country life mingle there as in a gently whirling vortex. Look there at that one-eyed dog crouching down! As far as his name is known is the extent of that suburb's territory. Look at that restaurant. There are the silhouettes of women, their voices raised, whether in tears or laughter I cannot tell. Outside is the night and an assortment of odours of smoke, earth and other things impossible to distinguish. Then there are two or three large wagons passing by, making a great noise as their wheels pass in and out of the ruts. Look at the two draught horses standing in front of the blacksmith's, their black shadows concealing two or three men having some secret discussion. The red-hot horseshoes are placed on the anvil, and as they are hammered sparks fly into the night sky, assaulting the darkness. Now the men involved in the discussion are laughing, and as the moon rises to the tops of the oak trees behind the houses, the roofs on the opposite side of the street begin to turn white.

Black soot is being emitted from the metal lamps and ten or so people, both villagers and townsmen, rush heedlessly through it. Here and there are piles of vegetables for this is a market place and auction house for such produce. You may think that the people go to bed when it gets dark, but until two in the morning, lights can be seen gleaming through the shop windows. To the back of the barber's shop are the peasants' dwellings where the lowing of cattle can be heard. Next door to the wine shop lives an old man who sells soya beans for soup and early each morning he sets off for the city, proclaiming his wares in a hoarse voice. In the summer when the nights are short and the dawn comes early, by sunrise the wagons are already beginning to pass by. All day long the rumbling wheels never cease. By nine or ten in the morning the cicadas have begun their chirruping from the high trees and it gradually grows hotter and hotter. The horses' hooves send up clouds of dust which are fanned into the empty skies by the wheels of the wagons, and flies flit from house to house, from horse to horse. Then one hears the distant boom of the noon gun and somewhere from the skies over the city one hears the midday siren. This is Musashino.

12

The Self-Made Man

Hibon naru Bonjin (The Self-Made Man) is in many senses the odd-one-out of this anthology for it is a story with an essentially optimistic message — no matter what the world does to you, if you apply yourself and use your human resources in the end you will overcome all obstacles. The literal meaning of *Hibon naru Bonjin* is 'the extraordinary ordinary man' which has been retitled here as 'The Self-Made Man', because the euphony of the Japanese phrase is not well reflected in the English.

The story is of a man named Katsura Shōsaku who despite the odds against him succeeds in life through the aid and application of the principles of Samuel Smiles' *Self-Help*. The *Self-Help* was one of the earliest western books to be translated into Japanese, by Nakamura Masanao in 1878, and it exerted a great influence over an entire generation. *Hibon naru Bonjin* was first published in March 1903 in vol. 6 no. 3 of the *Chūgaku Sekai* magazine. The literal meaning of the characters which make up the name Shōsaku is 'one who does the right(eous) thing', an interesting piece of symbolism.

A group of five or six young men were discussing their various acquaintances. One of them said:

'When I was a boy, I had a friend called Katsura Shōsaku. He's twenty-three now and works for some firm in Yokohama, in the electrical business I believe, but to me there is no man quite like him. It's not that there is anything very extraordinary about him, and yet he is not ordinary. He's not a crank or an eccentric or anything like that, and all things considered I think the most apt description of him would be to say that he is an extraordinary ordinary man.

'The more I get to know him, the more I am forced to admire him. I do not admire him in the same way as I do geniuses such as Hideyoshi or Napoleon, for they are men in a million, while Shōsaku is the type of man that ordinary, everyday society is always capable of producing. Indeed he is the very type ordinary society needs and is fortunate to have. I should like to tell you, though, why I think him "an extraordinary ordinary man".

'One Sunday while I was still attending junior school, four or five of us went up to Komatsuyama to play soldiers. I was Hideyoshi or Yoshitsune,* I don't remember which. Well, being boys, the game got

---

* Minamoto Yoshitsune (1159-89): a Japanese warrior, much celebrated in Japanese literature.

rather foolish and rough until in the end we became so tired and thirsty that we were obliged to run down to Shōsaku's garden which lay at the foot of the hill in order to quench our thirsts at his well. As we were drinking our fill I noticed Shōsaku looking out from a first floor window.

"Aren't you coming out to play?" I shouted.

'He shook his head and I could see that he was looking unusually serious. We did not press him, but hurried back up the hill. When we were thoroughly exhausted and could play no more, the others went off to their respective homes, while I walked back to Shōsaku's house alone. Without making a sound, I went up to the first floor where I found him seated at a table absorbed in a book. I say "table", but it was in reality just a Japanese style desk elevated by means of a box placed underneath it, and his chair was a similarly crude construction. He had carried out this painstaking labour because the school teacher had once said that Japanese style desks were unhealthy. Thereafter he always studied at this home-made table of his. On the table were school text-books and other books in neat piles, while even the stationery was all just so. Despite the fact that this was Sunday and the weather fine, Shōsaku sat with the book before him, oblivious to all else. I went up to him.

'I noticed that the book he was reading was a thick volume bound in western style.

"What are you reading?" I asked.

"A translation of Smiles' *Self Help*." His eyes were those of a man who has not yet awoken from a dream, and his mind seemed to be still in the book.

"Is it interesting?"

"Yes, it's a good book."

"Better than the *Nihon Gaishi*?"

'Shōsaku laughed, and then replied in his usual cheery voice:

"Much better, but it's a different type of work altogether. I borrowed it last night from Mr Umeda, and when I began to read it, it was so good that I just couldn't put it down. I shall most certainly buy myself a copy."

'Subsequently he did buy a copy, but it was so crudely bound that before he had read it even once, the pages were beginning to fall apart, and so he rebound it with thread in the Japanese manner. Once he had sampled the delights of the *Self Help*, he read it over and over again. Like me, he was only thirteen at the time, but he read the book with such devotion that he could almost recite it by heart, and even today he always has it by him. He has become a living incarnation of the principles taught by the book. Once he told me:

"If I had never read the *Self Help*, what would have become of me? What I am today I owe completely to that book."

'Many, many thousands all over the world must have read that book, but I wonder how many in the end could say in the words of Shōsaku, "This book made me what I am".

'As regards natural talent, Shōsaku was no more than average. His results as school put him in the middle of the class, and in fact many of his class-mates excelled him. He was, moreover, a mischievous boy and he and I got into many a scrape. In other words, neither at school nor in the village was he a boy who attracted very much attention. In character, however, he was open-hearted, frank and possessed of an indomitable spirit. At first impression, you might say that his spirit was simply adventurous, but on consideration you realised that it was rather ambitious and enterprising. His father came to ruin through being too enterprising and his brother was lost in seeking adventure. Yet Shōsaku was able to train his spirit by means of the *Self Help* so that he became both steadfast and resourceful.

'His father was no ordinary man. He was a *samurai* warrior who saw distinguished service in the war for the Restoration. He was a largely-built man, with glaring eyes, high nose and imposing countenance. He was every inch a warrior and not a man to be daunted by anything. If he had stuck to soldiering, he might well have become a great general, but, as it happened, he came back from the Restoration wars with only one idea in mind — farming. He wanted to make a fresh start and like many others who succumbed to the fashionable lure of agriculture, he lost all his money.

'The Katsura family mansion had once stood in the town, but with the decline in the family's fortunes, it had been moved and rebuilt beneath Komatsuyama. At the time my father and others said that it would have been far better to have sold the original mansion and built a new house with the money. Just this one instance serves to demonstrate the uncompromising nature of Shōsaku's father. Following this move to the foot of Komatsuyama, he became a farmer in real earnest and I often used to see him working in the fields.

'There is no doubt that at the time Shōsaku began to read the *Self Help*, the family were in real difficulties, but there was still plenty of spirit left in them. One day Shōsaku came to see me and told me triumphantly that they had received a letter from Tanaka Tsurukichi. Apparently his father had greatly admired the activities in the field of land cultivation of Tanaka, who was a man of great consequence in Japan, and had written to him expressing this admiration. Tanaka had sent a letter of thanks almost by return of post and this was something really special. On another occasion, Shōsaku came to me and said that in a few months' time they would be giving a great feast of clams, and when I asked how that could be, he said that his father had just gone in for the cultivation of clams and that soon there would be an abundant harvest to be had. From these incidents you can get a good picture of what type of family it was.

'Shōsaku's elder brother carried on the family tradition of enterprise.

At the age of fifteen, he had left home and gone no one knew where. Some said that he had gone to Hawaii and others to South America, but none knew for sure.

'After graduating from junior school, I entered the Prefectural middle school, and so was away from my native village for a time. Because of the lack of money, however, such a course was not open to Shōsaku who instead got a job in a bank at a salary of four or five yen a month. This left him with a five mile journey to and from work morning and evening which he had to do on foot. When the winter holidays came round, I set out for home in a rickshaw. When it reached a small slope near my village, I got out, and entrusting my baggage to the rickshaw man, I took up a stick and set out on foot. A little way ahead of me there was a young man wearing an old cloak and carrying a worn-out briefcase. He resembled Shōsaku, so I called out to him:

"Hey, is that you, Katsura?" He turned round with a broad smile on his face. It was indeed Shōsaku.

"Home for the winter holidays?" he asked.

"Yes. You still working at the bank?"

"Yes, but it's not very interesting."

"How come?" I asked, with surprise.

"Need you ask? If it were you, you'd be bored stiff in three days. No, banking's not for me."

'We walked along the road in conversation, with only the rickshaw man ahead of us.

"What do you aim to do with your life?" I asked.

"I'm going in for industry," he said with a smile. "I walk along this road day after day thinking what I should do. I can hit on nothing I'd like to do more than be an inventor."

'Watt, Stephenson and Edison. These were Shōsaku's heroes and still the *Self Help* was his Bible. I just nodded without saying anything, and he went on:

"And so, next spring I'm going up to Tokyo."

"Tokyo?" I queried in amazement.

"Yes. I've already got the money for the journey, but I was in a bit of a spot because I had only got enough to live on for about three months. However, I went to my father and he advanced me enough to cover my salary up until next March. So in April I shall be on my way."

'Like all young men, Shōsaku had his dreams, but in his case they did not stop at being mere dreams. He conceived his plans which had never changed from the time of his youth and was now putting them into operation, step by step, until in the end he would achieve his ambition. In this, of course, he was following the teachings of the *Self Help*. It seemed to me that his character resembled that of his grandfather, although I have time here to give only one anecdote connected with that remarkable man. Apparently, he set himself the ten-year task of making a beautiful manuscript copy of the three hundred chapters of the novel

Taikōki,* which in the end he completed. I saw the finished manuscript
once and even now I am still amazed at the patience it must have taken.
Shōsaku had the true blood of his grandfather beyond any doubt, or
perhaps he was just inspired by his example.

'Chatting all the way, we finally reached home at dusk and every day
during the holidays we met and discussed our ambitions for the future.
At last the winter vacation came to an end and on the evening before my
departure for school, Shōsaku came to visit me. He said that the next
time we met would be in Tokyo because he intended to be away there
for the next three or four years. And so I took my leave of him.

"In the spring of 1894, Shōsaku went up to Tokyo as he had planned
and from there he wrote me two letters which told me little more than
that he was safe and well, and gave me no details about how he was getting on. Nor did anyone at home have any idea of what he was doing,
certainly not his mother and father. However, there was one thing
which no one doubted and that was that he was laying his plans and
steadily moving towards the realisation of his ambitions. I went up to
Tokyo myself in the spring of 1897 where I visited him. We were both
eighteen at the time.

'It was about three o'clock in the afternoon and after making several
enquiries that I finally found where Shōsaku was living in Tsukiji. He
was living on the first floor of a poor house in a run-down part of town.
A woman answered the door.

"Does a Mr Katsura live here?" I asked.

"Yes, he does. Won't you please come in?"

'Hearing the sound of voices, he came down the creaking stairs and all
at once, it seemed, there he was whom I had last met three years before
— Katsura Shōsaku! We walked across two or three filthy mats, up
some steep and narrow stairs and into his room. It was a small room
with a low and soot-covered ceiling. The walls and mats were black
with dirt. There was one thing, however, that was not black and that
was his books. Few people are so careful of their books as Shōsaku. He
had placed all of them on his desk and it was quite obvious that none of
them were ever allowed to come into contact with any other part of the
room. He also took great care of everything about his person.

'As I looked round the room, I could see that the desk for a start was a
fine one and the box covers of the books were not that dirty at all. He
had none of the merits or vices of the typical great man of the East, but
to borrow a current vogue word, the way in which he derived his in-
spiration from the *Self Help* made him a man of "style", a man of the
times. I gave thanks to providence that this spirit of "style" had cap-
tured my friend as it had. As always the books on the desk were
arranged in neat piles and everything about the man himself was tidy

---

* A famous novel dealing with the life of Toyotomi Hideyoshi.

and smart. Do not grieve yourselves about the fact that the room itself was low-class, black and gloomy, for Shōsaku's principles and character had purified it and invested it with a dignity which was noble and admirable.

'His manner was as pleasant and open as ever and he answered all my questions about what had happened to him in Tokyo freely and easily, with no sense of either shame or boastfulness. Men as free from vanity as Shōsaku are a rarity. In his small corner of the world he diligently practised his beliefs and derived therefrom fulfilment and comfort. He never drew comparisons between himself and others and was just quietly progressing towards the fulfilment of his destiny. When he told me of all that he had done, I could not hold back my respect which grew and grew even as I listened.

'As he had planned, he had come up to Tokyo with just enough money to live for three months, but he was not the kind of man just to sit still and do nothing until his money ran out. He had started out by walking all round Tokyo in search of some interesting employment. He hit upon two possibilities, selling newspapers and sand writing which he had seen an old man doing in Kudan park. He had asked the old man what was involved and begged him to take him as his pupil. After two days' practice, he took to sitting beside the road and writing whatever came into his head for which people gave him a few coins. Eventually he had collected a tidy little sum. One day when he had no clients, he took to writing and erasing things just to please himself. He wrote the names Watt, Stephenson and others similar. Just then a well-dressed woman with her seven-year-old son passed by. The child spelled out the name "Watt" and his mother asked Shōsaku what it meant. He looked up and told the story of the great British inventor in a manner which the child could easily understand.

"When you grow up, be a great man like Watt," he told the boy. The woman thanked him and gave him a silver twenty *sen* coin, which was a great deal of money.

"I never spent that coin and I still have it now," he told me with an innocent smile. He lived in a cheap lodging house and in the evenings went to a Kanda night school where he studied mathematics principally. During the crisis of the Sino-Japanese war, he took to selling newspapers and made quite a lot of money from supplements. In the spring of 1895 he had the good fortune to get into some night-classes at an engineering school.

'What with all these questions I had to ask and the answers it was soon almost dusk.

"Let's go and have some rice!" Shōsaku said suddenly, taking his purse from his desk drawer and putting it in his pocket.

"Where?" I asked, slightly taken aback.

"There's an eating house nearby."

"I can eat when I get back to my inn, so please don't worry."

"Nonsense. Let's eat together, and then you can stay here the night. We still have lots to talk about."

'I fell in with these plans and we went out to the rickshaw rank. On the way Shōsaku chatted cheerfully and said that he had had news from the village and wanted to go back there during the course of the year. But as far as I could judge from his way of life, I thought that I could never see him travelling the six hundred miles back home. I didn't say that though, but just suggested that he should visit his mother and father.

"We're there!" Shōsaku led the way into a cheap-looking eating house, but I was rather alarmed by its appearance and hesitated outside.

"Hey, come on!" he said.

'There was nothing else for it so I went in where I discovered that he had already found a place and was waiting for me, a smile on his face. It was very quiet inside as there were only four or five men, apparently labourers, who were seated at the long dining table, eating and drinking. We took our places opposite them.

"I eat here every day," he said nonchalantly. "What'll you have?"

"Anything will do."

'Shōsaku went up to a waitress and ordered two or three items, but I had never heard their names before and did not know what they were. He set about his food with relish, but it seemed to me unclean somehow and I did not feel like eating. When I forced myself to take a few mouthfuls, tears came unbidden to my eyes. Now Shōsaku was the son of a *samurai* and even though the family had fallen on hard times, the son of a gentleman and here he was at table with working class people and making a great noise over his food. But it was not this that brought the tears to my eyes. Never. No, it was just that a thought occurred to me after I had eaten a few mouthfuls.

'This food was a treat for me, bought with money earned from labour by a man who was hard-working, capable, self-taught and who had learned to fend for himself. How could I say that this food I ate was tasteless! Did not Shōsaku himself come here to eat every day? Could I who hated this food I ate consider myself his childhood friend? This thought unconsciously checked the tears in my eyes and my heart felt much more at ease. We proceeded to make a good meal, after which we left the eating house. That night we lay together beneath his scanty bedding and lost all sense of time as by the hazy light of the lamp we discussed events back home, our other friends and our future aspirations. It was a happy night, one which remains vividly before my eyes.

'Afterwards we went our separate ways and I saw no more of him until the summer holidays when he paid a call on me at the rooming house where I was staying. What he had to say was unexpected.

"I'm thinking about going home. In fact I've made my mind up to it."

"That's splendid news, but ..." I hesitated, because I was worried whether he had the money for the trip.

"I've got the money. I've saved thirty yen and I think twenty will cover the fare and some presents to take home. When the rest is gone will be time enough to worry."

'When I heard this, I was deeply impressed that he was as prepared as he was, and I remembered how two years before he had planned to go home and had saved for that specific purpose. Well, my friends, how would you have fared in his situation! It sounds easy enough to do what he had done, but not so in practice. Shōsaku was certainly no ordinary man, and yet is it really so very extraordinary what he did? As you can imagine, I was overjoyed by his decision and I saw him off. He left Shinbashi in high spirits, having spent two-thirds of two years' savings quite happily on colour prints, material and so forth, presents to delight his mother, his brother and relatives' children.

'The next year in 1898, he graduated from school and was taken on by the electrical department of a Yokohama firm at the salary of twelve yen a month. Since then five years have passed, and in that time, what do you think he has been doing? Sticking steadfastly to his job and nothing more? Not a bit of it! He has two younger brothers called Gorō and Arao, both reckless like the elder brother who ran away from home. When Gorō heard that his elder brother had got into a Yokohama firm, he left home straightaway and went to Tokyo. For his brother's sake Shōsaku rushed about getting him jobs in shops or as a servant and so forth, but everywhere Gorō went he was an utter failure. However, Shōsaku kept his patience and stuck by him until in the end he took Gorō in with him, taught him, made him read the *Self Help* over and over again and finally got him into a craftsman's school. On his meagre salary he fed and clothed his brother until in the end after three years of hardship, Gorō became a craftsman and was taken on by a Yokohama firm where he pursued his work with diligence and earnestness.

'Arao also ran away from home and is at present suffering under the kindly, correcting hands of his two brothers. One evening this spring, I visited the house where Shōsaku now lives in Noge-machi, Yokohama. I was told that he was still at work, and minded to see what his workplace was like, I went there on foot. I know nothing of electricity so I can't give a satisfactory description of what was going on, but there was a group of men holding on to a thick iron pillar of some kind and Shōsaku was going round and round it doing something or other with great earnestness. The lights were on by now, illuminating the group almost as if it were daylight, and everyone was watching him. It seemed as if he was examining and repairing some piece of apparatus which had gone haywire, and the look on his face! He had forgotten me, forgotten the whole world. He was in a world of his own with body and soul completely thrown in to the work he was doing. Never have I seen such a look of intensity on anyone's face so that even as I watched, I was struck with a curious feeling that I was seeing something sublime.

'Everyone, please raise your glasses with me to toast my friend. May his future be bright and happy!'

13

Letter From Yugahara

Yugahara Yori (Letter From Yugahara) was first published in June 1902 in the magazine *Yamabiko* and is autobiographical in the sense that Yugahara was one of Doppo's favourite hot spring resorts. He often went there for short holidays and this particular story stems from a visit made in August 1901. In many ways it gives a foretaste of *Daisansha*. Like *Daisansha* it is written entirely in the form of a letter as the title implies and deals with the feelings of a man who is jilted by a maid in a country inn at Yugahara. In fact the course of events shows that this relationship with the girl only existed in his imagination. However, there is little doubt that, as in *Daisansha*, Doppo expressed in *Yugahara Yori* many of the emotions he felt at the time of the break-up of his marriage to Nobuko.

'My dear Uchiyama, no doubt you will be wondering why I ran away as I did, and now I feel that I must tell you everything although it distresses me to do so. What has happened may turn out to be my good fortune but, as I feel now, it is a tragedy and it will be a long time before I can see any good fortune in it. Even when such a time comes, if indeed it ever does, I shall still feel it as a personal tragedy.

'"There was a woman ...". All novels seem to begin in this way and although the critics profess themselves bored with romantic novels, this is how it really is to young people and nothing can be done about it. For my part I am thankful that the gods did not create humanity according to the demands of literary critics!

'On the evening of the 13th last, I was leaning on my desk deep in thought. It was past ten o'clock and all the people of the household were already fast asleep. There was a steady drizzle outside. Such evenings are not at all pleasant for someone like myself who has no family and to make matters worse I was living in a cheap boarding-house which was quite unbearable. Perhaps you can picture me gazing up at the lamp-shade with tearful face. Well, it was then that I suddenly began to think about O-kinu. O-kinu! O-kinu! You have probably never even heard her name and you are not alone in that for none of my friends has the slightest inkling what profound, tender and peaceful echoes that name has stirred in my heart. "There was a woman and her name was O-kinu." I put that in just by way of spiting the literary critics! When I thought of her my heart was flooded with the yearnings of love and a desperate

122

desire to see her. That's the truth of the matter, whatever you say, and there is no help for it. I began to feel that she was the only person in the whole wide world who loved me and whom I loved. Ah! Fickle heart! Why is it that the heart which is in love with nature is pure and noble, while the hearts of men and women in love are so fickle! No doubt the moralists will have an answer for that, but if I could have one wish granted now it would be to wipe from the face of the earth all moralists, critics and their kind. Oh, mighty volcano! Why do you not pour down your fiery wrath on the heads of all such men?! When I thought of my O-kinu bringing a pear for me to eat when I was alone in the bathhouse; when I thought of our walks together by the racing torrent at Yugahara; when I thought of her tender words, her innocence, her smile; ah, then I beat upon the table and declared aloud:

"Tomorrow I will go to her!"

'Who was my O-kinu? No, do not be alarmed. She was no geisha, no call-girl. She was not beautiful, neither was she ugly. She was just a woman! A maid in the Nakanishiya inn at Yugahara. A maid in the very inn from which I write to you now! She was just a country girl who thinks that Odahara is a big city, if you will believe! It was last summer I met her when, if you remember, the Red Cross doctor ordered me to take a couple of months' convalescence at the Yugahara spring after my illness.

'The very next day after making my resolve to go and see her, I finished all my preparations and took my leave of the lodging house. In the *Ginza*, I bought some hankies, some hairpins and such other things as I thought would please a woman, and then I boarded the train. It was the first time in my life I had ever bought anything for a woman, but when I thought how pleased O-kinu would be when I gave her my presents, my heart could scarcely contain its joy. What vanity! There are many men in the world who give women presents just for show and there are many who do not for the same reason, but I would give my poor gifts to my country sweetheart with all my love!

'The overnight rain had stopped, but the air was humid and the sky was heavy with cloud. I enjoy travelling in early summer more than at any other time of the year and have frequently made journeys at this season, but never with so much joy as I did then. My head was filled with pleasant fancies of how that very night I would see her and bathe in the pure, clear spring waters. This was indeed the season to travel, I thought. By the time I alighted from the train at Kokufuzu, the sun was peeping through the clouds and the fresh greenery of mountain, field and forest glittered before my eyes. What pleasure! The wonderful scenery rushed past my eyes as I rode in the train. Closer and closer drew the lofty and forbidding peaks of the Hakone range. Light, fluffy clouds floated over the coastal waters of the sea; the wild geese were on the wing; the waves were breaking on the shore. Now and then clouds flitted across the face of the sun casting faint shadows on the fields below until once more the clear rays of the sun emerged. At that moment I did not believe that I could ever be unhappy; never could the philosophy of pessimism hold any sway over me. When I arrived at Odahara I felt again, as I always feel, that if I could choose any place on earth to live, this would be it with its old castle, lofty mountains, the ocean stretching up to meet the sky and the profusion of trees. Surely it is not unreasonable that I who dream of making a career of painting, should want to live in such a place.

'At Odahara I decided to board the tram almost straight away. As I wanted to get to Yugahara as quickly as possible I gave up the pleasures of even an afternoon in Odahara and boarded the tram immediately after lunch. As I did so I felt as if I were already half-way to my destination. The tramway runs to the Yugahara hot spring belt via Atami and the Izu hills, so all who have travelled to these springs will appreciate the sense of contentment I felt at the prospect of the journey ahead of me. Slowly the tram pulled out of Odahara and I leaned out of the window in time to hear it sound its hooter and to see it begin to pull up the slope. As I looked back I could see the white banners fluttering over the inns of Odahara. Then I turned my attention to the track ahead of me where I saw three peasants walking along the rails towards Odahara. One was a girl dressed in red, one an old woman in white and the other a bowed, but sturdy-looking old man. Standing aside to let the tram pass, they all looked towards me. "It's O-kinu!" I thought as the tram drew level with them, and indeed it was her. "Hey, O-kinu!" I said, without thinking, raising my hand in greeting. She smiled and blushed slightly as she acknowledged me and then she receded into the distance as the tram drew quickly away. If there had been no one else in the carriage, I think I would have stamped my feet and hurled my hat into the air, but as there was a rather grave-looking man sitting opposite me who appeared to be a civil servant or the like, I merely folded my arms despondently.

'No one had to tell me; I knew that O-kinu was no longer working at the Nakanishiya. She had gone home to her parents to make arrangements for her marriage. I remembered having heard from other maids at the inn that previous summer that she was going around with some young man from Odahara. "It's finished," I thought, and my mood grew black. It was as if there were no longer any sea or mountains, and that offshore island — what was that to me?! The waves of the sea, great and small, what were they to me now? That very nature which up to then had been my delight had in that one moment lost all its appeal. I was a completely different person. I knew Yugahara very well and it was dear to my heart, so there was no reason why I should not have found something to amuse me there, even without O-kinu, but since I had known her any place where she was not was a place of sorrow for me. It was of great pain to me to be drawn along in that melancholy carriage through the gloomy gorges, but it was too late to turn back and in due course, at about five o'clock, I arrived at the inn. No one was expecting my arrival, but the innkeeper who was a good-hearted man made me very welcome. When I was in the bath one of the maids came in and said:

"It's a shame, isn't it?"

"What is?"

"That O-kinu isn't here," she gulped out, and then beat a hasty retreat. Ah! What sorrow! This is a memorial for my unrequited love. Unrequited love? I am weary of hearing about it. I was in love, but in a dream, yes even in a dream, I could never have made her mine. I've no doubt that O-kinu did not dislike me, but she never thought of me in any other terms.

'That evening all the maids and even the innkeeper's daughters came to my room. They talked of O-kinu and when I heard from them the final confirmation that she had arranged to go away and get married, I felt as if my fate were sealed and an unspeakable sorrow descended on my heart. This then was unrequited love. I had, without even realising it, allowed myself to become obsessed with the idea that she was mine and loved me only. I distributed the gifts I had brought her among the maids and the innkeeper's daughters, and they, to be sure, were delighted. But I got little enough pleasure from it.

'The next day it rained. There was a drizzle from early morning and it was very dull. The mountain stream had swollen and was very turbulent. One of the innkeeper's daughters waited on me at lunch and when I noticed her laughing as she watched me, I could not help but laugh also.

"Did you say you would like to meet O-kinu?" she asked.

"That's a peculiar thing to say. Is it so unnatural that I should want to see someone who last summer was very kind to me?"

"Shall I arrange for you to see her then?"

"Thank you. I'd be very grateful."

"She's sure to be coming here tomorrow."

"Well then, when she comes, please tell me."

'I did not take her seriously and she said nothing more, but just laughed. She was O-kinu's cousin. In the afternoon the rain stopped, but the clouds still hung over the land and it did not look like clearing up. The narrow valley seemed to be getting narrower and narrower and I felt as if I were sitting in a prison. I was just sitting there doing nothing but gaze at the world outside when my eye was caught by a figure in the shadow of the eaves of the house next door. It looked like O-kinu and I dashed outside to see.

'It was a lonely path strewn with stones. There were only about ten houses. A really desolate valley with just a few peasant dwellings and a few shops to serve their occupants. You can imagine how it looked with all the light and colour taken out by the rain clouds. I walked aimlessly along this path which ran along the banks of a stream. A little way downstream I came to a painted bridge; I sauntered across, in what mood I cannot tell. All the people leaning on the balcony rails of the inn and looking out seemed to be on the point of tears. A woman by the house-front with a child on her back seemed ill and the child was crying. Ah! The melancholy of it all! The long faces! The desolation! Everywhere I looked I seemed to see only the shadows of tragedy. I need not tell you, of course, that I did not see O-kinu.

'The next day, scornful of a threatening sky, I set out alone for Jukokutōge. The people at the inn tried to stop me from going, but I paid them no heed. Even when urged to take a companion with me on the road, I refused. The mountains were enveloped in cloud and recklessly I climbed towards those clouds. I have never seen such a desolate scene as I saw that day. Beneath my feet ashen clouds appeared and disappeared as quickly as they came. The wind sweeping across the grassy plains sang mournfully in my ears, and in the intervals between the clouds I could see nothing but mountains and more mountains. I was alone under the whole mantle of heaven as I sat for a while on a rock at the top of a mountain. There were no birds singing.

'At that time there was no awareness in my heart of love or unrequited love, just an unbearable feeling of desolation and I could not help myself but cry at the loneliness of my existence. On the way home I passed through a dark wood and my mind was engaged with gloomy thoughts. What would happen if I were to slip, plunge into the gorge and die? When I failed to return to the inn there would be a great hue and cry. They would engage a woodcutter to look for me; my body would be found at the bottom of this black gorge; a telegram would be sent to Tokyo and you or Awaji would come rushing here; I would be cremated and a student artist named Koyama would no longer exist in the world.

'As I thought all this, I unconsciously came to a halt. Raindrops were dripping from the thick, black branches overhead and from the gravel-like ravine I could hear the forlorn murmur of the fast-flowing stream. I could feel my hair standing on end. The people at the inn were surprised to see me return looking like a dead man, but even greater was my own surprise when that same day O-kinu came. However, she went away the same afternoon without my seeing her. That evening I went down with a fever and for the next two or three days there was no improvement. I suppose I must have caught a chill in the mountains.

'My dear Uchiyama, you at least are no literary critic and therefore I should like to tell you my thoughts about love during those three days I was confined to bed.

'Love is a power which no man can resist and he who thinks that he can overwhelm this power by ignoring it has not yet been truly touched by it. With the passing of time, a man who has suffered in love becomes himself again and then wonders why he was ever so tormented. This is because he is no longer touched by the power of love. If it is so with such a man how then can one who has never loved at all possibly understand the love of another? How can he understand the pleasures and torments? Love is the sincerest feeling a man can have and those of you who mock that feeling had better live as long as you possibly can. In the end the earth is waiting for you, for you are just dirt, my friends, if that is what you think of love.

'It makes me want to smile coldly when I see your faces as you try to make sense and order of this mysterious universe in which we live. Just for a moment I should like to get you to look at the problems of human life, of heaven and earth with a little more gravity and humility. When you laugh at love, ultimately you are laughing at man himself, for, contrary to what you think, man is a mysterious being.

'If you make fun of the love that is in a man's heart, in the final analysis what is human life worth? I say to you all that if on a moonlight night you hear the music of a flute and feel some semblance of awareness of eternity, then you must believe in love. If you are a follower of Nakae Chōmin* and are content to judge everything by his teachings, how can you interfere with the freedom of those who would sing "the spring is short, of what consequence is eternal life?" How can you interfere with the freedom of young men and women who desire the gratification of the flesh saying "youth comes only once"?

'My dear Uchiyama, this is how things are with me. I idolise and adore the concept of love perhaps because I myself have suffered from unrequited love. Tomorrow I return to Tokyo, but I am wondering how I shall feel when I pass through Odahara.'

---

* Nakae Chōmin (1847-1901). Writer, philosopher and devotee of the ideas of Rousseau.

14

Bird Of Spring

Haru no Tori (Bird Of Spring) was one of the last of Doppo's 'Saeki period' works and was written more than seven years after he left Saeki. The story was published in vol. 4 no. 4 of the magazine *Jogaku Sekai* in March 1904. As in *Gen Oji* the opening lines, 'Some six or seven years ago I was employed in teaching English and mathematics', are a reference to the year Doppo spent as a teacher at the Tsuruya Gakkan in Saeki, and the characters of the story, as Doppo later stated in *Waga sakuhin to kojitsu* (The Truth About My Works), are based on people known to him in the town.

Once again Doppo uses the idea of the tragic figure buffeted by fate, but in this case Rokuzō finds his release in accidental suicide while trying to fly away into the sky. Shiroyama, the hill which appears in many of the Saeki works, is located on the outskirts of the town and was a favourite spot with Doppo when he wanted to get away from the school. Wordsworth's influence on this story is made explicit by the reference to his poem *There Was A Boy*, the plot being in fact an imaginative extension of the poem.

Some six or seven years ago I was employed in teaching English and mathematics at a school in a Kyushu country town. On the edge of the town there stood a hill named Shiroyama which was covered in large, gloomy trees. I often used to climb this hill, because although it was not particularly high as hills go, its scenery and the view it commanded were of exceptional beauty. On the summit were the ruins of a castle whose high stone walls had an inexpressible charm with creepers trailing over them and staining them a deep red. Where the castle keep had once stood in ancient times, the ground was now levelled off and covered with a sparse scattering of dwarf pines, which had grown there in the dim past, amidst an unbroken sea of summer grasses. The whole scene had that atmosphere of pathos which comes with the memory of days gone by. Times without number I remember I just lay on the grass peering at the view of outlying gardens and fields over the tops of a wood to which no axe had been laid over hundreds of years.

I particularly remember one Sunday afternoon. It was late autumn and the sky was clear as water, but a wintry wind was blowing and the trees on Shiroyama were moaning violently. Following my usual custom I had climbed to the summit and was reading the book I had brought with me, from time to time pausing to watch the just past noon-day sun casting its red glow over the distant villages and outskirts of the town. Suddenly I heard the sound of voices and when I looked down over the stone wall I saw three quite ordinary-looking girls gathering dead branches for firewood. They already had large loads on their backs, but they were still pursuing their quest, perhaps because the violence of the wind had provided a harvest too good to miss. I watched them as they chattered and sang merrily and came to the conclusion that they must be about twelve or thirteen years old and probably came from some nearby village. Having made up my mind about that, I returned to my book and for the moment forget all about them.

'Aaah!' At the sound of a female cry, I looked down in surprise to see that the girls must have been frightened by something for they were flying in confusion with the firewood still on their backs. Almost immediately they were lost to view beyond the angle of the stone wall. Thinking this rather peculiar I looked carefully around me for the cause of their alarm and saw someone coming towards me from the murky wood, beating a path for himself through the trackless undergrowth. At first I could not see who it was, but then he finally cleared the wood and appeared beneath the stone wall. It was a boy, perhaps eleven or twelve years old, clad in a nevy-blue kimono fastened with a white cotton waistband; neither a farm lad nor a town boy as far as I could judge from his appearance. He was carrying a stout switch in his hand and was staring about him when suddenly he looked up over the stone wall and for an instant our eyes happened to meet. He gazed hard at me for a moment and then broke into a grin. But it was no normal grin, and from the way the eyes in his pale, round face goggled at me, I immediately perceived that this was no normal child at all.

'What are you doing, Sensei?' he called to me. I was slightly startled, but the place where I taught was an extremely small castle town, so even though I knew few people outside my pupils, the natives generally would be aware that a young teacher had arrived from the capital; thus it was not particularly strange for this child to address me as he did. I spoke kindly to him.

'I'm reading a book. Why don't you come up here?'

At once he put his hands on the stone wall and began to climb like a monkey. This rather took me aback as the wall was more than thirty feet high, but even as I reflected that I should make some effort to stop him, he was already half-way up. Grasping the nearest creeper as it came within reach, he agilely pulled himself up by it and in an instant was standing by my side, grinning.

'What's your name?' I asked.

'Roku.'

'Ah, Roku. It's Roku-san is it?'

He nodded, wearing the same peculiar grin. His mouth was slightly open and he was staring so hard at my face that I felt a little uncomfortable.

'How old are you?' I asked.

He looked puzzled, so I repeated the question, whereupon he twisted his mouth into a peculiar shape and moved his lips silently. Then, suddenly, he opened his hands and counted off on his fingers, 'one, two, three'; there he stopped and jumped suddenly to 'ten, eleven'. He regarded me gravely. He seemed to me just like a five-year-old child who had just learned to count.

'Well, you're pretty bright, aren't you?' I said instinctively.

'My mother taught me.'

'Don't you go to school?'

'No.'

'Why not?'

The boy hung his head and looked away, so I waited a moment, guessing that he was trying to think up an answer, but without any warning he just rushed off, making a croaking noise like a deaf-mute.

'Hey, Roku-san!' in amazement, I called for him to stop, but with a cry of 'Aaagh, aaagh!' he continued his headlong rush down the base of the keep without even looking back, and in a moment he had disappeared from sight.

* * *

At that time I was living in a lodging-house, but it was inconvenient and I decided to move. After making several enquiries, I eventually rented two upstairs rooms from a man named Taguchi who, it was arranged, would provide all the necessities. In earlier days Taguchi had been a principal *samurai* retainer and now he lived at the foot of Shiroyama in a splendid mansion which retained all the glory of the old style, so it was no small favour he did me by renting me the upper storey of his house and looking after me.

The morning after I moved in, I got up early to take a stroll and I was amazed to see the very boy I had met on the hill in the garden sweeping fallen leaves.

'Good morning, Roku-san,' I said. He looked at me with a grin and without making any reply, went on with sweeping the leaves.

As the days went by, I gradually came to know more of the story of this peculiar child, because I was careful to keep my eyes and ears open, discreetly of course. His real name was Rokuzō, and he was the nephew of my landlord Taguchi. He was mentally retarded. His mother a woman in her middle forties, had lost her husband early and had returned home with her two children to be cared for by Taguchi, who was her elder brother. Rokuzō's sister was called O-shige and from what I could see her plight was just as unfortunate as her brother's, for she was every bit as backward.

It seemed to me at first that Taguchi was trying to keep me unaware of their condition, but the truth will always out and so it came about that one evening he visited me in my room for a talk. He chatted a bit about education in general, finally working his way round to the subject of his nephew and niece. He told me what I knew already that both were mentally retarded and asked me whether it were possible for them to receive some sort of education. According to what he said, the father of this pathetic pair had been a very heavy drinker, shortening his own life in the process and squandering the family fortune. To begin with he had sent the children to primary school where both had proved singularly incapable of learning anything, no matter how hard the teachers had tried with them. Indeed, for the most part it had been impossible to teach them in the same classroom with the other pupils who made them the butt of their mischievous practical jokes. Finally the school authorities sympathetically suggested that they should be removed from the school.

As the details of the story became clearer to me, it was increasingly obvious that Rokuzō and O-shige were not merely a little backward, but truly mentally sub-normal. Also, although Taguchi himself did not admit it, general observation made it clear that the children's mother was none too bright, and I quickly perceived that while part of the cause of their condition was due to the father's alcoholism, it was also partly inherited from the mother.

I knew that there was such a thing as education for the mentally sub-normal, but specialised knowledge was necessary, so I avoided discussing the subject seriously with Taguchi and just said that it would not be an easy undertaking. However, as I came to see more of the two children, I could not help but feel great pity at their plight. I felt that no deformity could be more pitiable than theirs. After all, although there is a tragedy in being mute, deaf or blind, those who are unable to speak, hear or see are still capable of thought. They can think and feel, whereas the mentally sub-normal are afflicted with a muteness, a deafness and a blindness of the mind, so that to all intents and purposes they are no different from the birds and beasts. If a mind is balanced, even though somewhat lacking in depth, it is not too bad, but as the mind of the mentally sub-normal person is distorted and incomplete at the same time, he seems peculiar to all those around him. It does not matter if he is laughing, crying, rejoicing or being sad, because to normal people all of his actions will seem deranged. It is indeed a sorry plight.

Rokuzō I pitied doubly, because he had the innocence of extreme youth and so I resolved that, if it were at all humanly possible, I should like to somehow improve his mind, even though it might be to only a small degree.

Two weeks had passed after my talk with Taguchi, when, one evening at about ten o'clock, just as I was thinking of retiring to my bed, I heard a voice.

'Are you in bed, Sensei?' It was Rokuzō's mother, who had come into my room even as she asked the question. Short and thin with small head and prominent features, she was an old-fashioned woman who always blackened her teeth. Her mouth was slightly open and a benignly silly smile played perpetually in her eyes and on her lips.

'I was just thinking about it,' I said, and as I spoke she sat down by the brazier.

'I have a favour to ask you, Sensei,' she said, seeming to find it difficult to speak.

'What is it?'

'It's about Rokuzō. He's such a fool that it troubles me what the future holds in store for him. When I think about it, I forget my own stupidity. I just can't stop worrying about him.

'I understand, but there's really no need to worry so.' Simple human compassion for her feelings led me to utter these words of comfort.

★ ★ ★

As I listened that night to what Rokuzō's mother had to say, the thing which impressed me most strongly was her compassion for her child. As I have said before, it was apparent at a glance that the woman herself was not very bright, but her anxiety for her child was no different from that of a normal mother. Somehow it made the situation even more pitiable that she was retarded herself, and despite myself, I wept tears of sympathy. Eventually I sent the poor woman away with the promise that I would do my best for Rokuzō's education, and until late that night I racked my brains over what I should do.

Beginning next day, I started to take Rokuzō with me whenever I went out for a walk and, as the opportunity occurred, I tried to give his mind something to feed on. It was his inability to count that I was first aware of, because he did not even know the numbers from one to ten. However many times I taught him, he could never get beyond a verbal repetition of the numbers and if I put down some pebbles from the wayside and asked him how many there were, he would just contemplate them in silence. If I pressed him for an answer, he would just break into that weird smile of his at first, but it was never long before he was on the verge of tears. I stuck doggedly to my self-appointed task. Once we climbed the stone steps of the Hachiman Shrine, counting them as we went, 'one, two, three' and so forth until we reached the seventh step. When I asked him how many steps we had climbed at that point, he replied in a loud voice, 'Ten!' It was just the same when we counted pine trees and when I tried tempting him with sweets to teach him how to count them. In his mind there was no connection between the words 'one, two, three' and the numerical concepts the words implied. I had heard before that the mentally sub-normal have this inability to understand numbers, but I had never thought that it would be as bad as this. There were times when I felt like crying, and the tears would flow spontaneously as I watched the child's face.

Rokuzō was quite mischievous and there were times when he really startled people with his pranks. He was skilled at hill and mountain climbing and would run about Shiroyama just as if he were on level ground, bounding rapidly along even where there was no path. Thus it sometimes happened that he would disappear after lunch and suddenly, towards nightfall, come racing down from the crags of Shiroyama to Taguchi's garden. This habit was a cause of great anxiety to the Taguchi household. I did not take me long to realise that the reason the girls gathering wood had fled at the sight of Rokuzō was that they been frightened by his pranks many times in the past.

On the other hand, he was quick to cry. From time to time, out of consideration for her brother, Rokuzō's mother would administer severe scoldings, sometimes even striking the child with the flat of her hand. On such occasions, he would hang his head and shrink away screaming. Yet he was soon laughing again as if he had forgotten all about being hit.

From what I have said, you would probably be surprised to hear that Rokuzō knew such things as songs, but know them he did. He had off by heart such favourites as the wood-gathering song and he used to sing them in a low voice. One day I climbed Shiroyama alone. I had intended to take Rokuzō with me, but he could not be found. Even in winter Kyushu is a warm region and if only the skies are clear it can be very hot. Also the air is clear, and in my opinion winter is the best season for climbing in Kyushu. Treading among the fallen leaves, I reached the summit at my usual spot beneath the base of the keep. In the calm silence pervading the hill, I heard someone singing softly and when I looked up, I saw Rokuzō sitting astride the stone wall, dangling his legs and singing a popular song. His eyes were fixed far into the distance. It made quite a picture — the colour of the sky, the rays of the sun, the ruins of the old castle and this young boy. He seemed like a messenger of the gods. At that moment he did not seem subnormal at all. A sub-normal messenger of the gods — what a sad paradox! And yet I had the profound impression that for all his imbecility, this young boy was after all a child of nature.

One more of Rokuzō's strange characteristics was a fondness for birds. Just the sight of a bird was enough to make his eyes glow and he would shout aloud. Yet any bird he saw, he called a crow, and no matter how many times I taught him the proper names, he always forgot them. There was one amusing occasion when he saw an egret which as usual he called a crow — amusing because there is a popular saying 'to blacken an egret by calling it a crow' which means 'making a right into a wrong'. At least this is the meaning any normal person would attribute to the saying, but to this poor child it was a matter of literal truth. Whenever he saw a shrike singing from the top of a tall tree, he would look at it with mouth agape and it was strange to see him staring blankly at the place where the bird had been after it had flown away. To him the idea of birds flying freely in the air was a source of amazement.

* * *

I was doing my best for this sad child, but to no visible effect. What with one thing and another the next spring arrived and with it came an unforeseen disaster for Rokuzō. One day at the end of March, he disappeared in the early morning and still had not returned when midday had come and gone. When night fell and he was still not back, there was great anxiety in the Taguchi household and his mother particularly was upset. I decided that the best thing to do at first was to make a thorough search of Shiroyama. I took one of Taguchi's servants with me and, with a lantern at the ready, climbed by my usual path to the castle ruins — a strangely painful foreboding in my heart. I suppose my basic feeling when I arrived beneath the base of the keep was what people usually call premonition.

'Roku-san! Roku-san!' I called. The servant and I strained our ears for a reply, but there was none. What with being in the ruins of a castle and the child we were looking for not a normal one, I felt a quite indescribable sense of the macabre. When we emerged on top of the base of the keep and looked down over the parapet of the stone wall, we discovered Rokuzō's body lying directly beneath the highest angle of the wall on the northern side. It may sound like a ghost story, but as a matter of fact, after I knew it was past the time for Rokuzō's return, I had a feeling that he had fallen from this high stone wall and was already dead. You may laugh at this as idle fancy, but I confess it seemed to me that Rokuzō had thrown himself from the top of the stone wall with the intention of soaring into the sky like a bird. I do not doubt that if a bird had been flying about from branch to branch right before his eyes, then Rokuzō himself would have tried to fly up into the branches.

Two days after Rokuzō's funeral, I climbed up to the base of the keep alone. I was no longer able to bear the thoughts of the strangeness of life which occurred to me as I contemplated Rokuzō's fate. The difference between man and the other animals; the connection between man and nature; life and death — all these problems brought a profound sadness to my young heart. A famous English poet wrote a poem called *There Was A Boy* in which he tells how a child stands with hands clasped night after night by a lonely lake, enjoying the owls on the mountain on the other side of the lake, hooting in response to his imitation of an owl's cry. In the end, the child dies and is buried in a tranquil grave. His spirit returns to the bosom of nature. I was fond of this poem and read it often, but I felt that seeing Rokuzō's death and thinking on his life and retardedness made his story even more meaningful than that of the poem. The spring birds flew about as I stood watching from the top of the wall. Might not one of them be Rokuzō? Even if that were not so, how much did Rokuzō differ from these birds?

His wretched mother wept, despite protesting that Rokuzō's death was the best thing that could have happened to him. One day I went to the cemetery to the north of Shiroyama with the intention of visiting Rokuzō's fresh grave, but his mother was there before me. Apparently she was talking to herself as she walked repeatedly round the grave, and she seemed not to notice my approach.

'Why did you imitate the birds? Eh, why did you jump from the wall? That's what the Sensei said. He said that you jumped from the wall because you wanted to fly into the air. Is there anyone so foolish that he pretends to be a bird?' she said, but after a moment's reflection she continued, 'But it is better that you are dead. You are better off that way.'

Then she noticed me.

'Sensei, it is better for my Rokuzō to be dead, isn't it? she said, and burst into tears.

'That could never be so, but it was an accident that you could not foresee, so there is nothing but to resign yourself to it.'

'But why did he pretend to be a bird?'

'That's just my fancy. There's no way of knowing for sure how he met his death.'

'But isn't that what you said?' She raised her eyes and stared at me.

'Rokuzō was very fond of birds, so I just thought that might have been what happened.'

'Yes, he did love birds. Whenever he saw one, he would stretch out his hands like this.' She flapped her hands in imitation of a bird. 'He used to walk about trying to fly just like this. And he was good at mimicking the call of a crow.'

As she spoke her eyes kindled and at the sight I closed my own involuntarily. From the woods of Shiroyama a single crow flew leisurely past, cawing two or three times as it headed towards the beach. The woman suddenly stopped speaking and stared blankly after it, oblivious to everything else. What did she suppose that solitary crow was? I wonder ....

15
Meat And Potatoes

Gyūniku to Bareishō (Meat And Potatoes) was published in vol. 2 no. 3 of *Shōtenchi* in November 1901 and is regarded by Japanese literary historians as a turning point in Doppo's career on the road towards 'Naturalism' and 'Realism'. In its portrayal of the disillusioned idealist Okamoto Masao, who seems to take his disillusionment far more seriously than the others, there are strong overtones of Doppo's own life. Like Okamoto, he too went to Hokkaido as a Christian in search of the realisation of his ideals only to have his dreams shattered by the tragedy of his relationship with Sasaki Nobuko. Although later in his life he may not have felt quite the same disillusionment as Okamoto, there is no doubt that this story accurately reveals Doppo's thoughts at the time he wrote, perhaps even as far as his 'desire to be surprised' by the secrets of the universe.

If *Gyūniku to Bareishō* is a turning point in Doppo's thought, it is certainly a turning point in his style. Hitherto, he had been principally a narrative writer, but this story is almost entirely composed of dialogue which is penetrating and often witty. The symbolism of the title is particularly clever. Doppo always showed himself willing to experiment with styles of writing, as for example in *Daisansha* which is composed entirely of correspondence.

A long the moat in downtown Tokyo, there once stood a quite impressive western-style building which housed the Meiji Club. The building in fact still stands today, but its ownership has changed hands and the Meiji Club as such has ceased to exist.

One winter night when the Club was still in its heyday, lights were burning in the upstairs dining room and now and then loud laughter filtered through to the outside world. The Club seldom held meetings at night and generally speaking it was only during daylight hours that smoke could be seen rising from the chimney. The clock had already struck eight, but there was still no sign of the meeting breaking up. Six rickshaws were lined up by the entrance, but the rickshaw men all seemed busy gambling at the service entrance.

At that moment, a man emerged from the darkness. His collar was turned up and his felt hat was pressed down over his eyes. He gave a hard push on the door bell. The door opened and the man asked in a low, quiet voice:

'Has Mr Takeuchi come tonight?'

136

'Yes, sir, he has. And you?' the doorman answered politely, a thin-faced individual wearing Japanese clothes.

'Give him this, if you please,' the stranger said, handing the doorman a calling card which read simply 'Okamoto Masao'. It made no mention of title or rank. The doorman took it and hurried upstairs. In a moment he returned.

'This way, please, sir,' he said. The room to which he was led was suffocating for the stove had been going full blast. Three men sat in front of the stove, with another three sitting a little way away. A whisky bottle stood on a side-table accompanied by glasses, some empty and some half full. The men seemed in high spirits and were half drunk.

Takeuchi got up when he saw Okamoto and jovially thrust a chair at him. 'Here, take a seat.'

Okamoto, however, seemed in no hurry. Looking round, he saw that he knew five of the men, but there was one man, a light-skinned, well-dressed individual of medium height, whom he had never met before. Takeuchi noticed this.

'I believe you don't know this gentleman. Permit me to introduce you. This is Kamimura. He works for a coal-mining company in Hokkaido. Kamimura, this is Okamoto, a very old friend of mine.'

Before he had time to complete the introduction, Kamimura broke in and said cheerfully:

'Glad to meet you. I've read everything you've ever written, and I'm delighted to have the opportunity to meet you personally at last.'

'I'm pleased to make your acquaintance.' said Okamoto and sat down without another word.

'Go on with what you were saying,' said Watanuki, a short man with black side whiskers.

'Yes, Kamimura. What happened then?' demanded Iyama, a thin man with bleary eyes and balding head.

'It's not so easy for me to go on seeing as Okamoto here has put in an appearance,' Kamimura, the man from the coal-mining company laughed uneasily.

'What's it all about?' Okamoto asked Takeuchi.

'Well, it's really very interesting. Somehow we got talking about our personal views of life. Just you listen. Brilliant arguments. Really scintillating.'

'Well, I've said about all I have to say. You're the genuine article not a philistine like the rest of us. We'd like to hear your personal philosophy, eh, chaps?' Kamimura said, backing out.

'Oh no, you don't get away with it that easily. Finish what you were saying first!'

'Yes, I'd like that very much,' said Okamoto, taking a glass of whisky and downing it in one.

'Well, my views are the complete opposite of Okamoto's, I suspect. In other words, I believe that the ideal and reality are irreconcilable. Completely irreconcilable.'

'Hear, hear,' Iyama interrupted.

'If they are indeed irreconcilable, then my ideal is to submit to reality rather than pursue the ideal.'

'Is that all?' Okamoto snorted, a second glass of whisky in his hand.

'But the point is, you can't eat ideals,' said Kamimura, screwing up his face.

'Ha, ha. Of course you can't. They're not beefsteaks!' laughed Takeuchi, opening his huge mouth.

'But that's exactly it. Reality is a beefsteak. Or stew if you like.'

'Omelettes, perhaps!' said the hitherto silent Matsuki with a straight face. He was a red-faced man, the youngest there, and he had been half asleep. Everyone laughed.

'There's nothing in this to laugh about,' said Kamimura, a little agitated. 'It's just an analogy. If you pursue the ideal you'll have nothing but potatoes to eat, and you may not even have potatoes. Which do you chaps prefer — meat or potatoes?'

'It's meat for me!' said Matsuki in a dozy voice, serious this time.

'But potatoes are a side-dish for beef steak,' said the side-whiskered Watanuki, looking very pleased with himself.

'Precisely my point. Ideals are a side-dish for reality! You can't get by without potatoes, but to eat only potatoes ...' Kamimura turned to Okamoto with an air of self-satisfaction.

'Hokkaido is famous for its potatoes, is it not?' said Okamoto calmly.

'I've had enough of Hokkaido's potatoes to last me a life-time. Takeuchi knows what I'm on about. It may not look like it, but I'm an old graduate of Doshisha, and as you might expect, I was an ardent Christian like the others. You might say that I went in for the Potato Party in a big way!'

'You?' Iyama blinked his eyes in disbelief as he looked at Kamimura.

'There's nothing so strange about it. I was still young after all. I don't know how old you are, Okamoto, but I was twenty-two when I left Doshisha. That was thirteen years ago and I wish you could have seen what a keen member of the Potato Party I was in those days. Ever since my schooldays, I thrilled to my heart just to hear the name of Hokkaido. I fancied myself as a puritan. Quite unbearable I was!'

'He was some puritan!' piped up Matsuki again, but Kamimura cut him short and continued, sipping his whisky.

'I was resolved to leave this defiled part of the country and take my chance in the free lands of Hokkaido.' Okamoto watched Kamimura's face intently as he spoke. 'I took every chance I could to hear about Hokkaido and whenever there was any missionary who had been to Hokkaido, I was quick to go and hear what he had to say. Some marvellous things they used to tell! They kept saying that nature was this or that, or talking about how wide the River Ishikari was, or how

forests extended as far as the eye could see. It was all too much for me. I
fell head over heels in love with it. Piecing together all I had heard I imagined myself clearing forests with the sweat of my brow, felling trees
and planting Azuki beans ...'

'Ha, ha. I'd like to have seen you as a farmer!' Takeuchi laughed.

'The thing is, I really did it. Wait a bit and I'll get round to it. As time
went by, I'd bring more fields under cultivation and plant things,
potatoes mostly. I reckoned that as long as I had potatoes, I'd never
starve.'

'Aha! Potatoes rear their ugly heads again!' It was Matsuki again.

'And there, in the middle of the fields, is a house. Crudely constructed of course and obviously American-style — an imitation of New
England colonial style. The roof slopes steeply, like this, and to one side
an ostentatious chimney. It gave me much food for thought how many
windows I should put in.'

Iyama blinked again. 'You actually built this house?'

'No. This is how I imagined it when I was in Kyoto. Let me see.
That's it! It was on my way home from a stroll to the Nyakuō temple
that I thought about the windows.'

'And what did you do then?' Okamoto earnestly urged him to continue.

'I marked off a belt of trees to act as a windbreak, wanting to keep as
much of the woods as I could. A small stream with crystal water would
wind from the right side of the windbreak, flowing past the house. Of
course, purple-winged geese and ducks with white backs would swim
in the stream over which I would build a bridge made of three-inch
planks. I wondered whether I should attach railings to the bridge, but
decided against it. Much more natural without railings. This is how I
imagined it, but my imagination wasn't content to leave it at that. When
the first winter came ...'

'Excuse me interrupting, but didn't the very sound of the word
"winter" carry you away?'

'How on earth did you know that? How interesting. I can see why
you're a member of the Potato Party! Yes, I was over the moon at the
very sound of the word. Somehow it seemed to me that winter and
freedom were synonymous. Add to that the fact that I was a Christian,
one of the band who celebrate Christmas. Of course, Christmas just
wasn't Christmas without deep snow and icicles hanging from the
eaves. I did not so much think of winter in Hokkaido as that winter was
Hokkaido. Whenever any one was talking to me of Hokkaido and ut-
tered the words "when winter comes", I shivered with excitement.
Whenever I imagined the winter coming, I thought of my house buried
in snow and at night a red glimmer of light from my window. Now and
then a gust of wind sweeping the snow from the branches of the trees.
And a cow lowing in the barn, of course!'

'The man's a poet!' someone shouted, stamping on the floor. It was a man named Kondo who had said nothing since Okamoto had come into the room. A tall, sinister-looking man, he had been drinking alone sunk in his own thoughts.

'That's right, Okamoto, isn't is?' he added. Okamoto simply nodded his agreement, making no comment.

'A poet? Yes, I suppose I was, then. "Now fades the glimmering landscape on the sight." I loved to read that line from Gray's Elegy, albeit in translation. I used to write things of my own as well, I reckon I can call myself one of the modern "free verse" poets.'

'I've written some free verse myself,' said Matsuki, now taking a greater interest in proceedings.

'Well, I've written two or three poems,' said Iyama earnestly, not to be outdone.

'And how about you, Watanuki?' asked Takeuchi.

'I'm ashamed to admit it, but there's nothing of the poet about me. I lack the feminine spirit, as you well know. My life is based on rights and duties, do you see. That's all there is to it. I suppose I must seem pretty boorish to you,' said Watanuki, running his hand through his hair.

'No, it's me who should feel ashamed. After all, I wrote some poems as well. Even had some published in a magazine. Ha, ha, ha, ha!'

Everyone burst out laughing.

'So everyone here has had a go at it! This is rare!' shouted Watanuki.

'Well, so everyone has. What a surprise! You were all potato eaters in those days, then,' said Kamimura, looking very pleased with himself.

'Go on with your story, won't you,' Okamoto urged Kamimura.

'Yes, tell us the rest!' said Kondo, as if he were giving an order.

'All right, I will. For about a year after my graduation, I hung around Tokyo not knowing what to do with myself, but finally I made up my mind to go to Hokkaido. I cannot tell you how happy I felt then. I felt like shouting "Fools! Idiots!" I boarded the train at Ueno station, and when the whistle went and the train began to move, I leaned out of the window and spat in the direction of Tokyo. Unutterable joy came over me so that I secretly shed tears into my handkerchief. And that's the truth!'

'Hold on a minute. Just now you said something about feeling you wanted to shout "Fools! Idiots!" to everyone. I don't get it. What did you mean by it?' asked the man with obligations, Watanuki, seriously.

'Oh, I meant those poor fools in Tokyo, with their constant hankering after wealth and fame. "Fools! Idiots! Look at me, I'm not one of you!" That's the feeling I mean,' Kamimura added earnestly, by way of explanation.

'I won't tell you about the journey. At any rate, I arrived safely at Sapporo in Hokkaido, the heart of potato country. I acquired 200 acres of land without any trouble and got going right away, saying to myself,

"Now for it, now to start working with the sweat of my brow." Of course, I had a friend who had shared my ideals from the very beginning. He's working for the same company as me now. Well, together we began to clear the land. Takeuchi, I think you know him. Kajiwara Shintarō.'

'What? Old Kajiwara? Was he a potato man as well? He's as fat as a pig now, isn't he?' Takeuchi seemed taken aback.

'Yes. He'd gobble up a bloody steak in a couple of mouthfuls now, like a hungry devil. He was smarter than me from the outset. We had been persevering for perhaps a couple of months, when one day he suggested we give up our crazy idea. His argument was that there was no point in carrying on thinking the way we did and making ourselves into recluses. Why battle against nature? Wouldn't it be better to enter the fray of the social world. "There's more nourishment in meat than in potatoes," he said. At the time I had a lot to say against him. "If you want to quit, go ahead," I said, "I'll go through with it, even if I have to do it alone." Then he said, "If that's what you want, it's up to you, but it won't be long before you see the light." His point was that ideals are an illusion, the dreams of a fool. Well, he went on and on to that effect and finally packed his bags and left. I put a brave face on it once left to my own devices, but at heart I felt let down. I teamed up with a couple of tenant farmers and persevered for about three months. Some achievement, eh?!'

'You were a fool!' said Kondo as if rebuking him.

'A fool? Not a fool, I think. In retrospect I agree I was a very great fool, but at the time I felt myself to be really something.'

'You were a fool for all that. You were never cut out for the life. You're not the type to live in Hokkaido with nothing but potatoes to eat. What else can I call you but a fool if you stuck it for three months without realising the fact?'

'You're right. I was a fool and gradually I woke up to the truth of what you said about my not being the type. I'm glad that I wasn't cut out for it. Well, anyway, summer passed and winter came closer and closer. You remember I said I was looking forward to it. Autumn of course came first and that did not live up to my expectations. The early autumn rains pattered on the treetops in the hush of the forest, and the sun seemed weak somehow. I had no one to talk to and nothing to eat apart from a small supply of rice and, of course, potatoes. All I had to sleep in was a hut with walls made of bark.'

'Surely you had anticipated all that!' Okamoto interrupted.

'That's the point. A pleasant reality is better than ideals. Sure, I had indeed anticipated what would happen, but when it came to it, I didn't like it very much. Well, for starters, I got thin.' Kamimura moistened his lips with a drink. 'I never thought that I would get thin!'

Everyone roared with laughter.

'Well, I thought it over. "Kajiwara was right," I thought, "I'm behaving like a fool. Well, I'll give it up." And give it up I did. If I'd stuck it out the winter, I'd have been done for.'

'What's your present position, if I may make so bold?' asked Okamoto, half in scorn, but half in earnest.

'Well, because of what happened, I'd grown fed up with potatoes. So now I'm a realist. I make money, eat good food and drink with you like this by a warm stove. And I say exactly what I like. When I'm hungry, I eat meat ...'

Watanuki exclaimed enthusiastically, 'Hear, hear! I'm with you in that. Loyalty, patriotism or whatever, they are all compatible with meat. Anyone who says otherwise is just not capable of making them so. They are the fools!'

'I don't agree!' shouted Kondo. He sat astride his chair with his back to the stove. He looked about him with a ferocious gleam in his eyes, and continued:

'I've never been a member of either the Potato Party or the Meat Party. Kamimura and the rest of you were members of the Potato Party at first, but later changed your allegiance to the Meat Party. In other words, you're all weak-willed. Poets the lot of you, with all the degeneracy of poets and that's why you go around willy-nilly twitching your noses, sniffing for the smell of beef! You make me sick!'

'Hey, before you go insulting others, you must tell us what you believe in. In what respects are we "degenerate"?' Kamimura interrupted.'

'Degenerate? To be degenerate implies descent from a lofty place to a low one. Fortunately, I've never been in a lofty place, so I don't have to behave as ignominiously as the rest of you. You all ate potatoes for the sake of it, not because you liked them. Because of that you were hungry for meat. People like me eat meat because they like it and that's why we never hunger for it. Never!'

'I don't get it at all,' shouted Kamimura. Kondo was just about to elaborate when a waiter came straight up to him and whispered something in his ear.

Kondo roared, 'Tell them that Kondo's generosity does not run that far!'

'What's up?' one of the company asked in amazement.

'That idiot of a rickshaw man. He's lost at gambling again and wants me to lend him something ... So you don't get me, eh? It's abundantly clear. You're all members of the Meat Party — "Meatists" if you like. It's a principle with you. Now me, I've liked meat from the start and it has nothing to do with principles I can tell you!'

'I absolutely agree,' someone said in a calm and quiet voice.

'Of course you do,' Kondo laughed, with his eyes on Okamoto.

'I agree completely; that principles have nothing to do with it, that is.

There's nothing in the world so stupid as all these "isms".' Okamoto turned his bright gaze on those about him.

'Say what you mean. I'd like to hear what you have to say,' said Kondo, thrusting out his square jaw.

'Which side are you on, meat or potatoes? Potatoes, I suppose,' asked Kamimura, as if he already knew what Okamoto was going to say.

'I'm not a member of the Meat Party, nor do I subscribe to the Potato Party. However, I'm not sure that I like beef as Kondo here does. Naturally I scorn these home-made "isms" we've been talking about, but I find myself unable to indulge my tastes for either beef or potatoes.'

'Well, what, then?' asked Iyama gravely, blinking his bleary eyes.

'There's nothing to it, really. I'll skip the analogies and speak plainly. I can't submit to any particular ideal, but neither can I find satisfaction in giving myself over to the lusts of the flesh. It's impossible, I tell you. It's not a case of not doing it. To tell the truth, as it makes no difference one way or the other I sometimes wish that I could make a definite choice, but because of some twist of fate I am clinging to one unusual wish. It is because of this wish that I am unable to choose.'

'Well, what is this unusual wish, eh?' Kondo demanded in his usual aggressive manner.

'I can't explain it in a word.'

'You're not suggesting you'd like to eat a roast wolf with your drinks?'

'Something like that. Actually, I once fell in love with a woman.' Okamoto began his story on a serious note.

'I say! This is beginning to warm up. What happened?' said the young Matsuki, pulling his chair nearer the stove.

'This is all rather sudden, I know, but if I'm going to tell you about this unusual wish of mine, I had better begin with this. She was really beautiful.'

'My, my!' said Matsuki, almost dancing with joy.

'Her face was quite round and her skin was pale. Her shoulders were full and round like a westerner's. Her eyes had a sleepy cast, not bright, as if she were lost in her own thoughts. They had charm, those eyes, and could usually melt the heart of the hardest man once she fixed him with her gaze. I was an easy mark. I didn't notice this charm so much when I first set eyes on her, but one meeting led to a second and by the time of the third I felt myself strangely drawn towards her. She began to obsess me, but I had no idea as yet that I was in love with her.

'One day, when I went to call on her at home, her parents were out; only the maid, the girl herself and her eleven-year-old sister were in the house. She was depressed and told me that she wasn't feeling very well. She sat alone in an inner room lost in her own thoughts while I sat on the veranda listening to her as she sang softly.

"O-ei, it makes me feel so sad when you sing like that. I can't bear it,"

I said, before I knew what I was saying.

"I don't understand why I should have to live in such a world as this," she said beseechingly. Her words seemed more real to me than any great philosophical treatise on pessimism. I'm sure you'll understand what I mean, even if I don't go into detail.

'Before we knew it, we had become slaves of love and it was then for the first time that I knew the joy and misery of love. I passed the next two months as if in a dream. A couple of things happened in that time which I might tell you. One began in this way:

'Around five o'clock one evening I attended a farewell party for a friend and his wife who were going abroad. My darling was also there with her mother. The party was quite an affair and there was even a count's daughter among the guests. It gradually began to break up about ten o'clock and as there was such a fine moon, I decided to walk back with the girl and her mother from the hotel to their home in Shiba Sannai. On the way the girl's mother chattered a lot about the couple who were going abroad, praising them no end and sounding very envious. I detected in her words that she regretted her daughter's tendency to hold herself aloof from the affairs of the world, and she even hinted here and there that this was due to the kind of company she kept. At this, my love who was walking close beside me clasped my hand tightly. I clasped hers in return. It was by way of an empty gesture of protest against her mother.

'When we entered a grove in Sannai, the moonlight filtered wanly through the trees enhancing its effect. Her mother walked about five paces ahead of us. It was late and there were few people around. It was very quiet and only the sound of my shoes and their sandals broke the silence, creating a weird echoing effect. The two of us walked in silence, for her mother's words had made a profound impression on us, while her mother walked quickly along in equally sad-faced silence. We came to a place where the dark shadows of the trees excluded the light of the moon, and suddenly the girl clasped me to her and whispered, "Don't take any notice of what mother says. You mustn't forsake me." She put her hand on my shoulder and suddenly I felt something hot brush against my cheek and a fragrance sweeter than that of flowers assailed my nostrils. Suddenly we emerged into the moonlight again and I saw that her eyes were brimming with tears and her face was ghastly pale. It was perhaps partly due to the flood of moonlight, but as soon as I saw it I experienced a sense of chill and my heart was assailed with feelings that were partly fear and partly sorrow. It's difficult to describe. I felt just as if a lead weight was oppressing my soul.

'I went as far as the gate that night. Her mother invited me in for some tea, but I declined and set out for home. I felt as if I had been presented with a difficult puzzle and that once I had solved it, I would be able to understand the full bitterness of my fate. I am not speaking in analogies; it is how I really felt and I couldn't help myself. I did not go straight home, therefore, but wandered aimlessly around the lonely spots in the area and before I knew where I was I had reached the top of Maruyama. I sat on a bench and gazed intently for a while at the sky over Shinagawa. "Supposing she should soon die?" The idea flashed like lightning across the darkest corners of my heart, so that I jumped to my feet and walked backwards and forwards in a trance, my eyes glued to the ground. "It'll never happen. It just won't!" I shouted as though to rebuke the devil in my heart. But the devil would not depart. Occasionally I stopped and stared at the ground and then the girl's pale face would appear vividly before my eyes, the paleness of her face clearly indicating that she was not of this world. Finally, I calmed down and set off down Maruyama, persuading myself that I was confused and had better get a good night's rest. It was then that I ran into a second incident which threw me into further confusion. I hadn't noticed it on the way up, but there was a body hanging from a branch of a tree by the road-side. It was quite a shock. I stood rooted to the spot feeling as if someone had poured cold water over my head. When I had plucked up the courage to go closer to it, I saw that it was the body of a woman. I couldn't see the face of course, but I could tell that she was young by the discarded sandals lying in the road. I was in a complete trance as I ran to the police box at the head of the road as you go down towards Sannai from the Koyokan, to report what I had seen.'

'You're going to tell us that it was the woman you loved, I suppose,' said Kondo icily.

'That only happens in novels. It wasn't at all like that.'

'Two days later I saw an article in the newspaper about her. She was nineteen and she had had an affair with a soldier, getting herself pregnant. It appeared that she had got to the end of her tether and hanged herself. Well, anyway, I didn't get much sleep that night.

'But I was lucky and when I saw my girl next day she was back to normal. When she greeted me with laughter in those languid eyes, all the sorrow of the previous night vanished like a mist. All went well for the next month or so; it was pure joy.'

'This is rare indeed!' said Watanuki, kicking the floor.'

Matsuki spoke up very gravely. 'Be quiet and listen to what he says. What happened then?'

But Kondo said seriously, 'I'll tell you what happened next. In the end the girl got fed up and that was that as far as your great love was concerned. Am I right?'

Two or three of the group burst into laughter.

'At least, that's what love was like for me,' Kondo went on.

'What do you know about things like love, then?' Iyama asked, stepping out of character.

'Okamoto hasn't finished his story yet, but let me tell you about my love. It'll only take a minute. I had an affair with this woman and we were in ecstasy. For a while everything was wonderful, but after three months she got fed up, we separated and that was that. That's how all love ends. Every single member of the female species gets bored with a man after three months. If she happens to get married she keeps the relationship going simply because there is nothing else for it. A married woman just has to stifle her boredom. Don't you agree?'

'Well, perhaps you are right, but unfortunately our relationship didn't last long enough for her to get bored. Listen and I'll tell you the rest.

'In those days, like Kamimura, I was hung up on an enthusiasm for Hokkaido and to tell you the truth I still think life on Hokkaido would be pretty good. I had all sorts of images in my mind about Hokkaido, and my love and I were never happier than when we were discussing it. Again like Kamimura, I drew up plans on a large piece of paper for an American-style house. It differed in one respect, however, in that besides the red glimmer of light from the window on winter nights, I wanted to hear the sound of happy laughter from time to time; the clear ring of a girl's voice singing.'

'But I didn't have a woman,' said Kamimura with feeling. Everybody laughed.

'That no doubt is one of the reasons you swapped over to the Meat Party,' said Watanuki.

'That's a lie,' roared Kondo. 'If Kamimura had had a woman he'd have been a turncoat before he'd ever set foot on Hokkaido. Women can never get on with a diet of potatoes. They're born meat eaters, just like me. It's a lie to say that women like potatoes.' Everyone laughed again at this last shot of Kondo's.

'Well, anyway, the two of us ...' Okamoto went on not a whit disturbed, and this brought silence again.

'We decided to go and live in Hokkaido. When our plans matured, I first returned to my village. I had some land which my family were looking after for me. I intended to sell all this and use the proceeds to open up some new land on Hokkaido. I had intended to spend no more than ten days at home, but in the first place my family were something of a stumbling-block and then I had to agree on a price, so although I hadn't intended it, I ended up spending twenty days there. Then, one day I received a telegram from the girl's mother. I was shocked and rushed back to Tokyo, but by the time I arrived she was already dead.'

'Dead?' shrieked Matsuki.

'Yes, so all my hopes had come to nothing.' Almost before Okamoto had time to finish what he was saying, Kondo spoke up, just as if he were making a speech.

'We who have just had the pleasure of listening to this fascinating love story are deeply grateful. However, for Okamoto's sake, I celebrate the death of his love. If that word is improper then I will say that I am glad, glad to my heart. Yes, I prefer to say glad, for if she had not died I believe beyond all doubt that the outcome would have been much more tragic than the tragedy of mere death.' Thus far Kondo had been in dead earnest, but feeling no doubt a little foolish, he swiftly changed his tone; lowering his voice, he said with a smile, 'When all's said and done, women do get bored. There are many types of boredom. Two of these are particularly tragic and hateful. With one, you weary of life and with the other you weary of love. It is usually men who weary of life, and women of love. The first is the most tragic and the second the most hateful.'

Kondo then returned to his more solemn tone, 'Women seldom weary of life, although young girls sometimes show signs of it. This however is a mere abnormality arising from their desire to be loved. When they have the luck to find love, they seem for a while supremely happy, and truly they are happy. The very meaning of the word "happiness" is represented in the state of mind of such girls. However, they soon become weary of their love and surely there is nothing more difficult to deal with than a woman who is tired of love. I said just now that this kind of boredom was hateful, but perhaps it should rather be pitied.

'It's different for men. They often weary of life and if they encounter love in such a state, they find in it a means of escape. For that reason they throw their whole hearts into the fiery furnace of love. When a man is in this condition, love to him is life itself.' He glanced at Okamoto, 'Well, that's it, isn't it? Does my theory fit the facts in your case?'

'I don't get it all!' shrieked Matsuki.

'You don't get it? Well, neither do I to tell the truth. I just felt like saying it. Well, Okamoto, that is what I think. You're a member of neither the Potato Party nor the Meat Party. You have one unusual wish and that is to meet the dead girl. Am I right?'

'No!' cried Okamoto, rising from his chair. He was already quite drunk. 'I deny that. If you'll listen, I'll tell you my unusual wish.'

'I don't know about you fellows, but I definitely want to hear,' said Kondo, raising his hand. Everyone else kept silent and looked at Okamoto. Matsuki and Takeuchi looked solemn, but Watanuki, Iyama and Kamimura were smiling.

'Once again I shout "no!" Kondo was right when he said that I was a man who sought through love to escape from the boredom of life and that's why her death was such a blow. As I said before, almost all my hopes were dashed. If these were a kind of incense to bring back the dead, I'd like to buy three or four hundred pounds of it. I want to have her back again and so intensely do I feel about that that I don't care what happens to me. I freely admit that I've cried over her many times.

Over and over again I've called her name and looked up at the sky. Of course I wish that she would come back to life.

'But that is not my unusual wish. Not my one, real wish. I have an even profounder wish, a more ardent desire. If only this were granted, it would not matter so much if she didn't come back to life. And even if she did and sold me before my very eyes I wouldn't care. I wouldn't care even if her ghost stuck out its red tongue and mocked me. The words "if I learn the right path in the morning, I shall gladly die in the evening" are not identical in substance to my wish, but the feeling is the same. If my wish be not granted, I could live to a hundred and it would avail me nothing. I would know no happiness; rather I would be living in agony. It does not matter if I am the only person in the world who has this wish. Alone I will go in quest of its fulfilment and if in the process I have to commit burglary, murder or arson, I won't give a damn. If there were a devil and he said to me, "Give me your wife that I may rape her; give me your child that I may eat it, and then I shall grant your wish," then if I had a wife, gladly would I give her, and if I had a child, him would I also give.'

'This is really interesting. Hurry up and tell us your wish. I want to hear it,' exclaimed Watanuki, tugging furiously at his beard.

'I'm coming to it now. I'm sure you're all fed up with our unstable government. You want to combine the talents of people like Bismarck, Gladstone and Hideyoshi to forge a government of steel. Of course, you'd like to build such a government. I too in fact have that wish, but this again is not my unusual wish. I'd like to be a sage, a prince or compassion incarnate, a Christ, a Buddha or a Confucius. I truly wish these things. But if my unusual wish be not granted then I will have nothing of sages or gods.

'Life in the mountains and forests! My blood runs hot at the very sound of these words and this is what makes me think of Hokkaido. Sometimes I walk the suburban streets when the winter skies are clear. At such times when I look over the distant horizon at the snow-capped peaks which surround the landscape, my blood surges like the waves of the sea, until I can't endure it. Yet once my thoughts turn to this wish of mine. Such things count for nothing. If only my wish be granted, I could work as a rickshaw man in the dusty streets of a busy city and not mind at all.

'There have been all sorts of carping arguments about the mysteries of the universe, the mysteries of human life and about the origins of heaven and earth. Science, philosophy and religion investigate and explain these things and then go through agonies trying to fit these phenomena into a peaceful and enlightened system. I too should like to become a great philosopher or a scientist such as would put Darwin in the shade, or a great religious figure. But this again is not my real wish. If my wish weren't granted and I were to become a great philosopher, I should mock myself and brand my face with the word "liar!"'

'Do hurry up and tell us your wish!' said Matsuki impatiently.

'O.K. But don't be suprised.'

'Come on, out with it. Quickly!'

Okamoto was calm. 'My wish is that I should like to be surprised.'

'What's that? Absolute nonsense!'

'What did you say?'

'Is that all you were getting at?'

They all spoke as if they were disgusted. Only Kondo said nothing, apparently waiting for Okamoto's explanation.

'There's a line of poetry which goes,

> "Awake, poor troubled sleeper; shake off thy torpid nightmare dream."

My wish, in other words, is to rid myself of the demon of my dreams.'

'I don't understand what you're on about,' said Watanuki, as if to himself.

'I don't want to know the mysteries of the universe. I just want to be surprised by them.'

'It seems more and more like a riddle.' Iyama rubbed his cheek.

'I don't want to know the secrets of death; I just want to be surprised at the fact of death!'

Watanuki jeered, 'Go ahead and be surprised as much as you like. That's not difficult.'

'Faith itself is not something I necessarily want. But I do want to be plagued with doubts about the mysteries of man and the universe to the point where without faith I can have no peace even for a moment.'

'This gets more and more difficult to understand,' murmured Matsuki, gazing intently at Okamoto.

'What I really want is to gouge out my worn-out grape-like eyes!' Okamoto thumped the table without realising what he was doing.

'Hear, hear!' shouted Kondo, without thinking what he was saying.

'I don't desire the courage of a Luther who at the Diet of Worms defied the power of the princes. When he was nineteen Luther had a chance meeting with the mysteries of death itself when his schoolmate Alexis was struck dead by lightning before his very eyes. That's the part of his heart I desire. Watanuki said just now, "Go ahead and be as surprised as you like." Very interesting words, but you can never be surprised to order.

'My love died, vanished from this world. Because I had loved her with all my being, I was terribly upset. But my grief was that of a bereft lover. I was unable to face up to the remorseless fact of death. Nothing can rule a man's heart so much as love. Yet there is one thing which presses down on a man's heart with a force many times greater. I refer to the power of custom. "Our birth is but a sleep and a forgetting." That line expresses it perfectly. We are born and come into this world. From our childhood, we encounter all sorts of things. Every day we look up at the sun and every night at the stars. Thereby even the mysteries of the earth lose their mystery. Life and death and all the phenomena of the universe become commonplace in the end. Those who invoke philosophy and science look at the universe as though they were standing outside it.

'Full soon thy soul shall have her earthly freight,
And custom lie upon thee with a weight,
Heavy as frost, and deep almost as life.'

These lines go right to the heart of the matter. My wish is somehow to shake off the frost. Somehow I want to be free of the pressure of old worn-out customs. I want to stand on my own feet in this universe and be capable of surprise. I don't give a damn if this means that I am a meat eater or a potato eater, or even if I end up a pessimist and despise life.

'I don't care about the results. I don't want to set up false causes. I don't want to set up premises on the basis of studies for amusement based on habit. Take phrases like, "the light of the moon is beautiful"; "evenings when the flowers are in bloom"; "starry nights are like ..." and so forth. These eloquences of poets are a form of hobby for them. They never see what's for real. They are merely looking at phantoms through eyes which are blinded by triteness. It's a game of the emotions. Philosophy and religion, what they were in the beginning I know not, have through the centuries come to the same thing. I have a friend who mocks at people who give themselves pain by asking such foolish questions as "What am I?", and says that you can never know what is unknowable. From a worldly point of view this is true, but people who raise these questions don't necessarily expect an answer. It is a cry of the soul which comes spontaneously when we acquire a deep awareness of the mysteries of the universe. The question itself is a grave expression of the soul. To scorn people who ask it is an admission of the paralysis of the soul itself. My wish is to raise this question from my heart. But though I can put it into words, it will not come from my heart.

'You often hear the questions, "Where do I come from? Where am I going?" The well of religion springs from the heart of a man who cannot help raising these questions, no matter how hard he tries not to. It is the same with poetry and that is why anything not related to these questions is false and a waste of time.

'I'd better stop now. It's no use; no use. It's useless however much I talk. I'm so exhausted, but I'll say one last word. I should like to divide mankind into two categories; people who are capable of being surprised and those who are indifferent.'

'To which do I belong?' Matsuki laughed.

'To the indifferent category, of course. All seven of us belong to the most indifferent of the indifferent category. Of the millions of people in the world, how many are not indifferent, I wonder? Look at the poets, the philosophers, the ministers of religion, the scientists and the politicians. They all bandy about their theories, look enlightened and weep for the sorrows of the world. A pretty indifferent crowd!

'Last night I had a dream.

'I dreamed that I was dead. I was alone and walking down this dark path. Without thinking what I was saying, I cried out, "I never thought that I would die!" Yes, it was I who cried out. This is what I think. Suppose that today a hundred people attend a funeral or experience the death of a parent or child. Now when they are dead and stand at the Gates of Hell, they too will cry out, "I never thought that I would die!" And they will be mocked by the Devil. Ha, ha, ha, ha, ha!'

'They say that you can be cured of hiccups by someone giving you a shock. But you have to be pretty unusual if you want shocks when you can live indifferently and dine on meat. Ha, ha, ha, ha!' Watanuki clutched his fat belly he was so overcome with laughter.

'No, I say that I want to be surprised, but it's just for the sake of saying it. Ha, ha.'

'It's just for the sake of saying it, is it?'

'I see. You go so far as expressing the wish and that's all.'

'Yes, it's just a way of passing the time. Ha, ha, ha, ha, ha!' Okamoto joined in the others' laughter.

But Kondo noticed an expression of profound anguish on Okamoto's face.

定価2,900円
in Japan